The tractor steals the show—and a client's house—in the 1936 film Earthworm Tractors. *(Wisconsin Center for Film and Theater Research)*

Alexander
BOTTS
Rides Again

More *Mayhem* on the *Earthworm Tractor!*

By William Hazlett Upson

Voyageur Press

Edited by Danielle J. Ibister
Designed by Maria Friedrich
Printed in China

05   06   07   08   09   5   4   3   2   1

Library of Congress Cataloging-in-Publication Data

Upson, William Hazlett, 1891-1975.
  Alexander Botts rides again : more mayhem on the earthworm tractor! / by William Hazlett Upson.
      p. cm.
  Stories originally published in the Saturday Evening Post between 1927 and 1975.
  ISBN 0-89658-672-3 (pbk. : alk. paper)
  1. Botts, Alexander (Fictitious character)—Fiction. 2. Tractor industry—Fiction. 3. Humorous stories, American. 4. Sales personnel—Fiction. 5. Tractors—Fiction. I. Title.

  PS3541.P74A78 2005
  813'.52—dc22

                          2004019054

Distributed in Canada by Raincoast Books, 9050 Shaughnessy Street, Vancouver, B.C. V6P 6E5

Published by Voyageur Press, Inc.
123 North Second Street, P.O. Box 338, Stillwater, MN 55082 U.S.A.
651-430-2210, fax 651-430-2211
books@voyageurpress.com
www.voyageurpress.com

Acknowledgments

Voyageur Press thanks the following people for their generous help with this book: Robert Dike Blair; Connell B. Gallagher, Jeffrey D. Marshall, and Sylvia Bugbee at the University of Vermont Bailey/Howe Library; and Dorinda Hartmann at the Wisconsin Center for Film and Theater Research.

On the front cover: In 1936, Hollywood merged with the tales of William Hazlett Upson to create the film Earthworm Tractors, *starring comic actor Joe E. Brown as Alexander Botts, tractor salesman extraordinaire.*

Alexander Botts explains his way out of another disastrous tractor demonstration in this Earthworm Tractors *film still. (Wisconsin Center for Film and Theater Research)*

Contents

Introduction

Alexander Botts, everybody's favorite Earthworm tractor salesman, delighted readers of the *Saturday Evening Post* for nearly
half a century. Starting in 1927, children and parents alike
looked forward to the newest tales, each packed with endearing
humor and satisfying twists of fate.

The creation of author William Hazlett Upson, Botts is a
braggart, a buffoon, and a darn good salesman. Upson based
the series on his own experience as a mechanic with the Caterpillar Tractor Company, a job that had him following traveling
salesmen around the country—and gaining a remarkable
amount of insight into what it takes to be a salesman. In the
case of Botts, Upson hit on a winning formula: plenty of energy
and resourcefulness, a forgiving nature, and a healthy dose of
rebelliousness.

At the heart of these stories lies the temperamental correspondence between Botts and his embattled boss, Gilbert
Henderson. In the opening tale, Botts famously offers his services to the Farmers' Friend Tractor Company, maker of Earthworm tractors. Henderson employs Botts as a mechanic, with
disastrous results—though Botts does manage to sell three tractors. Thus Botts' illustrious career as a tractor salesman is born.

Throughout the years, we learn that Botts is an ordinary
hero from small-town Iowa with a pull-yourself-up-by-your-boot-
straps philosophy but a soft spot for helping folks in trouble.
He originally discovered Earthworm tractors as a private in
France during World War I and has made a couple of smart decisions in his life, namely signing on with the Farmers' Friend
Tractor Company and marrying his wife, Mildred Deane: "I always call her Gadget because she is one of the most valuable
accessories I have ever picked up."

Despite little to no sales experience, Alexander Botts lands a job selling Earthworm tractors through sheer gumption, as illustrated in this comic. A spinoff of Upson's tales in the Saturday Evening Post, *the "Alexander the Great" strip ran from 1936 to 1938. (University of Vermont Bailey/Howe Library)*

In all, "America's magazine" published 112 Botts stories, starting in 1927 and staying strong through the Depression, World War II, and post-war America. The series finally came to a close in 1975, but readers would not soon forget Alexander Botts or his Earthworm tractors. Behind the light humor is a compassionate and creative mind, behind the craziness is a sound business acumen, and behind the burlesque is robust storytelling.

Though Botts is best remembered as a character of literature, he took on other forms as well, including a short-lived comic strip titled "Alexander the Great," a radio show, and the 1936 Hollywood production *Earthworm Tractors*, which has recently been re-released on DVD. The lead actor is Joe E. Brown, a comedian whose trademark is an "air of amiable idiocy"—perfect for the characterization of Alexander Botts.

Over the years, Upson's tales have been collected into several books, though they have all fallen out of print. In 2001, Voyageur Press corrected that wrong by publishing *The Fabulous Saga of Alexander Botts and the Earthworm Tractor*. That book was so well received that we decided to present loyal fans with another hilarious selection of Botts tales.

In these stories, Botts battles a sea captain, a magician, a duplicitous contractor, an inept farmer, a discouraged tractor salesman, several unreasonable commanding officers, and a tractor dealer with some newfangled ideas about salesmanship. Botts' amazing Earthworm tractors topple over waterfalls and into the Grand Canyon with happy results, and they plow through everything from a Florida jungle to snowdrifts equal to the Himalayas. All the stories here first appeared in the *Saturday Evening Post*; two, "Botts' Folly" and "Botts and the Bag of Tricks," have never been reprinted in any other collection.

Perhaps you recall haunting the mailbox for your *Post* subscription and Botts' latest exploits. If so, please, sit down and let Botts recapture your heart. If, on the other hand, you've never experienced Botts, prepare yourself. You're in for a wild ride!

Joe E. Brown mugs for this 1936 Earthworm Tractors *film lobby card. The comic actor played the role of ever enthusiastic salesman Alexander Botts with perfect panache.*

The Indirect Method

FARMERS' FRIEND TRACTOR COMPANY
MAKERS OF EARTHWORM TRACTORS
EARTHWORM CITY, ILLINOIS

June 1, 1920.

Mr. Alexander Botts,
Muller Hotel,
Kansas City, Mo.

DEAR MR. BOTTS: We are informed that the Road Commissioners of Silica County, Kansas, are considering buying a tractor for grading and general road work. We want you to go at once to Sandy Forks, the county seat, and sell these Commissioners an Earthworm Tractor.

Salesmen from other companies will probably be there. In addition, it is possible that you may encounter a little sales resistance due to the fact that Mr. Joseph Ripley, a wealthy farmer of Silica County, has been having trouble with his Earthworm Tractor—due entirely to his own negligence—and has been blaming everything on the company.

However, we have every confidence in you, and feel sure you will put over this deal. Advise us fully in your daily reports as to what progress you make.

> Very sincerely,
> GILBERT HENDERSON,
> Sales Manager.

FARMERS' FRIEND TRACTOR COMPANY
SALESMAN'S DAILY REPORT
Date: June 3, 1920.
Written from: Sandy Forks, Kansas.
Written by: Alexander Botts, Salesman.

I got your letter yesterday, and it is a good thing you are putting onto this job a real high-powered salesman like me, rather than one of your ordinary men. When I explain the situation here, you will see that any ordinary man would have quit cold. But not Alexander Botts.

I left Kansas City bright and early this morning in my new flivver roadster, and about the middle of the afternoon—when I had gotten to within about two miles of the town of Sandy Forks—I saw something that I can only describe as a sickening sight. Right beside the main road as you approach Sandy Forks is a little bluff looking out over a very pretty lake. And right on top of this bluff, in plain sight of anybody coming along the road was a large ten ton Earthworm Tractor with a big sign on it reading as follows:

I WILL SELL THIS EARTHWORM TRACTOR VERY CHEAP OWING TO THE FACT THAT IT IS ABSOLUTELY NO GOOD, NEVER WAS NO GOOD, AND THE COMPANY THAT MADE IT WON'T STAND BEHIND IT.—JOSEPH RIPLEY.

Parking my car by the road, I walked up and looked at the tractor. It was old, weather-beaten and rusty, and the carburetor and magneto were gone. One of the side plates was off the crank case, so that I could look in and see that the bearings were all loose and wobbly. Running my hand up into the cylinders, I could feel that they were scored and pitted in a scandalous manner.

As I sadly returned to my car, there came walking along the road a young man in overalls, whom I rightly guessed to be a native of these parts.

"Yes," he said, in answer to my questions, "Old man Ripley has had a lot of grief with that tractor, and he sure is sore at the company that made it. He has just got himself elected to the County Board of Road Commissioners so he can make sure that when the county buys a tractor it will be something else besides one of these Earthworms."

"Won't the other members have something to say about that?" I asked.

"Well," he said, "Old Joe Ripley is the richest and most influential farmer in the county. Most of the other members have worked for him at one time or another, and they'll probably want to work for him again. They aren't apt to go against what he says."

"Where does this Mr. Ripley live?" I asked.

"Straight ahead. First house on the right."

"Thank you," I said.

After the young man had left, I pondered the situation, and as I have a quick mind I soon realized that you were right when you said in your letter that Mr. Ripley has been having trouble with his tractor. Apparently you hadn't heard that he was the main guy on the Board of Road Commissioners, or that he was putting on this pretty little tractor show out beside the state road. But I decided you were right when you said I might possibly encounter a little sales resistance. And that is why it is lucky you sent the kind of a man that it takes to overcome sales resistance.

I didn't waste any time. I decided I would take this bull by the horns; I would beard this lion in his den. Accordingly, I drove on up the road to the first house on the right, which turned out to be a nice looking white farm house with trees all around it and big red barns behind. In the front yard stood an old gentleman who appeared to be gazing down a well. In his hands he held a large mirror.

"Howdy, neighbor!" I said cordially, as I drew up beside the road. "What seems to be the trouble?"

"There seems to be something the matter with this well," he said, "but I can't find out what it is. It's so dark down there I can't see a thing."

"Well," I said, "it just happens that I am an expert on wells, so perhaps I can help you."

(NOTE: As a matter of fact, all I know about a well is that it is a hole in the ground with water at the bottom. I have never even been able to figure out just how the water gets there. But I felt it would be wiser to approach his guy by the indirect method and to introduce myself as a well expert rather than as a salesman for Earthworm Tractors.)

"My name," I said, "is Alexander Botts, Expert on Wells."

"My name," said the old gentleman, "is Joseph Ripley."

"Pleased to meet you," I said. "And now we will see what is the matter with this well. First of all, what is the idea of that mirror?"

"Everybody knows," said Mr. Ripley, "that the way to look down a well is to hold a mirror at the top and shine the sunlight down into it. But this tree, right over the well here, makes such a dense shade that there isn't enough sunlight to do any good."

"Yes," I said, "that tree complicates matters. I will have to think it over and see what we can do."

At first I was going to suggest cutting down the tree, but I doubt if the old gentleman would have approved. Then, all at once like an inspiration, I got one of the most brilliant ideas that has come into my mind for a long time.

"Have you another mirror in the house?" I asked.

"Yes," he answered.

"Fine," I said, "go in and get it."

Somewhat doubtfully he went into the house and came out with another large mirror. I then had him go out by the road in the bright sunshine and reflect a beam of light over to where I was standing at the top of the well. With the other mirror I reflected this beam of light down into the depths. The results were extraordinarily gratifying. The inside of the well was brilliantly illuminated, and far below floating in the water I could see, just as plain as day, a large and probably once very handsome cat.

"Beautiful!" I said. "Splendid! I have discovered what is the matter with your well."

I then walked out into the sunlight with my mirror and had Mr. Ripley look down into the well with his. He agreed with me at once that we had discovered what was the matter with the well, and declared that the unlucky animal was no doubt a cat by the name of Cicero, which he had kept at the barn, and which had disappeared some weeks before. He said he would call a couple of men from the fields to get busy and clean the well.

"No!" I said, "I am an expert on wells, and I will go down for you and take out this unfortunate cat."

(NOTE: I will admit that I did not particularly enjoy the idea of going down into a well after a cat, but it seemed to me that this was a splendid opportunity to get in strong with the old guy.)

I immediately let the bucket down into the bottom of the well, and after removing my coat I went down the rope hand over hand. As I am fairly agile, and as the force of gravity was working in my favor, it did not take me long to descend to the level of the water. Standing with my feet on projecting stones at opposite sides of the well, I reached down, placed all that was left of poor old Cicero in the bucket and yelled to Mr. Ripley to pull it up.

This he did. And as Cicero was mounting upwards there suddenly came to me, just like an inspiration, a plan by which I could extend my visit with Mr. Ripley, and have a better chance to get in strong with him. Acting upon this inspiration, I at once climbed down into the water of the well, bracing my feet against the projecting stones at the sides, until I was up to my neck in the icy water. Many men would have shrunk back from the terrible coldness of that water. But not Alexander Botts. As soon as I was completely covered by the water I began splashing, and yelling as loud as I could that I had fallen in and was drowning. Mr. Ripley at once let down the bucket, and I proceeded to scramble up the rope, assisting myself by stepping on the projecting stones on the sides of the well.

When I reached the top I tumbled out on the grass and lay on my back, gasping, coughing, choking, and rolling my eyes, imitating as nearly as I could a person who is half-drowned. Mr. Ripley set up a great hollering, and a couple of farm hands came running from the barn. He had them carry me into the house, and after they had laid me on the bed in the spare room he gave me a drink of some liquid which produced a pleasant feeling of warmth over my entire body. By the time I had had two or three drinks of this excellent stuff, I was feeling very comfortable, and I was able to accept very gracefully Mr. Ripley's invitation to spend the night. He saw that my car was put in the barn, and I remained in bed for the rest of the afternoon while old Mrs. Ripley dried and pressed my clothes. Meanwhile Mr. Ripley had his men pump all the water out of the well and give it a thorough cleaning.

So far, I had not mentioned tractors, but after supper I brought up the subject in a casual and indirect way—without spilling the news that I was a salesman for Earthworms. Mr. Ripley was very willing to talk. He said that he bought the tractor last year, and that after he had used it only two weeks it quit on him. He had then asked for a service man from the factory, and the service man had told him it was all his own fault for not putting oil in the machine, and the Company had refused to repair it for free. That made him so mad he had run it out by the road and put that sign on it so as to knock the company as much as he could.

"Did you really run it for two weeks without oil?" I asked.

"I can't remember for sure," said Mr. Ripley; "very possibly I did. But that doesn't let the Tractor Company out. That machine was guaranteed for a year, and it went bad after only two weeks. So it was their business to fix it up for me free. What if I did forget about the oil? Anybody is liable to forget a little thing like that. I know that I gave it plenty of gasoline and plenty of water, and anybody is liable to forget a little minor thing like oil. No, sir, these Earthworm Tractor people are nothing but a bunch of crooks."

"Well," I said, "you certainly have had a most unfortunate experience."

"Right you are," said Mr. Ripley, "and the worst of it is all the people around here are kidding me about it. I suppose I got bit once, but I ain't going to get bit again. I am a member of the Board of County Commissioners, and we're going to buy a tractor for road work, but you can bet your bottom dollar it won't be one of those damn Earthworms. Salesmen for several other makes of tractors are going to do some demonstrating for us down around town, and we'll take whichever one of them shows up the best. There was a man here trying to sell us an Earthworm, and we told him we wouldn't even consider it."

"I didn't know there were any Earthworm salesmen around here," I said.

"This man," said Mr. Ripley, "is a contractor by the name of Casey. He's just finished up a dirt-moving job over in the next County at Johnsonville. He's moving out to Oregon for his next job, and he has a second-hand Earthworm tractor that he is willing to sell cheap. But I told him I wouldn't take it as a gift, so that's all there is to that."

"And what are you going to do with that old tractor of yours," I asked, "just leave it out there beside the road?"

"Sure," he said, "unless somebody comes along and wants to buy it, but I haven't had any offers for it yet. I paid $6,000 for it, and I'll let it go for $1,000 just as it stands, including the carburetor and magneto which I've got up here in the barn."

"Sold!" I said.

"You mean you want to buy it yourself?" he said.

"Exactly so."

"But I don't want to stick you."

"I'll risk that."

"It's absolutely no good," he said. "I have had several mechanics from town come out and look at it, and they tell me it is completely shot to pieces."

"Don't worry about me," I said. "In addition to being an expert on wells, I am also an expert on tractors, and I figure I can fix it up and maybe sell it at a profit. You said you would sell it for $1,000. You certainly aren't going to be a cheap sport and back down on your promise, are you?"

"No."

"Fine," I said, "the deal is closed."

I at once got out my check book and wrote him a check for $1,000 on the First National Bank of Earthworm City.

"I am dating this check June 10th—a week ahead—" I said, "to give me time to transfer that much money into my checking account, but I won't take the tractor away until the check has been cashed. That will be all right with you, won't it?"

"Absolutely," said Mr. Ripley.

Shortly after this, I said good-night and came up to my room, where I have been spending the rest of the evening writing up this report.

From what I have related you can see that you made no mistake in sending me to handle this very difficult job. Instead of blatting out the news that I was an Earthworm salesman, and thus getting myself thrown off old man Ripley's farm, I have proceeded by the indirect method, and—thanks to my energy in taking advantage of the fortunate incident of Cicero in the well— I have already gotten in very strong with this old gentleman, who is the main guy on the Board of Road Commissioners. Furthermore, by purchasing this old tractor I have taken the first step toward carrying out a very deep plan which I have evolved for the purpose of carrying through this matter in my usual brilliant manner.

I will now close and get myself some sleep, but tomorrow I am going to start some real action around this neck of the woods.

Cordially yours,
ALEXANDER BOTTS,
Earthworm Salesman.

P. S.—In looking over the stubs in my check book, I find that my balance in the First National Bank of Earthworm City is $21.30. As I have no funds of my own to bring up this account, I must ask you to have the cashier of the tractor company place $1,000 to my credit in this bank at once. Otherwise the highly important operations which I am conducting in this region are liable to be somewhat hampered.

A. B.

FARMERS' FRIEND TRACTOR COMPANY
SALESMAN'S DAILY REPORT
Date: June 5, 1920.
Written from: Sandy Forks, Kan.
Written by: Alexander Botts.

I was so busy all day yesterday, last night, and today that I haven't had time to write you any report until just now. But when you read what I have been doing, you will realize that I have been right up on my toes all the time. I have got things moving along something swell.

Bright and early yesterday morning I got my car out, and told Mr. Ripley I was going to get some tools to repair the tractor, and that I would be back the next day. He gave me the magneto and carburetor, which I placed in the car, and then I started toward town. I chucked the carburetor and magneto into some thick bramble bushes beside the road. Then instead of getting any tools I drove twenty miles over into the next county, and just outside the town of Johnsonville I found the camp of this contractor Casey. Most of the equipment of the camp seemed to be packed up ready to move. The only man there was a young guy with red hair who told me that Mr. Casey had gone to town, and would be back in about half an hour. So I had to wait; but while waiting I did not let any grass grow under my feet. I talked most pleasantly with this young red-headed guy, and I got him to show me the tractor, which turned out to be exactly the same model as the one owned by Mr. Ripley. I was also pleased to see that it had been out in the weather long enough to make it just about as rusty-looking as Mr. Ripley's old wreck. The red-headed guy told me, however, that it was in A-1 condition, and he proved it by cranking it up and driving around a bit for me. Then thanked him, and gave him a few cigars, and patted him on the back, and talked to him so pleasantly that he finally blurted out the good news that Mr. Casey was so anxious to sell the tractor he would let it go for $2,000, although he was asking and hoping for $4,000.

Pretty soon after that, an automobile came driving up and out stepped a rather nervous-looking guy, who proved to be Mr. Casey himself. I don't know why it is, but pretty near all these contractors are nervous-looking guys—they seem to have a whole lot on their mind.

I at once offered Mr. Casey $600 for his tractor, at which he let out a loud laugh, and told me he wouldn't take one cent less than $4,000. So we jawed around a while. I came up a little, and he went down a little, until finally I told him that if he would include a big chain that was hanging on the tractor, and if he would have his man drive the tractor over to the town of Sandy Forks for me, I would pay him $2,000. As he saw that he couldn't make any better bargain, and as he had already (according to the red-headed guy) decided to let her go for that, he accepted.

But when I started to write out a check on the First National Bank of Earthworm City he began to look even more nervous than before.

"How do I know," he said, "that your check will be good?"

"Oh! don't worry about that," I said. "Anybody around Earthworm City could tell you that Alexander Botts is good for a hundred times as much money as this paltry $2,000."

"That's all right," he said, "but is there anybody around here that knows you?"

"No," I said, "I am afraid there isn't. But listen," I said: "this check will go through in a few days, and in the meantime I am only taking this tractor as far as Sandy Forks. You are a reasonable man and you ought to know that I couldn't skip out of the country with a great big thing like a ten ton tractor."

"Well," he said, "I guess maybe that's right."

"Sure it's right," I said, "but, of course, if you want to call off the sale,–"

"No," he said, "I'll take a chance."

So he took the check and made me out a bill of sale.

(NOTE: As Mr. Casey was so suspicious about my check, I did not like to ask his permission to date it ahead, consequently it is very important that the cashier of the Farmers' Friend Tractor Company place an additional $2,000 to my credit at the First National Bank of Earthworm City. Be sure and have him do this AT ONCE, as Mr. Casey will probably send in the check right away, and it is possible that if this check came back marked "No Funds" it might very seriously cramp my style in my present undertakings and result in considerable embarrassment and detriment to myself and to the best interests of the Farmers' Friend Tractor Company.)

The young red-headed guy filled up the tractor with gas and oil and we started out for Sandy Forks with me leading the way in my car and him following with the tractor. I had him drive very slow, and we stopped a long time for lunch at a little village, so we didn't get to Sandy Forks until dark. I led the way along a road that went around the town so as not to attract too much attention, and I had him drag the tractor into a field about a mile from Mr. Ripley's farm. Then I drove him back to Casey's camp at Johnsonville in my car, after which I returned to Sandy Forks.

I had supper at a little restaurant, and about midnight I drove out to where I had left Casey's tractor. I cranked it up and then I drove it along the road until I came to Mr. Ripley's old tractor. It didn't take me more than five minutes to remove the big sign, hook onto the tractor with the big chain, and drag it down to the shore of the little lake. Then I unhooked, drove around behind it with the Casey tractor, and gave it a good healthy push that sent it over the steep bank and into the deep muddy water beneath. Next, I drove back and stopped Mr. Casey's tractor exactly where the other one had been, and I put Mr. Ripley's sign on top of it. After this I walked back to where I had left my car, drove to town, got myself a room at the hotel, and went to bed about 2 A.M.

Bright and early the next morning I drove out to Mr. Ripley's farm and found him inspecting his well, which, after being cleaned out, was now once more full of fine fresh water.

"Good morning, Mr. Botts," he said, as I drove up. "What is the news with you?"

"Very good news," I said. "I have just been down the country a ways to my brother-in-law's farm, and my brother-in-law has promised me that if this tractor runs as well as I expect to make it, he will buy it from me for $5,000.

(NOTE: I will admit that this statement was somewhat exaggerated. As a matter of fact I have no brother-in-law, and even if I had I doubt very much if he would have $5,000 to spend on a tractor. However, I felt that the delicacy of my manoeuvers in the matters of all these various tractors justified the use of a certain amount of strategy.)

"If you can get $5,000 for that bunch of junk," said Mr. Ripley, "you're welcome to it."

"That's fine," I said. "I was sure you'd be a good sport about it. You know that when I bought that tractor, I took an awful chance, and I was ready to stand the loss in case it turned out worse than I thought it was. But now that it turns out to be in a really swell condition, I figure that I am entitled to whatever profit I can make on it."

"Sounds fair enough to me," said Mr. Ripley. "But I think you are fooling yourself. The best automobile mechanics in town have told me that the machine is a wreck."

"The best automobile mechanics," I answered, "at some-times none too good on tractors. But I am a tractor expert. I stopped off this morning and put on the carburetor and mag-neto, and filled the old baby up with gas, oil, and water. And I find that lack of oil was really the only thing the matter. Now that I have filled her up with plenty of good fresh oil, she's prac-tically as good as new."

"Important," said the old guy, "if true."

"If you have any plowing or any other work you want done," I suggested, "we'll crank up the tractor and try it out."

"All right," said Mr. Ripley, "I want to plow that forty-acre patch across the road. There is an eight-bottom gangplow in the barn, and if you can get that tractor up here you can hook on and start in. But I doubt if you can make the tractor run three feet. The only way I could get it to where it is now was by hook-ing onto it with all the horses on the place."

"Let's go," I said, "and see what we can do."

We walked down to the tractor and I removed the handsome sign. Then I gave the crank one flip, and the motor started with a roar. I climbed in and drove up to the barn as fast as I could, with Mr. Ripley trotting along behind,—the most surprised-looking old geezer I have ever seen in my life. By the time he reached the barn I had already hooked up to the plow, taken it across the road, and started a deep furrow down the middle of his forty-acre field. At the end of the first round I stopped and cut off the motor, and I was very much pleased to note that I was making quite an impression on old Joe. He came up and stood behind the machine, and for a while he couldn't say a word or do anything except open and shut his mouth in a foolish sort of way.

"I never seen the like," he said, after a while. "I wouldn't have believed it possible. Those mechanics all told me the machine was a wreck."

"Those mechanics must have been trying to fool you," I said. "The idea of telling a smart, intelligent man like you that you were a dumb tractor operator! From the looks of this machine I would say that you were one of the best tractor operators in the country. You have kept it in fine shape."

"Do you really think so?" he asked.

"Sure I do," I said. "Stick around and wait until we make a few more rounds."

Mr. Ripley looked at his watch. "I wish I could," he said, "but I just happened to think I have to get to town to see a tractor demonstration that these other guys are putting on today. There are three different machines down there and they are all going to demonstrate what they can do on road-grading and moving dirt."

"Where is this demonstration going to be?" I said.

"Oh, just up and down some of the main roads," he said.

"Listen," I said. "I don't want to butt in on anybody else's business, but I am an expert on all kinds of tractors, and I can give you a tip on how to find out which one of these machines is the best."

"How is that?" he asked.

"Any of these machines," I said, "can pull a grader on a nice dry road, but when you get a tractor for road work, you want one that will go through all the deep mud holes that come in the bad weather in the spring and fall. So if I were you I would pick out a nice wet swamp and make them all go through that."

"Sounds like a good idea," said Mr. Ripley; "there's a nice soft swamp just north of town."

"Make 'em go through that," I said. "And in the meantime I'll see if I can't get a little plowing done for you."

I cranked up the machine and started across the field again, and looking over my shoulder I saw Mr. Ripley climb into his car and drive off toward town.

All the rest of the morning I kept that tractor running wide open, and I certainly have got to hand it to Casey and his red-headed operator for keeping the old baby in fine shape. She went sailing back and forth across that field as smooth and steady as a ferry boat. The ground was loose and sandy and turned over just as easy as could be. I took a half an hour off at noon to eat some lunch that Mrs. Ripley gave me, and then went back and plowed all the afternoon, and at half past five I finished up the last headland and dragged the plow back to the barn.

At six o'clock, when Mr. Ripley got back from town, I was all washed up and sitting comfortably in a rocking chair on the porch. When he saw how I had plowed forty acres in one day with a machine that he supposed was nothing but a bunch of junk, I thought the poor old gentleman was going to faint. It also seemed to me that he looked just a little bit sore, so I started in to talk right way. And I will admit that I am a good talker.

"It certainly is lucky, Mr. Ripley," I said, "that you are such an intelligent, fair-minded man. Some people would be low-down enough to be mad because I am going to make such a nice profit on this tractor deal. But I know that you are a gentleman, and a real good sport."

"Yes," he said, "of course I want to be a gentleman and a good sport. But at the same time I almost wish I hadn't sold you that machine. I'd almost be willing to buy it back from you for twice as much as you paid for it."

"I wish I could let you have it, Mr. Ripley," I said, "but really don't see how I can without going back on my promise to my brother-in-law. You see I told him he could have it for $5,000, and, of course, you are too fine a man, Mr. Ripley, to want me to break my word to my brother-in-law."

"I suppose you're right," said Mr. Ripley, shaking his head very sad, "but this business has gotten me all confused. I don't know whether I am going in or coming out."

"There is one thing to be thankful for anyway," I said. "You know now that you were a good judge of machinery when you bought this machine, and you also know yhat you are a perfectly competent tractor operator. And by the way, how did the big tractor demonstration come off down in town?"

"The tractor demonstration in town," said Mr. Ripley, "was a joke."

"Did they go through the swamp?" I asked.

"They went into the swamp," said Mr. Ripley. "At first none of them would try it, but I told them that we wouldn't buy any tractor that couldn't go through soft ground. So they all started out, and all three of them are mired down so deep in the swamp that it looks like it will take a week to get them out."

"But which one of them are you doing to buy?" I asked.

"I don't know," said Mr. Ripley. "We have a meeting of the Board of County Commissioners tomorrow afternoon to decide what to do, but I don't know as I want to buy any of those machines."

"I'll tell you how you could have a lot of fun," I said, "and show up a lot of those town people for the boobs that they are. You know that they have been saying around town that you are a bum tractor operator. Now is your chance to show them all that you are the best there is."

"How can I do that?"

"In the morning," I said, "we will both get in that old Earthworm tractor, and you will drive. We will go down there and drive right through that old swamp and pull these three machines out of the mud. I guess that will show them what a real operator like you will do when you are driving a real machine like this Earthworm."

"Do you honestly think we could do it?"

"Sure we can," I said. "These three machines are nothing but ordinary tractors, and of course they sink right down in the mud just the same as an automobile would. But this Earthworm has tracks on it like a wartime tank and it can stay right up on top of the mud as nice as you please. And I would be glad to let you use the tractor because I promised you I wouldn't take it away until the check came through."

"It sounds like a good idea," said old Mr. Ripley. "I believe we will do it."

"Fine," I said.

Soon after that we had supper, and as Mr. Ripley had invited me to spend the night I came up to my room, and I have been writing this report ever since.

From what I have told you you can see that everything is going swell, and that you made no mistake in sending me to handle this very delicate situation. By the use of the indirect method I have now gotten Mr. Ripley eating out of my hand. Tomorrow morning I intend to sell him back his own old tractor—which, as I have explained, is not really his own old tractor at all. And tomorrow afternoon I will go before the Road Commissioners, tell them that I have just taken over the Earthworm agency, and I will then count on Mr. Ripley's help to sell them a machine for the county.

Please let me know right away whether or not you have deposited that $3,000 to my account in the First National Bank of Earthworm City.

Cordially yours,
ALEXANDER BOTTS.

FARMERS' FRIEND TRACTOR COMPANY
SALESMAN'S DAILY REPORT
Date: June 6, 1920.
Written from: County Jail, Johnsonville, Kan.
Written by: Alexander Botts.

As you may guess from the heading of this letter, my operations in this region are not proceeding in as felicitous a manner as I had hoped they would, but when I explain matters you will see that it is not my fault. I will admit that I was very much shocked and disappointed when I visited the Post Office this noon and received such a chilly letter from Mr. Gilbert Henderson, Sales Manager of the Earthworm Tractor Company. I notice that Mr. Henderson says that the salesmen of this Company are expected to sell tractors and not to buy them, and that the Company cannot finance unauthorized purchases of second-hand tractors. Also I see that he has turned down my request that $3,000 be deposited to my account at the First National Bank of Earthworm City. I suppose Mr. Henderson thinks he knows how to run a sales department, but I nevertheless wish to point out that his action in this matter has probably cost the Company the sale of a tractor, and has also put this particular salesman in a somewhat embarrassing position,—as you may judge from the heading of this report. This is particularly unfortunate in view of the fact that I had already managed—by employing all my energy and intellect and sales experience—to bring matters almost to the point of a brilliant and highly successful conclusion.

When I think of the splendid things I accomplished this morning, it almost makes me weep to think of the depths to which I have sunk this evening. Immediately after breakfast I cranked up the good old tractor, told Mr. Ripley once more what a splendid operator he was and had him take his place on the driver's seat. I then climbed in beside him and we started for town. Mr. Ripley—although probably one of the worst mechanics in Kansas—is nevertheless perfectly capable of going through the simple procedure of starting and stopping a tractor, and also steering it to the right, left, or straight ahead as the case may be. We rolled down the road very nicely and before long we had reached the swamp where the three tractors were mired down.

The salesmen and mechanics in charge of these tractor were all out with shovels and timbers trying to get them out, and there were also a great many of the townspeople who had come to observe the excitement. I have never seen a prouder man than old Mr. Ripley as he drove that splendid Earthworm tractor out over the soft swamp in front of all the admiring townspeople. I coached him up on just what to do and we put on a beautiful show. The salesmen for these other tractors were none too pleased to have us come out there, but they could not offer to refuse the assistance that we so kindly offered them.

First of all, we drove out to the nearest tractor—a big hulk of a machine known as the Behemoth tractor. I had told Mr. Ripley to take up our machine up to the front of it, and then I hooked on the big chain and told him to go ahead. It was a hard pull, but we finally got it out of its hole and dragged it up onto the firm ground at the edge of the swamp. Then we went after the other two. And just as I had predicted, the old Earthworm stayed right up on top of the soft ground, and performed in a really splendid manner. After about an hour's work we had all three of these clumsy machines out of the swamp and up on the high ground.

By this time it looked as if practically all of the town was out to see the show, and when we had at last finished they all began waving their hats around and shouting with the greatest enthusiasm. Old Mr. Ripley was tickled absolutely pink. He stood up and bowed gracefully to the crowd, and when he finally sat down I told him once more that he was one of the best tractor operators in the entire United States, and also a very good sport.

"Yes, sir," he said to me, "I guess I have shown you and all the rest of them that I am a pretty swell operator, and now I am going to show you that I am also a very good sport. I will buy this tractor back from you and I will pay you exactly what you said you could get for it from that other guy down in the country. I will pay you the full $5,000."

"No, Mr. Ripley," I said, "you are such a good friend of mine that I could not think of asking you that much. I am making a profit on this tractor myself, and I am such a good sport that I am going to let you also make a profit of $1,000 on this transaction. I will make it up to my brother-in-law in some other way, and I will sell you this tractor for only $4,000. I know that you are offering me 5,000, but you are such a good friend of mine that I am willing to let you take it *for only $4,000.*"

It was really touching to see the gratitude with which old Mr. Ripley received my very generous offer. He shook me by the hand, and there actually seemed to be tears in his eyes as he accepted the proposition. I persuaded the old gentleman to get down out of the tractor at once, and I took him over to the bank in town while the cheers of the crowd were still ringing in his ears. With a smile on his face he wrote me out a check for $3,000 and handed me over my own check for $1,000 which he had been carrying around in his pocket. I then handed him back the bill of sale on the tractor, which he had given me, and we shook hands once more in the most cordial spirit imaginable.

(NOTE: I wish to point out—in view of my somewhat unfortunate situation this evening, as indicated in the heading of this report—that my financial operations in respect to this tractor were rather good, if I do say so myself. You will have to admit that it takes a guy with a quick mind—and a good talker too—to buy a man's tractor for $1,000, and then sell back to him what he thinks is the same machine for $4,000, and make him think that you are doing him a favor. And in a way I was doing him a favor; I could have soaked him $5,000 easy.)

As soon as our little transaction was completed, Mr. Ripley started back to look after his tractor, and I at once turned his check into the bank, opening an account in my own name for the $3,000. I felt that if Mr. Ripley calmed down from the warm glow which had been induced by the applause of the crowd, and if he then changed his mind, it would be just as well to have the check cashed so he could not stop payment.

After leaving the bank I stopped in at the Post Office and received Mr. Henderson's most unwelcome letter, which seemed to indicate that I had no funds at the First National Bank of Earthworm City to back up the $2,000 check I had given Mr. Casey. As I am a very good business man, it at once occurred to me that it might be wise to get in touch with Mr. Casey to prevent the possibility of there being any misunderstanding. Consequently I called his camp at once on the long-distance telephone. Unfortunately, Mr. Casey was out, and the red-headed tractor operator with whom I talked did not know when he would return. As I am very conservative, I decided to take no more chances than I could help. So I told the red-headed operator to inform Mr. Casey when he came back that I was coming over to Johnsonville at once to see him. I then went back to the bank and had them give me a certified check for $2,000, after which I hired a car to take me out to Mr. Ripley's place, where I got into my own machine and drove at once to Johnsonville.

As I am always the soul of honor in all business transactions, I was resolved to avoid even the appearance of evil in my dealings with Mr. Casey. If he had not yet sent in the check on the First National Bank of Earthworm City, I would redeem it with the gilt-edged certified check on the Sandy Forks bank. In case he had already sent in the check, I was prepared to place the certified check in the care of the cashier of the Johnsonville bank, to be paid over to Mr. Casey when my other check should come back.

But unfortunately all my good intentions went for nothing. When I arrived at Mr. Casey's camp I was met, not by Mr. Casey, but by a tall gentleman with a very disagreeable face. As soon as I had told him my name he pulled back the flap of his coat and showed me a cheap-looking, nickel-plated star, which was pinned to his vest, and which bore the words "Deputy Sheriff." He then drew a large paper from the side pocket of his coat and informed me that it was a warrant for my arrest.

"I would advise you to come quietly," he said, "and I must warn you that anything you say may be used against you."

"But why," I said, "would anyone want to arrest a law-abiding citizen like me?"

"This warrant," he said, "was sworn out by Mr. Casey, who charges you with passing a bad check for $2,000."

"It is all a mistake," I said. "Take me to Mr. Casey and I will straighten everything out."

"Mr. Casey," he said, "left about a half an hour ago for Kansas City to see his lawyer. He said he would be back in the morning, at which time you will have a hearing before the Judge."

"But I have to be back in Sandy Forks this afternoon for a very important meeting," I said. "I can't stay until tomorrow."

"Oh, yes, you can," he said.

I then gave that man all the arguments I could think of. I told him it was all a mistake. I showed him the certified check. I threatened to sue him for false arrest. I even gave him two very good cigars—which he took—and asked him as one gentleman to another to let me go for the afternoon on my word of honor to come back the next day. I talked with that man for a good half hour—and I am a pretty good talker, if I do say so myself—but it seems as though these guys with the stars on their vests are pretty hard birds to talk to. I didn't seem to get anywhere at all and finally he even had the nerve to make me drive the both of us back to town in my own car, after which he locked me up in the Johnsonville jail.

In all fairness, I must admit that this is a very handsome jail. It seems to be a brand-new, and the bars of my little cage seem to be of as good quality steel as anything used even in such a high grade machine as the Earthworm tractor. I have been scratching away on one of the bars for half an hour with a piece of a hack-saw blade which I happened to have in my pocket, and which they missed when they took my money and everything else away from me, but I haven't been able to make any impression on it.

So I have been sitting around in this dump all the afternoon, and now, after supper, I am writing this report with pencil and paper which the Jailer's wife was kind enough to let me have. I am fairly comfortable in here, but it just makes me sick to think that I got the chief county commissioner over at Sandy Forks all worked up ready to buy an Earthworm tractor, and then I was unable to attend the meeting and put over the deal. As no Earthworm salesman was present at that meeting this afternoon, I suppose they have probably bought one of those other tractors.

Yours,
ALEXANDER BOTTS.

FARMERS' FRIEND TRACTOR COMPANY
SALESMAN'S DAILY REPORT
Date: June 7, 1920.
Written from: Sandy Forks, Kan.
Written by: Alexander Botts.

Well, I am out of jail again.

When Mr. Casey showed up at the hearing this morning I learned that right after he had taken my check some days ago, he had become even more nervous than usual. And as he seems to have a peculiarly low, suspicious type of mind, he had pulled a very dirty trick indeed. Instead of sending my check through in the regular way, he had had his own bank telegraph at once to the First National Bank of Earthworm City to inquire whether my account was good for $2,000. When the word came back that it was not, he had at once sworn out a warrant for me. However, when I explained that it was all a mistake and produced the certified check, he at least had the decency to say he would drop the charges if he was sure to get his money. So as soon as they had telephoned to the bank in Sandy Forks and found that the certified check was O. K., they turned me loose.

I drove back to Mr. Ripley's house outside Sandy Forks with a heavy heart. I was somewhat reassured when that gentleman met me with a smiling face, and I was greatly pleased when I heard what had happened at the meeting.

It seemed that the Commissioners had unanimously turned down the three other tractors. And, as there was no Earthworm salesman present, they decided—on Mr. Ripley's motion—to write in to the Farmers' Friend Tractor Company and order two ten ton Earthworm tractors to be used in county road work. Their letter will, no doubt, be in your hands by the time this report reaches you. I am leaving tonight for Kansas City, and I wish to point out that although I have used the indirect method in this transaction so that my name does not appear on the county order, and although nobody around here suspects that I am a salesman for the Earthworm Company, nevertheless I am entitled to my regular commission on this sale.

As I look back on the events of the last three days I am very much impressed with the energy and resourcefulness I employed in bringing this transaction to such a successful conclusion.

Very cordially yours,
ALEXANDER BOTTS.

P. S.—I have been wondering what I ought to do about that extra $1,000 in the bank that seems to be left over. If the Earthworm Company had put $3,000 into this financial operation I would feel that this $1,000 profit belonged to the company. But as long as the company did not do so, I have decided, after long thought, to keep the money myself.

I'm a Hard Boiled Bozo

FARMERS' FRIEND TRACTOR COMPANY
MAKERS OF EARTHWORM TRACTORS
EARTHWORM CITY, ILLINOIS

January 3, 1921.

Mr. Alexander Botts,
Whitestone Hotel,
Chicago, Ill.

DEAR MR. BOTTS: At your earliest convenience we would like you to go to Centerville, Wisconsin, and call on Mr. Edward Beekman, a farmer who lives near that place. Last spring Mr. Beekman bought one of our ten ton Earthworm tractors at six thousand dollars, paying three thousand cash, and giving us his notes for three thousand balance, secured by a chattel mortgage on the tractor.

One of these notes for one thousand dollars came due last September, and in response to our letters requesting payment we have received evasive replies, but no cash.

You will call on Mr. Beekman and demand payment, failing which you are hereby authorized to take possession of the tractor, which you will have shipped back to the factory for overhauling and re-sale, as per our agreement.

Although we do not usually ask our salesmen to undertake collections, we are asking you to do it in this case because we have no one else available at the moment, and we feel sure you will be willing to undertake this job, and will carry it through with your usual energy.

We enclose Mr. Beekman's note and the mortgage.

Very truly,

GILBERT HENDERSON,
Sales Manager.

―――――――――

FARMERS' FRIEND TRACTOR COMPANY
SALESMAN'S DAILY REPORT
Date: January 5, 1921.
Written from: Centerville, Wis.
Written by: Alexander Botts, Salesman.

I received your letter in Chicago yesterday. I have come right up here to Centerville, and I wish to state that I am perfectly willing to tackle this little job of collecting. What it takes to get money out of these lowdown dead beats, I've got. In general I try to cultivate a polite and ingratiating manner, but on a job such as this, I'm a hard boiled bozo. I will go after this Beekman guy like a mad bull, and before I leave I will either have the money or take the tractor away from him.

And it certainly is lucky you sent a guy like me who is not afraid of difficulties, because when I explain the situation up here you will see that any ordinary man would have been helpless.

I suppose when you sit in your swell steam-heated office in Earthworm City and dictate a letter telling me to call on a bird who lives just outside of Centerville, Wisconsin, you think you are asking for something very simple and easy. But you don't know what this country is up here. It is practically a suburb of the North Pole, and yesterday and last night they got one of the biggest blizzards in the memory of man.

When I got off the train this morning—four hours late—I found the town practically covered up except for one little path that had been shoveled from the station across the street to the hotel. The snow seemed to be about up to my neck on the level, and where it was drifted it looked like the pictures of the Himalaya Mountains. It is so cold I don't dare look at a thermometer to find out what it really is.

I followed the little path across to the hotel, and asked the clerk if he knew where Mr. Edward Beekman lived. He replied that Mr. Beekman lived about ten miles south of town on the main road leading to a place called White Creek. But when I asked how I could get there, he said he didn't have the faintest idea.

"When the roads are open," he said, "there is a bus line that runs all the way down to Milwaukee; you can hop a bus at the hotel here and get off right in front of his house. But the busses have been tied up since November, and now you can't even telephone, as the blizzard has broken down the lines."

"Can't I hire a car?" I asked. "Or a horse and wagon?"

At this the clerk let out a loud laugh. "Nobody ever tries to run a car around here in the winter time," he said. "We all put our machines in storage in the fall and don't take them out till spring. Usually the farmers break out the roads with horses after every storm. But there is so much snow this time that it will be several days before you can get out into the country."

"Several days, my eye!" I exclaimed. "I can't wait that long. I am going to find some way to get out there today."

And it gives me great pleasure to report that this remark was no idle boast. I have bought myself—in a store next the hotel—a pair of high grade snow shoes, together with all necessary accessories. Although I had never used these contrivances before, I have—in ten minutes' practicing behind the hotel—discovered that I am a natural born snow shoe artist. I have been told that Mr. Beekman's house is straight south on a direct road, and I figure that if the road is concealed by drifts, I can follow the telephone poles, which ought to be high enough to stick up through the snow. You see I think of everything. And now that I have had dinner at the hotel and practically finished this report, I am all ready and raring to go.

I have given you this very full account of the snowbound situation here, so that you will cheerfully O. K. my expense account, which will on this occasion contain charges for my arctic outfit, consisting of one pair snow hoes, one pair leather moccasins, one fur cap with ear laps, one pair leggins, one pair fur mittens, one Mackinac coat, one pair lumberman's socks, and one suit extra heavy red flannel underwear. By beating down the store keeper, I was able to get the whole business for the very moderate price of $93.49.

Cordially yours,

ALEXANDER BOTTS.

FARMERS' FRIEND TRACTOR COMPANY
SALESMAN'S DAILY REPORT
Date: January 5, 1921, 9 P.M.
Written from: The Beekman Farm, outside Centerville, Wis.
Written by: Alexander Botts.

Well, I followed the telephone poles and I got here. I will not describe my trip in any way except to state that my splendid new clothes kept me comfortably warm, and that the snow shoes are not so good, after all. Even for a born expert like myself, it is impossible to walk in anything like a natural manner with a couple of tennis rackets strapped to the feet. The only thing a guy can do is to waddle along like a duck, and a pretty fat old duck at that. A very fatiguing procedure.

After I had waddled the first mile, I was very tired. After I had waddled the first five miles, I will admit that I was practically all in. But I never thought of turning back. Calling upon every ounce of my will power, I kept bravely on, and just at evening I had covered the entire ten miles and found myself in front of a very pretty little white farm house, set in amongst the snow-covered hills. Behind the house was a large red barn, and in front, sticking up through the snow, was the top of a red gasoline filling station pump.

I tottered up to the door of the house, knocked somewhat feebly, and was admitted by a young lady. Even in my exhausted condition, I could not help noticing that she was what I would call very good looking. She was medium size and slender, but with a gracefully athletic build. She had blue eyes, and beautiful golden hair of about the same color as the very highest grade of light cylinder oil.

As I am a hard boiled bozo, however, I scarcely noticed these points, but came directly to the business in hand.

"I wish to see Mr. Edward Beekman," I said.

"Come right in," she replied, smiling very cordially, "and sit down by the fire. You must be terribly cold. How far have you come?"

"I have come from Centerville," I said.

"You poor thing!" she went on. "What a frightfully long trip. You must be pretty strong and husky, or you never would have made it."

"Yes," I admitted, "that is true." But as flattery such as this has no effect on me, I at once brought the conversation back to the matter in hand. "I wish to see Mr. Edward Beekman," I repeated.

The young lady called upstairs to someone whom she addressed as "Ted," and there shortly appeared a man who was large and powerful, but very young looking—nothing but a kid.

"I want to see the man who owns the Earthworm tractor," I said.

"I guess I'm the one," he replied.

"All right," I said. "My name is Alexander Botts."

"Glad to meet you, Mr. Botts," he remarked. "My name is Edward Beekman, and this is my wife."

I then shook hands with both of them, and I will admit that it is not as easy as you might think to get hard boiled with mere children such as these people seemed to be, especially when they were such nice looking children. However, with me business is always first.

"I represent the Farmers' Friend Tractor Company," I said—"the people who sold you your Earthworm tractor. And I have come to collect the thousand dollars which was due on this machine last September, and which has not yet been paid."

At this the two children looked very much embarrassed, and Mr. Beekman said, "I am sorry, but I just haven't got that much money."

"How much have you got?" I asked, in my practical way.

"Eight hundred dollars."

"Isn't there some way you can raise the other two hundred?"

"I'm afraid not," he replied. "I really need this eight hundred for a lot of overdue local bills; but I would be willing to let you have it if you would trust me till next fall for the rest."

"By the next fall there will be two thousand dollars more due," I reminded him.

"If you would only let me off now, I might be able to pay the whole business by that time."

"I am sorry," I said, talking as hard boiled as I could, "but I have no authority to grant you any such extension. I have the mortgage and your note here in my pocket, and if you cannot pay, I will have to take the tractor."

"What are you going to do," he asked—"drive it back to town tonight?"

"To tell the truth," I replied, "I haven't figured out yet just what I'll do."

"Better spend the night with us," said Mr. Beekman, "and in the morning you can see how the weather looks and decide what to do. I hate like the devil to lose the tractor, but I can't blame you for taking it, so I might as well be a good sport. You can have it any time you want."

After rapidly considering the situation, I came to the conclusion that I did not like the idea of starting out again in all the snow, so I decided to spend the night. Mrs. Beekman soon set out a most excellent supper, that proved she was a swell cook as well as an ornament to the household. And my long waddle through the snow had given me an appetite that permitted me to absorb a really surprising amount of food.

After supper we sat around a large open fire. As the hard boiled business part of my visit had already been completed, and as these people were treating me so much better than I could have expected, I decided to be as agreeable as possible. I entertained them with some of my very best Swedish jokes. And afterward we talked of one thing and another and became very good friends indeed, considering the nature of my visit. By the end of the evening they were calling me "Alex," and I was calling them "Ted" and "Anne," and I had found out how it happened that they were stuck way up here in Wisconsin with a tractor they couldn't pay for.

It seems both of them are just twenty-two years old, and they were born and brought up in Chicago. Ted had been in the army in France, and when he came back he had worked in some office where he had met Anne, who was a stenographer in the same place.

Like lots of other city people, they hated city life and wanted to live in the country and run a farm. They decided to try it. Ted had inherited five thousand dollars from his father, and they spent practically the whole thing in making down payments on the farm and on various pieces of equipment, including the big ten ton Earthworm. And early last spring they threw up their jobs, got married, and came up to their farm.

"How big is your place?" I asked.

"Fifty acres of cultivated fields," said Ted, "and a hundred acres of woods."

"Holy Moses!" I said. "You bought a great big ten ton tractor to cultivate fifty acres! You are a bigger sap than I took you for, Ted. You could plow your whole farm in two days easy, and then you would have that great big expensive machine sitting around idle the rest of the year."

"I know," said Ted. "I hoped I could get work plowing for other farmers, or grading the roads. But all the farmers around here do their own plowing, and the road commissioners are so old fashioned they won't use anything but horses."

"Too bad I wasn't here; I could have talked them into giving you a job," I said. "But probably you are not much of a salesman. Did you know anything about running a tractor when you first bought your machine?"

"I sure did. I ran an artillery model Earthworm when I was in the army. I decided then that an Earthworm was the finest tractor in the world. And maybe that is the real reason I bought one—just for the pleasure of having such swell piece of machinery around."

"I know just how you feel," I said. "The Earthworm is indeed a wonderful machine. But your admiration isn't going to help you pay for it. Haven't you made any money out of your farming?"

"Not much. We've made enough to keep ourselves alive, but we haven't saved a cent. That eight hundred dollars I spoke of is what is left of the five thousand we started with. And we have lots of debts. Besides what we owe on the tractor, we have a five hundred dollar payment on the farm mortgage that is past due. Then there are a good many little bills, and we owe the oil company two hundred dollars."

"What's that for?"

"That was another good idea gone wrong. We thought we could make a lot of money out of all the automobile traffic that goes along this road. But we didn't get our filling station installed until late in the fall, just before the snow came and blocked the road, so we have over five hundred gallons of gasoline and a whole lot of oil on hand, with no chance of selling it until spring."

As I am rather quick on business matters, I was beginning to suspect that Ted's financial situation was not as sound as might be desired. "It seems to me," I said length, "that you are in rather bad shape."

"I'm afraid we are," said Ted. "You are going to take the tractor away, and I suppose they will foreclose the farm mortgage in the spring. Then Anne and I will have to go back to Chicago, and I'll probably have to work about five years in some filthy office before we can save enough to come back here and try again."

"So you aren't completely discouraged with farming?"

"I should say not," spoke up Anne. "We've been happier here than ever before in our lives. We are both crazy about the country, and we think it is the only place to bring up children. You see, we hope—that is, we think—I mean, we expect that next summer we will have—that is, there will be an addition—there will be three of us."

I have put in all the above dashes to indicate hesitation so you can see that Anne is really a very nice, old-fashioned kind of girl, and is properly somewhat reluctant to discuss these delicate subjects—even with such a friend of the family as I have become.

After I had congratulated them on the coming event, I tactfully changed the subject by asking if I could see the tractor.

"Sure," said Ted. "Old Betsey—that's what we have christened her—is right out in the barn." He lit a lantern and Anne and I followed him out.

I was pleased to see that Betsey was in fine condition—as bright and shiny as the day she left the factory. Ted and Anne both seemed very proud of her, and it filled me with sorrow to think that I was about to take this beautiful machine away from these two excellent people. After we had finished looking over the tractor, we returned to the house and Anne showed me up to my room. Since then I have been writing this report, which I will mail as soon as I get a chance.

I have made a very full report of the situation here you can see just what sort of a problem I am up against. And I wish to point out that you did very well in sending a hard boiled bozo like myself to handle things. If you had sent a soft hearted, sentimental guy, he would have been so overcome at seeing such nice young people as Ted and Anne in such a hard fix, that he would have let them hang onto their tractor whether they paid for it or not. This would have been very wrong, as it would have made them into dead beats, and would have left the company holding the sack.

On the other hand, I must admit that I rather hate to take the tractor away. I always try to look at things from all points of view, and it occurs to me that it is not good for the reputation of the Farmers' Friend Tractor Company to have it know that an Earthworm owner had gone busted because he could not find enough profitable work for his machine to do. The problem as I see it is to find some way by which the Beekmans can get hold of enough money to climb out of their financial hole and keep their tractor. At present it does not look as if there was any way to do this. But if there is a way, you may be sure that Alexander Botts will find it.

I will now go to bed, and while I am asleep I will let my subconscious mind tackle this problem. And tomorrow morning when I am rested and refreshed from my long waddle through the snow, it is my intention to start things moving around here, and stir things up in such a way as to get some real results.

Very truly yours,
ALEXANDER BOTTS.

FARMERS' FRIEND TRACTOR COMPANY
SALESMAN'S DAILY REPORT
Date: January 6, 1921, 9 P.M.
Written from: The Beekman Farm.
Written by: Alexander Botts.

It gives me great pleasure to report that I have put in a very busy day, and have made a good start toward bring matters to a satisfactory conclusion.

You will remember that last night the prospects looked very gloomy indeed. Here were these two excellent young people on the way to losing their tractor and their farm. Here was the entire countryside presenting the most disheartening picture: all the roads blocked with snow, all the automobiles put up for the winter, and all the merchants of Centerville so snowbound that they had practically no business at all. Everything seemed all wrong.

But when I sprang from my bed bright and early this morning, my heart was full of joy and hope. For, just like an inspiration, there had come into my mind a scheme for doing away with all this sorrow and grief.

The scheme was simple but magnificent. The chief thing that the inhabitants of this benighted land need is to have the snow plowed off their roads. The chief thing that these splendid Beekman children need is a good paying job for their tractor. The answer is self evident.

As soon as I could get into my clothes I rushed downstairs.

"Ted!" I yelled. "It is all settled. We are going into the snow-plowing business."

"How do you mean?" he asked.

"We are going to put a snowplow on old Betsey's nose, and we are going to plow the roads, and we will make all kinds of money."

"Who is going to pay us?"

"The county road commissioners."

"I doubt if they will," said Ted. "I made a proposition to them last fall that I would keep the roads cleared for them this winter. But they said it wouldn't be practical, they never had done it, and they didn't intend to do it."

"That's what they think now," I said. "But wait till they see what sort of work we can do. We will plow the main road all the way from Centerville to this town of White Creek free of charge. And when they see how good it is they will give us a regular job."

"I tried to talk them into it last fall," said Ted, "but they are too stubborn and set in their ways."

"Wait till I get after them," I said. "With a sample of our work to show them and a flow of language such as I have got, they will soon be eating out of our hand."

"I'm not so sure about that," said Ted, "but I would just as soon try."

So, immediately after an excellent breakfast—which proved once more that Anne is a swell cook—I started things moving in my usual energetic fashion. With Ted and Anne to help me, I gathered together a lot of timbers and planks from around the barn. Then we all worked fast and furious, and by noon we had a rough, but large and imposing locomotive-type snowplow rigged up on the front of old Betsey. We filled the old lady up with gas and oil from the filling station, after which we had lunch. As I said before, this little girl Anne certainly understands the art of cooking.

After lunch, Ted cranked up, and we both climbed aboard and started. The grousers on the tracks gave us splendid traction, and as Ted had taken very good care of the motor we had all the power we needed. We nosed our way through a tremendous drift in front of the barn, swung out into the road, and opened her up wide, while Anne waved encouragement from the

front porch. The snowplow worked to perfection—great mountains of snow rolled off to the right and left—and with the motor
roaring like an airplane we moved majestically forward at three
miles an hour in the direction of White Creek.

As this was strictly a money making venture, I was deter-
mined to pick up as much on the side as I could. Consequently I
stopped opposite the first farm house I came to and floundered
through the drifts up to the door. An old gent with a beard answered my knock, and I asked him if he would like to have his
driveway plowed back as far as the barn.

"The main road is going to be plowed all the way from
Centerville to White Creek," I explained, "and if you have your
driveway plowed also you can take your car out and drive to town
just as easy as if it was summer time."

"It's a fine idea," said the old, gent. "Go ahead and plow her
out."

"The charges," I said, "will be ten dollars. Just slip me the
cash, and the work will be done in the twinkling of an eye."

"'Ten dollars!" said the old gent. "I should say not. I'd rather
shovel it myself."

"Very well," I said. "Good bye."

The old gent shut the door, and I returned to the tractor. As
I am quick at sizing up a situation, I soon came to the conclusion that ten dollars was perhaps a little too much to ask. Consequently I quoted a price of five smackers at the next farm
house. But even this seemed to be more than they cared to pay.
So at successive houses I dropped down to four, three, two, and
finally one dollar. At this last price, I picked up jobs from about
half the people interviewed.

This stopping at each house delayed us a good deal, so it
was five o'clock in the afternoon, and already getting dark, when
we arrived at White Creek. Accordingly, after I had dropped my
yesterday's report into a mail box, we turned around, put the

machine in high, and came clattering back along that beautifully plowed road as fast as we could—arriving at the Beekman
place at about eight o'clock.

I had no use for my snow shoes on this trip, but—as the
weather was distinctly cool—my newly purchased arctic garments, including the red flannels, were all that saved me from
freezing to death. I mention this fact so that you may recognize
my wisdom in buying these articles, and so that it will be easy
for you to O. K. the expense account on which I have charged
them.

Upon arriving at the house we were warmly welcomed by
Anne. That girl has one of the most attractive smiles I have ever
seen, and she also puts out a wonderful meal of victuals.

On counting up the money we had made by plowing driveways, I found we had fifteen dollars—just about enough to pay
for the gas and oil.

"But we haven't really made expenses," I said. "We ought to
figure about ten dollars a day for interest and depreciation on
the machine, and quite a bit more than that to pay us for our
valuable time."

"Yes," said Ted. "Considering that this machine will do the
work of eighteen or twenty horses, we ought to get at least fifty
dollars a day. And at that price we would really be making
money."

"Right you are," I said, "and I figure that the amount of plowing we can do in a day ought to be worth at least a hundred dollars a day to the inhabitants of this snow-infested region. Consequently," I went on, "we will clear the road to Centerville
tomorrow, and we will put it up to the county commissioners
that it is their duty to pay us that much for our services. One
hundred dollars a day, or, if they prefer, three dollars and a half
a running mile."

"I hope you can convince them," said Ted.

"Trust me," I replied. "I am one of the best little old talkers in the whole United States. As a persuader, I am good, and I admit it myself."

With these words I came up to my room, and now that I have finished my daily report I will retire with high hopes for the morrow.

Yours enthusiastically,
ALEXANDER BOTTS.

———————————

FARMERS' FRIEND TRACTOR COMPANY
SALESMAN'S DAILY REPORT
Date: January 7, 1921, 1 P.M.
Written from: Centerville Hotel, Centerville, Wis.
Written by: Alexander Botts.

It gives me great pleasure to report that the day's activities are proceeding in an unusually auspicious manner. Bright and early, after a really swell breakfast, Ted and I went out and twisted Betsey's tail. As was to be expected, she started up with a beautiful roar. Waving good bye to Anne, we swung out into the road and headed for Centerville. On the way we collected twenty dollars for plowing out driveways, arriving in town at about eleven o'clock.

On this trip I did the driving myself, and it is lucky that this was the case, as we very nearly had a serious accident which was only averted by my coolness and skill. The near-accident was caused by the fact that the weather was not as cold as yesterday, so that—after we had driven about a mile—my arctic garments began to be a little I warm. This warmth, in conjunction with the somewhat rough, woolly texture of my red flannels, produced a condition which made it absolutely necessary for me to twist about in my seat and scratch various parts of my person.

While I was reaching with my left hand for a point on my right shoulder blade, and while as a consequence my eyes wandered momentarily from the road, there came sudden, sickening crash. Quick as a wink I grabbed the levers, stopped the tractor, and then backed up a few yards. A single glance of my practiced eye told me what had occurred: the machine had veered to the side, and had run into the railing of a concrete bridge over which we chanced to be passing at the time. Had I been a less skillful driver, or had I waited one-tenth of a second more before stopping, we would have gone right on through the railing and dropped to the frozen surface of a street twenty feet below. As it was, I escaped with no damage at all to the tractor or the sturdy plow, and without knocking off more than about fifteen feet of the concrete railing.

When we got to Centerville we were most fortunate in finding the county road commissioners gathered at their regular monthly meeting. I at once introduced myself, explained what I had been doing, and persuaded them all to come out and look at the tractor and the results of the plowing. I then brought them back to the Court House and offered to plow as many of the county roads as they wanted for a flat price of one hundred dollars a day or three dollars and a half a running mile.

As they seemed a little hesitant, I started in and made one of the finest orations I have ever put across. I compared the paltry three dollars and a half that I would charge with the hundreds of dollars it would cost to shovel a mile of road through these drifts by hand. I told them that a plowed road would dry out so quickly in the spring and be in such good condition that the plowing would pay for itself ten times over by saving most of the spring road scraping. I pointed out the tremendous loss suffered by the merchants of the town through the inability of the farmers to come in and do their trading when the roads were impassable.

And after going into these and other economic aspects of the case with great thoroughness, I concluded with a tremendous emotional appeal on sentimental and humanitarian grounds. In the choicest English at my command, and with many graceful gestures, I pictured the case of a beautiful child taken suddenly ill in a farm house far out on one of those snow-blocked roads. I pictured the weeping mother, and the desperate attempts of the father to telephone the doctor. In vain! For the telephone wires are down, and owing to the condition of the roads it, is impossible to repair them. Furthermore, even if a message could be sent to town, the doctor would not be able to make his way out to the farm through the terrific drifts that block the way. I then pictured the heroic father rushing out into the storm and the night to seek help in this great emergency. But again in vain! For the father freezes to death in a great snow drift, while his beloved little one perishes for lack of proper medical attention.

"But if the roads had been plowed," I said, "the father could have telephoned, the doctor could have sped out in high-powered car, and two precious lives would have been saved."

As I finished this recital I was practically in tears, and I noticed that several of the commissioners were using their handkerchiefs. The chairman said he was much impressed, and requested me to withdraw while they deliberated.

I accordingly took Ted over to the Centerville Hotel, where we have had a dinner that was not so good, and where I have been writing this report. As it is now mail time I will close, and in my next communication I expect to report that Mr. Ted Beekman has started to make so much money that we need have no further worry about the payment of his notes. And thus will come to a close another brilliant chapter in the record of my services to The Farmers' Friend Tractor Company.

Cordially yours,
ALEXANDER BOTTS.

FARMERS' FRIEND TRACTOR COMPANY
SALESMAN'S DAILY REPORT
Date: January 7, 1921, 9 P.M.
Written from: The Beekman Farm.
Written by: Alexander Botts.

It gives me great pain to report that a train of distressing circumstances entirely outside my control has for the moment delayed my activities in this region. I will explain exactly what
has occurred so that you can appreciate what I am up against
and see that the present regrettable situation is not in any way
my fault.

The first unfortunate incident was the almost incredible
action of the road commissioners. You will scarcely believe me
when I tell you this, but it is nevertheless a fact that these men—
after listening to my masterly address, which had them all practically in tears—proceeded to put away their handkerchiefs and
unanimously vote against spending any of the county money
on such an unheard-of activity as plowing the roads.

By the time Ted and I called at the Court House, the commissioners had already adjourned and gone home, and there was
nobody there except the County Clerk, who told us this shock-
ing news. He further informed us that the commissioners had
in some way been informed that we had knocked off fifteen feet
of railing from the bridge outside of town. And they had directed
the County Clerk to hand Ted a bill for two hundred dollars to
cover the cost of repairs. This last unkindest cut of all was almost more than I could bear. But I never faltered. I decided to
save what I could from the wreck of our lost hopes.

"Let us drive Betsey back to your house," I said. "Then you
can give me that eight hundred dollars before these worthless
commissioners get hold of any of it, and I will see that you are
allowed to keep your tractor till spring. As soon as the weather
opens up you may be able to get enough work for the machine to
pay the rest you owe. It is a slender hope, but all we have."

Ted at once agreed to this proposition, so we drove back to the farm, where Anne greeted us with a glad, happy smile, and reported that the filling station had been doing a rushing business. Apparently the news that we had cleared the road had spread rapidly; people had gotten out their cars; the motor bus had started running; and Anne had sold twenty-eight dollars' worth of gasoline and oil.

But our joy of this news was short lived, for Anne proceeded to tell us that there had been other visitors besides the customers for gasoline. The man who owns the mortgage on the farm had had so little sense of decency that he had actually taken advantage of our snowplowing and come out in his flivver to demand a payment of five hundred dollars which was a month overdue. Furthermore, the manager of the oil company had had the bad taste to appear with a demand for two hundred dollars due him since last fall for gas and oil. And poor Anne, although she is a splendid girl, a swell cook, a dutiful wife, and (will be next summer) a loving mother, seems to have no business sense at all. She had actually signed checks to pay both these bids, so that eight hundred dollars bank balance was now reduced to one hundred.

This was a stunning blow, but I could not very well bawl out Anne about it, as I had already refused this eight hundred dollars when I first came, on the ground that I would take a thousand or nothing. And Anne, in her innocence, had supposed that I really meant it.

The whole deplorable incident proves what I have always contended—that there ought to be a law against this insidious modern practice of husbands keeping their money in a joint account and letting their wives have a check book.

Ted offered me the remaining hundred and remarked that if I wanted it I had better take it at once as there would probably be other bill collectors after it first thing in the morning. I said

I would think it over. After carefully pondering the situation, however, I finally came to the conclusion that it would be useless for me to take this paltry hundred berries. If these people could not even make a decent start toward paying for their tractor the most merciful course would be to end the agony as soon as possible and take the machine away from them. But as it was getting late, and as there was no way get back to town, I resolved to take no action for the moment. I accordingly partook of an excellent supper hiding my dreary thoughts under a jovial exterior, and cheering up poor old Ted and Anne with an entirely new bunch of Swedish wise cracks.

I have now come up to my room, where I have been writing this report. And tomorrow morning, although hate to do it worse than anything I have ever done in my life, I will take possession of that tractor like the hard boiled bozo that I am.

Yours,
ALEXANDER BOTTS.

FARMERS FRIEND TRACTOR COMPANY
SALESMAN'S DAILY REPORT
Date: January 8, 1921.
Written from: The Beekman Farm.
Written by: Alexander Botts.

Well, I have been hard boiled. I have carried this matter through to a conclusion, and I am leaving for Chicago on the noon train. When I relate exactly what occurred, you will see that I have done my duty, and done it pretty damn well, if I do say so myself.

Bright and early this morning I went down stairs all ready to announce that I was taking the tractor away. But Ted and Anne greeted me so cordially that I decided it would be better to wait until after breakfast. And by the time I had finished this meal—

which was as usual most excellently cooked—I felt in such a kindly frame of mind that I decided to wait a little longer. Consequently, leaving Ted and Anne in the kitchen, I walked into the front parlor and spent about five minutes scowling at myself in a mirror so as to get worked up into a mean state of mind.

About the time I had completed this exercise and gotten myself all ready for some real dirty work, but before I had had a chance to go back and start in on Ted and Anne, I chanced to glance through the window. A luxurious motor car had stopped just outside, and a large and important-looking man in a tremendous, expensive fur coat was coming up to the house. I promptly opened the door and he asked to see Mr. Edward Beekman. As I was—as I have explained—in a hostile frame of mind, I lost no time in telling him exactly what I thought of him.

"You dirty bill collectors make me sick and tired," I said. "Why can't you leave these poor people alone? Isn't it enough that you are already lousy with wealth? Look at your elegant car! Look at your disgustingly expensive coat! Think of the money you have probably extorted from widows and orphans! Then think of these two splendid young people you are hounding, and if there is a spark of decency left within you, your fat face will be suffused with a blush of shame!"

I have repeated exactly what I said, so that you can see I am still one of the best talkers in your whole organization—although in this particular instance it appears that I did not know what I was talking about.

The man in the fur coat appeared somewhat taken aback. "Let me explain," he said. "Let me explain."

"Very well," I replied, "but make it snappy."

"My name is George Westerville," he said. "I am the president of the Central Wisconsin Autobus Company, and I wish to hire Mr. Beekman to do some snow plowing for me."

"Step inside, Mr. Westerville," I said.

He entered and took the chair I offered. Ted and Anne came in from the kitchen at this moment, but I motioned them to keep out of the discussion.

"I am Mr. Beekman's partner, Mr. Westerville," I said, "and I am the guy you talk business with."

I sat down, and he explained that he ran five hundred miles of bus lines, covering a good portion of the state, and that he suffered tremendous losses when the roads were blocked. The snow in Wisconsin, he said, was too heavy for horse drawn plows, and for plows on trucks and busses. He had never heard of the Earthworm tractor before, but since he had seen the work we had done he was convinced it was the only thing for him. He had tried to get the state and county commissioners to buy some of the machines, but he had had no luck, so he had decided it would pay him to do the plowing himself.

He had tried to buy an Earthworm, but the dealer in Chicago had wired that he couldn't promise delivery for several weeks. He wanted action at once—he was losing money every day—and he wanted to buy Mr. Beekman's tractor or else hire him to plow out the roads.

While Mr. Westerville was explaining these things I was watching him very narrowly, and as I am a wonderful judge of men I detected that my aggressive greeting had forced him into a somewhat apologetic frame mind. His manner betrayed that he actually thought we would be doing him a great favor to work for him. I at once decided that it would be just as easy—now that I had started the day as a hard boiled bozo—to keep on the same way. I recalled the words of General Hines in the Battle of the Argonne: "Now is the time to strike and strike hard."

"I am sorry, Mr. Westerville," I said coldly, "but the tractor is not for sale. Furthermore, we have taken a contract to haul logs for The Eureka Wooden Box, Barrel, Kitchen Cabinet, and Furniture Manufacturing Corporation up in the northern part of the state. If we are behind hand in this work we will forfeit a bond of thousand dollars which we have posted with them. So that is that. Kindly close the door as you go out."

(NOTE: Perhaps I should explain that, as far as I know, there is no such company as The Eureka Wooden Box, Barrel, Kitchen Cabinet, and Furniture Manufacturing Corporation. But I thought that as long as I was evolving a name, it might as well be a good one.)

For a moment I was afraid that Mr. Westerville might actually go out—closing the door as I had suggested—but such was not the case. He became even more apologetic and pleading than before. He stated that he absolutely MUST have this plowing done.

But, as I contemplated that elegant fur coat, and figured on the money it must have cost, I became more and more disagreeable. And when I finally yielded, I wrote out and made him sign one of the prettiest little contracts I have ever seen.

It provided that Ted was to hire extra operators and run three shifts, so that he could plow day and night and get over the whole five hundred miles of bus lines in something like a week. Payment was to be made every Saturday night at the rate of six dollars a running mile—which was not so bad in view of the fact that the day before we would have been glad to get three and a half from the county commissioners. Furthermore, the contract was to be in force two years—Ted to plow the roads after every snowfall exceeding six inches in depth, U. S. Weather' Bureau figures. And in addition to all other payments, Mr. Westerville was to give us at once his check for one thousand dollars as a bonus to cover the bond to The Eureka Wooden Box, Barrel, Kitchen Cabinet, and Furniture Manufacturing Corporation.

When Mr. Westerville read this contract, he let out a faint groan. But I pointed out that his increased profits would more than cover his payments to us; and I further cheered him up by telling him that out of pure generosity we wouldn't charge him anything for the thirty miles we had plowed already—and he finally signed the contract and the thousand dollar check like a man.

After he had gone, Ted endorsed the check over to me, so he is now all paid up to date. As he will take in about three thousand dollars on this first plowing; as there will undoubtedly be other snow storms both this year and next; and as the gasoline filling station is now doing a brisk business, he will have no trouble in paying the two thousand dollars which he still owes on old Betsey.

It is now time to leave for the railroad station, so I will not be able to go into any greater detail regarding the energy and resourcefulness I have displayed in handling this little collection affair. In conclusion I wish to state that I am leaving these two splendid young people in the best of good spirits, and I may add that they have quietly informed me that they hope it will be a boy so that it can bear the brave name of Alexander Botts Beekman.

Proudly yours,
ALEXANDER BOTTS.

Sandy Inlet

FARMERS' FRIEND TRACTOR COMPANY
MAKERS OF EARTHWORM TRACTORS
EARTHWORM CITY, ILLINOIS

June 27, 1925.

Mr. Alexander Botts,
Hotel McAlpin,
New York City.

DEAR MR. BOTTS: On your forthcoming trip into New England we want you to call on Mr. Caleb R. Hubbard, at Hubbardston, Maine. He has just written us that he is thinking of buying a tractor, and we will count on you to get his order for an Earthworm.

   If he wants to see a machine in action, you can take him over to Castle Harbor, ten miles from Hubbardston, where our records show that the Maine State Highway Department has a ten ton Earthworm at work on the roads.

Very sincerely,

GILBERT HENDERSON,

Sales Manager.

FARMERS' FRIEND TRACTOR COMPANY
SALESMAN'S DAILY REPORT
Date: Wednesday, July 1, 1925. 9 P.M.
Written from: Hubbardston Hotel, Hubbardston, Maine.
Written by: Alexander Botts, Salesman.

I arrived here early this afternoon. And I am up against a tough proposition. I have had competition before from other makes of tractors and from horses and mules, but this time I have to compete with boats and airplanes.

However, I am going swell. I am getting ready to put on such a wow of a demonstration that it wouldn't make any difference if I was competing against the whole British Navy and a fleet of all-metal dirigibles besides. When I explain what I am going to do you will realize that I am getting better and better all the time.

I hopped off the train at one this afternoon. I checked in at the Hubbardston Hotel, ate lunch, and called on Mr. Hubbard a little before two. Mr. Hubbard turned out to be very intelligent and businesslike, and explained at once what he wanted.

"I own a tract of land on the seashore about ten miles north of here," he said. "At the present time I have a small hotel there called the Seaside Inn. It has been so successful that I am going to build a much larger hotel—which means that I will have to take over a whole lot of building material such as lumber, cement, plumbing supplies, and so forth."

"When it comes to hauling freight," I said, "the Earthworm tractor can't be beat. If it is only ten miles we could make two or three trips a day."

"The trouble," Mr. Hubbard went on, "is that the place is very inaccessible. If you will step over here I will show you what I mean."

He led me across the room and pointed to a map which hung on the wall. "Here is Hubbardston," he said, "where we are now. On the sea coast just north of town is Hubbard's Point, which is about five miles wide, and which extends eastward out into the sea about twenty miles."

"Exactly," I said.

"Just north of Hubbard's Point," he continued, "is Sandy Inlet, which is about five miles wide at the mouth, and which extends inland to the west about twenty miles. The Seaside Inn is right here—on a rocky hill just to the north of the mouth of Sandy Inlet. Is that clear?"

"I follow you exactly," I said.

"The inn," Mr. Hubbard went on, "is thus only ten miles north of here as the crow flies, but it is very hard to reach. If you go by sea you have to sail out around the point. If you go by land you have to circle around the inlet. Of course I could go by air, and there is a man in town now trying to sell me a small airplane. I may buy it. I have a field over there big enough to land on, and I could transport the guests of the inn by air very nicely."

"But you couldn't carry much freight on a small plane," I said.

"No," he admitted, "I couldn't."

"How have you managed in the past?" I asked.

"We've been using a rented motor boat," he said. "That means we have to take a fifty-mile trip way out around the end of Hubbard's Point. It takes almost all day. We can't use a large motor boat because we don't have a deep-water landing place at the inn. So, if we have to transport all our building materials on a small motor boat it will be a very slow and a very expensive process. And whenever there is a storm we can't make the trip at all."

"I see," I said. "You want to haul the stuff overland. Is there a road?"

"There is a good road," said Mr. Hubbard, "which leads five miles across the base of Hubbard's Point to the south shore of Sandy Inlet. From there you can see Seaside Inn. It's only five miles farther on, but it's on the other side of the inlet, and to get there by land you have to take a fifty-mile drive on very poor wood roads clear around the inlet."

"Why not haul your stuff across the point by tractor," I suggested, "and then take it over the inlet by boat?"

"The inlet is full of rocks," said Mr. Hubbard. "The tide sweeps in and out at about ten miles an hour, and at low tide it's practically dry—nothing but an expanse of mud and sand, with here and there a bunch of rocks. So it's a bad place for boats.

But I thought perhaps we could drive straight across with one of your tractors."

"What!" I said. "With that water running in and out at fearful speed?"

"We would go over when the tide is out," said Mr. Hubbard. "At each low tide we have at least four hours when the sand flats are uncovered. Of course the sand is wet and pretty soft in places. But I have walked out a mile or two at low tide and the sand is solid enough to bear the weight of a man. So if your tractor can run on fairly soft ground, if it can pull a reasonable load in a wagon behind it, if it can make the five miles in less than four hours, and if it is reliable and won't break down and get caught by the tide, I think it will be just the machine I need."

"Mr. Hubbard," I said, "your troubles are over!" And at once I explained to him just exactly how good the Earthworm tractor is, and how it would fulfill all of his requirements. I got out my order blanks, and I got out my fountain pen. But unfortunately Mr. Hubbard is a very skeptical Yankee. He absolutely demanded a demonstration before he would do business.

"All right, Mr. Hubbard," I said; "if you want a demonstration, you'll have a demonstration."

I hurried back to the hotel. I hired an automobile. I drove across the base of Hubbard's Point to the south shore of Sandy Inlet. Fortunately, it was low tide, and I was able to walk out and inspect the sand. It was plenty solid enough for an Earthworm tractor and a wagon.

On the shore was a building with a sign, "Down East Canning Company," and out in front on the sand were a lot of men digging clams and taking them into the factory to be canned. These men pointed out the Seaside Inn—a mere speck of a building on the wooded shore far away to the north over the flats.

It looked like a cinch to haul a load over to the inn. An Earthworm tractor, making three miles an hour, could cross in less than two hours. And the tide stayed out for four hours.

Immediately I drove my hired automobile back to town and then ten miles down the coast to Castle Harbor, where I found the State Highway Department's ten ton Earthworm tractor pulling a twelve-foot blade grader along the road. The tractor was in charge of an elderly guy with a walrus mustache by the name of Andy Meiklejohn. After a long discussion Andy agreed to drive the tractor to Hubbardston early tomorrow morning and work for me one or more days at a flat price of thirty-five dollars a day. Whether the State Highway Department will get this thirty-five per, or whether Andy will knock it down for himself, I do not know. And I don't know that I care.

After arranging for the tractor I went back and called on Mr. Hubbard.

"Mr. Hubbard," I said, "I have just got hold of an Earthworm tractor. I am going to drive it across the sands of Sandy Inlet tomorrow. I want you to have a wagon loaded up with at least five tons of building material for me to drag along. And I hope you can come yourself."

"Fine!" said Mr. Hubbard. "I'll have them load up a wagon this afternoon at the lumber yard. But I can't go with you myself. I have arranged to fly to the inn day after tomorrow morning with the man who is trying to sell me the airplane."

"I will probably see you over there then," I said. "Where can I get an exact time-table of the tides?"

"You had better see Captain Dobbs. He owns the motor boat which I have been using for trips to the inn. He knows more about the tides in Sandy Inlet than anybody else in town."

"Thanks," I said.

I found Captain Dobbs down on the water front, shining up the brass on his motor boat. I explained exactly what I was going to do, and he told me the morning low tide would be from five thirty to ten thirty, and the afternoon low tide from six until ten. As the morning tide is pretty early, I have decided to go in the afternoon.

I thanked Captain Dobbs, and came back to the hotel, arriving just in time for supper. After supper, while sitting on the porch of the hotel, I got to talking with a gentleman from New York who had arrived on the afternoon train. He was a little guy, with a timid and somewhat harassed look on his face. And he said that he and a party of five others were going over to the Seaside Inn tomorrow.

"The inn has a wonderful location," he said, "between the primeval forest and the sea."

"But it's a hell of a place to get to," I said.

"Yes," he agreed. "The women in my party were so seasick in that little motor boat last year, that they almost refused to come this year."

"You don't have to go by motor boat any more," I said. I then explained how I was going over by tractor, and suggested that he and his friends ride along on the wagon. The gentleman from New York at once went up stairs to consult with the rest of his party, and soon returned, saying that they would accept my invitation with the greatest pleasure. I warned him that the wagon would not be luxurious, but he said anything would be better than bobbing along all day in a sickening little motor boat. So it was agreed that we would all meet tomorrow afternoon a little after four.

Thus you see that I have arranged a splendid demonstration. As usual, I am doing more than anyone could have asked or expected. Not only am I going to show Mr. Hubbard that the Earthworm tractor is the best means of hauling freight over to his inn, but I am also going to take a load of his hotel guests and thus prove to him that the Earthworm is the best means of transporting passengers.

By tomorrow night, I expect to have Mr. Hubbard's order.

Very sincerely,

ALEXANDER BOTTS.

FARMERS' FRIEND TRACTOR COMPANY
SALESMAN'S DAILY REPORT
Date: Friday, July 3, 1925.
Written from: Hubbardston, Maine.
Written by: Alexander Botts.

I did not send you any report yesterday because I was too busy. And when I say busy that is exactly what I mean. After I tell you what has happened you will see that I have handled everything in my usual competent and efficient manner. And it was only due to treachery of the basest sort from a quarter whence no one would have suspected it that the situation today is not as bright as might be desired.

Yesterday morning everything started out very propitiously. The weather was fair, sunny, and perfect. At about nine o'clock Andy rolled up to the hotel in his ten ton Earthworm. As I am very careful and thorough about everything, I had him drive around to Smith's garage where the two of us spent several hours greasing the machine, changing the crank-case oil, filling up with gasoline and water, and checking over the distributor, the breaker-points, the valve timing, and everything else we could think of. The tractor had evidently been given very good care, and by the time we had checked it all over it was as near perfect as a machine could be.

After a late lunch we drove over to the lumber yard and hooked onto Mr. Hubbard's wagon. It was loaded with a lot of heavy planks and timbers, on top of which were tied a number of kegs of nails, a lot of picks and shovels and other tools, and a big road plow. We drove onto the lumber yard scales and found that our load weighed a little over four tons including the wagon—not much for a ten ton tractor, but all right for a trial trip over unknown ground.

When we got to the hotel, the gentleman from New York was waiting for us with the other members of his party—whom I had not seen up to this time. It turned out they were all women. One of them was good looking. The other four were very large and imposing. By way of baggage, they had four trunks, eighteen suit cases, a lot of bundles, blankets, sweaters, coats, umbrellas, one dog, one canary bird in a gilded cage, and a large box of fireworks intended—I suppose—for the approaching Fourth of July. Fortunately there were no parrots, cats, goldfish, or monkeys.

As the four important females swarmed about the wagon, I began to understand that harassed look on the face of the little gentleman from New York. All four of them began telling him where to put the suit cases and other junk, where to have the hotel porter put the trunks, where they themselves wanted to sit, and how everything was to be done. As they all had different ideas, and as the gentleman from New York was trying to please everybody, he was soon in a completely dazed condition.

Accordingly, I took charge of things myself. I had Andy open up the throttle so that the tractor motor—which had been idling quietly—started up with such a roar that the ladies' conversation was completely drowned out. Then I had Andy shut down the throttle very quick, and before the ladies could start up again I told them with brutal directness that unless they kept quiet they would have to travel by motor boat. They kept quiet.

And in my usual decisive manner I directed the loading of the extra cargo. There was room for most of the smaller bundles in the grouser box of the tractor. The hotel porter got some extra ropes and we lashed the trunks and suit cases on top of the lumber behind the plow and the other junk. Then I had the four large females and the gentleman from New York sit on the suit cases, using the blankets and sweaters as cushions. As soon as they were settled I tossed them the dog and the bird cage.

This left only the fifth lady—the good-looking one—who all this time had been standing around very modestly without attempting to boss anybody. As a reward for this good conduct I allowed her to ride on the wide, comfortable seat of the tractor with me and Andy.

(NOTE: I have described my handling of this party from New York in order that you may see that I am more than a mere salesman. I am an executive. And it would be a good thing to remember this in case there should ever be a vacancy in some of the higher executive positions in the company.)

By the time we were ready to start, the four large ladies on the wagon had begun to chatter once more. They wanted to know how long the trip would take, and what they could do if it rained, and was the wagon perfectly safe, and so on.

"All right, Andy," I said, "let's go."

Andy stepped on the gas, the motor let out a splendid roar, and we rolled off up the street. And that was the last I heard from the four important ladies for some time.

The noise of the motor, however, was not so loud as to drown out all conversation on the seat of the tractor. And I learned from the young lady beside me that her name was Miss Mabel Cortlandt. She was the niece of the gentleman from New York. The four imposing females were her aunts.

The tractor ran beautifully, and we arrived at the canning factory on the south shore of Sandy Inlet a few minutes after six o'clock—just as I had planned. The tide was out—just as Captain Dobbs had said it would be—and Andy drove straight out onto the vast expanse of slimy sand that stretched away toward the wooded shore line and the Seaside Inn, five miles to the north.

I was delighted to observe that the tractor hardly sank in at all. The wagon wheels cut into the soft sand to some extent, but we had a light load—even though it included the four heavyweight ladies—and we moved along as nice as anyone could wish.

We passed very close to a bunch of clam diggers from the factory. They looked at us as if they thought we were crazy, and shouted and waved for us to stop—but we had no time to bother with them. And soon they were left far behind.

As I am always polite and aim to make a good impression on everyone, whether they are prospective purchasers of tractors or not, I started in and explained the advantages of the Earthworm to Miss Mabel Cortlandt. And after I had touched on all the high points of this subject, I began to point out the beauties of the sunset. The orb of day was fast going down on our left, lighting up the water-soaked sands far up the inlet with a beautiful golden glow. It reminded me of a song I had once learned, and at once I began to sing it: "Out on the Deep when the Sun Is Low." But just as I started, Andy stopped the tractor.

"What time did you say the tide was due to come in?" he asked.

"Ten o'clock," I said. "Why?"

"Look over there," he said. He pointed toward the east. The flat sands stretched out white and bare.

"You see that black line about a mile or so away?" he asked.

"Yes," I said. "It looks to me like the edge of the water."

"It is the edge of the water," said Andy, "and what's more it's moving toward us all the time. The tide is coming in."

"That's impossible," I said. "Captain Dobbs told me the tide wouldn't come in until ten o'clock."

"And who is Captain Dobbs?" asked Andy.

"He is the man," I said, "who owns the motor boat that Mr. Hubbard hires to make trips over to the Seaside Inn. He is supposed to know more about the tides in Sandy Inlet than anybody else in Hubbardston."

We sat still for a minute more and watched that black line. It was getting nearer, and it was getting nearer fast. Finally, Miss Mabel Cortlandt spoke up.

"This Captain Dobbs probably knows a lot about the tides," she said, "but that isn't all he knows."

"All right," I said, "what else does he know?"

"He knows that if you get across here with this tractor his job with the motor boat will be gone. So he might have decided that he didn't want you to get across."

"Why, the dirty bum!" I said. "You don't suppose he would really act as low down as that!"

"I don't know," said Andy, "but if you ask me, I would say we had better turn around and head back toward that canning factory. We're only about a third of the way across, and if we hurry we maybe able to get back before we're swamped."

I took another look at the black line of water. It was now less than half a mile away and it was coming fast. By this time the four ladies on the lumber wagon had noticed it too. They were waving their arms and pointing at it and yelling at me.

"All right," I said to Andy, "let's turn around and go back."

Andy started up, made a wide swing over the sand and headed for the canning factory, which was on the nearest high ground in sight.

All this time the dark line of water was coming on with incredible speed. Before we had gone a hundred feet it had reached us. A half a minute later it was way beyond us, racing up the inlet toward the setting sun. Andy put on all the speed he could and the tractor and the wagon went splashing along in swiftly flowing inch-deep water. In almost no time at all the water was two inches deep.

"Do you think we can make it?" I asked Andy.

"I'm afraid not," he said. "It looks bad."

And he was right. It looked very bad indeed. In such a situation many people would have given up to panic and despair. But with me it is different. I have always noticed that my mind works at its highest efficiency when I am confronted by a great emergency.

With lightning-like rapidity my brain began to analyze the situation. I knew that the tractor could run through water about two feet deep. But if it got much deeper than that it would reach the magneto and the whole machine would go dead. We were about a mile and a half—or half an hour's drive—from shore. At the rate the water was rising I knew we could never make it. I remembered that I had noticed the high-water marks on the rocks near the canning factory about six feet above the level of the sand. If the water eventually got six feet deep we would be in a bad way. Possibly we could make a raft by tying together some of the lumber on the lumber wagon. But that would have its disadvantages.

And then suddenly I got one of my brilliant ideas. And at once I proceeded to put it into effect. I had Andy stop the tractor and back it up a few inches to loosen the hitch. Then Andy and I got out into the ankle-deep water and unfastened the tractor from the wagon. Next we climbed up on the load of lumber, moved the trunks, the suit cases, the blankets, the four women, the canary bird, the dog, the gentleman from New York and all the other junk up to the forward end. Then we loosened the chains and ropes that held the lumber, and laid a half a dozen long six-by-eight timbers from the rear end of the load of lumber down to the sand. By this time the water was about six inches deep.

Andy then got into the tractor, drove it around to the back of the wagon, and started up the timbers. It was a steep climb, and the tracks were wet and slippery, but Andy was a splendid driver. And finally—to the accompaniment of encouraging shouts from the young niece, hysterical screams from the four other females, shrill barking from the dog, weak chirping from the canary bird, and silence from the poor little gentleman from New York—Andy got the tractor up on top of the load of lumber.

We lifted the six-by-eight timbers back in place, tightened the chains and ropes so that none of the lumber would be washed away, and made everything ship shape by lashing the trunks, the suit cases, and other perishable baggage on top of the big tractor hood as high above the water as possible. Then Andy and I helped the four fat ladies and the gentleman from New York up on to the tractor. As the seat was already reserved for Mabel and Andy and myself, it was necessary for these other people to perch around on the grouser box and the gasoline tank. One of the ladies held the bird cage in her lap, and another took charge of the pup.

At once I made a short speech.

"Ladies and gentlemen," I said, "I wish to assure you that you are perfectly safe. If you will do as I tell you and keep quiet no harm can befall you. Our present situation is somewhat inconvenient, I will admit, but it is not due to any negligence on my part. I was treacherously and infamously given false information as to the time of the tides by a man, who posed as my friend but who has turned out to be my enemy.

"When I started to cross these flats I had every reason to believe that I had ample time to get to the other side. When I discovered that the tide was rising I attempted to get back to shore. But it was too late. Consequently I have placed the tractor as you see on top of the lumber wagon, and I have placed my passengers on top of the tractor. We are perfectly safe. All we have to do is wait until the tide goes out again when we can proceed on our way."

"But the tide isn't going out," said one of the fat ladies. "It's still coming in. And it's going to get so deep that it will go right over the top of this machine and we'll all be washed away and drowned. It's terrible! Oh, why did I ever come? I demand that you take us ashore at once."

"Madam," I said, "I had not finished my talk. If there were any way to take you ashore I would take you—if only for the sake of getting rid of you. But it can't be done. You will have to stay here, and while you remain you will have to do exactly as I tell you. We are now upon the high seas. Legally speaking this tractor, is now a boat. I am the captain, and under the maritime law of the United States of America I have complete authority over my crew and passengers. If there is any insubordination or disobedience of any kind I can shoot you or have you tried for mutiny."

As I finished this talk I scowled as darkly as Mussolini himself. And I was gratified to see that the four hysterical females from New York appeared to be completely awed. Andy and the gentleman from New York said I could count on them. And the young niece somewhat surprised me by telling me privately that she was having a swell time, and wasn't it too exciting for words, and she thought my address was wonderful because it was the first time she had ever seen anyone who could shut up all of her four aunts at the same time.

I thanked her and then borrowed an umbrella from one of the aunts and took a sounding. The water was about a foot and a half deep. Furthermore the wind was freshening, and little waves were beginning to dash against the wheels of the wagon. As the sun sank lower the tide rose higher; and just as the sun disappeared the water reached the bottom planks of our load of lumber. As the darkness deepened the water crept up further and further. The wind blew in stronger and stronger from the sea and the spray from the breaking waves began to drive over the top of the lumber. The fat ladies, although I had them too much awed to make a disturbance, nevertheless kept up a continuous chattering. One of them suggested that if we could signal to the shore somebody might come out in a boat and rescue us.

"It's a splendid idea," said Mabel. "I'll light off some of these fireworks. Maybe they'll send a boat and maybe they'll shoot us a line and we can all go ashore in a breeches buoy."

And right away she climbed out over the suit cases on top of the hood, pulled out the box of fireworks, and amused herself for an hour or so sending up rockets and shooting off Roman candles. But nobody came out from the shore. Probably nobody saw us. Or if they did they thought we were just having a premature Fourth of July celebration.

At ten o'clock the waves were washing right over the top of the lumber, and we all began to get pretty anxious. The current was strong. It was still flowing in from the sea. There was a pale moon, but it was a dark night just the same. It was cold and none of us really knew how high the water would rise before it started down again.

"When I studied geography," one of the aunts said, "I was taught that the tide in the Bay of Fundy rises seventy feet. What if it gets that high here?"

"It won't get that high," I said.

"What if it rises only half that far?"

"It won't," I said, although I wasn't sure. "And what is more I don't want any more pessimistic remarks like that out of anybody."

At eleven o'clock the water had risen at least another foot, the wind was still strong, the waves were sloshing against the side of the tractor at a great rate, and the spray was dashing in onto the floor in front of the seat.

"If it comes much higher," said one of the aunts, "we're lost. And I think it is time you did something, Mr. Captain. This lumber is the only chance we have of saving our lives. But as long as this heavy iron tractor is on top of it holding it down it can't do us any good. What you ought to do is run the tractor off of here while there is still time. Then the lumber will float up to the surface and we can use it as a raft."

"Not on your life," spoke up Andy. "This tractor belongs to the Maine State Highway Department and I am responsible for it."

"And what is a tractor," asked the lady, "as compared to our precious human lives?"

At this point I decided to end the discussion. "The tractor will stay where it is," I announced very decisively, "and this discussion will cease at once. If you people don't shut up I will have you prosecuted for mutiny, lèse-majesté, and piracy on the high seas."

They shut up. At half past eleven it looked as if the water was going down. And at midnight we began to see the uppermost planks of the lumber under the tractor. We knew then that all was well.

And the next two or three hours were really not bad at all. Mabel and I climbed out over the trunks and suit cases and sat on top of the radiator at the extreme front end of the tractor and admired the stars and the moonlight on the waves. We had one interruption when one of the aunts protested that I was getting too familiar with her niece—which was absurd because I was only protecting her from the cold and the damp sea air. After I had threatened to put the aunt in irons for the rest of the voyage, she quieted down.

Gradually the water sank lower and lower until finally—just as the sky to the northeast began to brighten with the dawn—I looked down and saw wet shiny sand all around us.

Andy and I put the big timbers in place at the back of the wagon. Andy backed the tractor down onto the sand and drove around and hitched onto the wagon once more. As far as I was concerned I was ready to go on to the Seaside Inn. And Andy and the gentleman from New York and his niece were game. But the four aunts set up such a roar, and demanded so loudly to be taken back to the nearest dry land, that I decided the easiest thing to do would be to humor them. Consequently we set off full speed for the canning factory, and in about half an hour we had almost reached the shore line. I had decided to dump my passengers at the factory, where they could telephone for a taxi to take them to town, and I was then going to turn right around and head for the Seaside Inn, which I was certain I could reach before the tide came in again.

But about a hundred yards from shore we ran into a patch of mud which was much softer than the sand. The tractor stayed on top very well but the wagon began to sink in so deep that I was afraid it would be completely stuck.

"Whoa!" I said to Andy. "I think we had better unhook the tractor, drive it around and hook onto the rear so we can pull the wagon backward out of this mud. As soon as we get the wagon onto the firm sand we can hook on in front again and circle around this soft spot."

"All right," said Andy. "It's a good idea."

Unfortunately it was not a good idea. We had no trouble

hooking onto the rear of the wagon, but as we pulled it back-wards we must have backed the nut off the end of one of the axles. When we were just about halfway out of the mud hole the left hind wheel came off, the left hind corner of the wagon dropped down, and the four ladies, the gentleman from New York, the four trunks, the eighteen suit cases, the road plow, the nail kegs, the dog, and the canary bird all slid off gently but firmly into the mud. It certainly was lucky that Andy, Mabel, and I happened to be on the seat of the tractor.

For some reason or other the four aunts seemed to blame me for this accident, although it was nothing that I could have foreseen or prevented and was obviously due to faulty design in the wagon. They shook their umbrellas at me and told me ex-actly what they thought of me—which apparently was not much. After what they said it would have served them right if I had let them waddle ashore through all the mud. But I am naturally chivalrous and kind-hearted, so I had Andy make several trips with the tractor and carry them and their belongings over to the canning factory.

You might have supposed that this kind treatment on my part would have earned their gratitude. But such was not the case. They all trooped into the factory—which was not locked, although the workmen had not yet appeared—and one of them called up Mr. Hubbard on the telephone. She told Mr. Hubbard to come out and get them at once, and she said that they had been thrown in the mud, insulted, kidnapped, and half drowned by a crazy tractor salesman. After the telephoning was over they all stood around and glared at me—that is, all but the gentle-man from New York who was too timid, and his niece who was too sensible. As there didn't seem to be much I could do for these people, and as some of them did not seem to be enjoying my com-pany, I withdrew and went out with Andy to work over the wagon. After hunting around a while we were fortunate enough to find the nut which had come off the axle.

"If we were on a hard road," said Andy, "and if we had a good jack, we could lift up this axle and put the wheel back very easy. But as it is I'm afraid we'll have to take off the whole load of lumber."

"I'm afraid you're right," I said.

Pretty soon we saw Mr. Hubbard driving up to the canning factory. He had come in a hurry. At once the four excited females gathered around him, talking fast and furious, and apparently giving him their version of what had happened. They must have poured him out a good earful, because very shortly we saw him coming across the sand like a cavalry charge. Andy and I walked forward to meet him and he was positively foaming at the mouth.

"This is the damnedest proceeding I ever heard of," he said. "What do you mean by pulling off such a stunt? You told me you were going to haul a load of lumber over to the Seaside Inn. Instead of which you kidnap a lot of my guests. You take them out into the middle of the bay. You pretty near drown them. You scare them half to death. Then you wreck my wagon and dump them all into the mud. It's an outrage."

"But, Mr. Hubbard," I said, "you don't understand. I can explain everything."

"I don't want to hear another word," interrupted Mr. Hubbard, "and I don't want any explanations. I don't want anything more to do with you. I wouldn't take your tractor as a gift. The best thing you can do is get out of town as fast as you can. If you ever even speak to me again I'll knock your block off."

And before I could answer he turned around and went back to his automobile. The party from New York all piled in. I heard Mr. Hubbard tell them he would send back a truck for their trunks and suit cases. Then they drove off toward Hubbardston.

Andy and I sat down on the shore to consider the situation. I will have to admit that I was not completely satisfied with the way things had been going. Of course I was not to blame for the treachery of Captain Dobbs, nor for the unfortunate loss of the wheel from the lumber wagon. But I realized, nevertheless, that I was to a certain extent in wrong with Mr. Hubbard. I knew that if I was to sell him a tractor I would have to overcome a certain amount of sales resistance. And I decided that the only thing to do was to take that load of lumber across to the Seaside Inn as soon as possible. This would give me a talking point with which I could once more approach my prospect.

"Andy," I said, "if we are able to get this wagon repaired, are you willing to try another trip?"

"Sure," said Andy.

By this time it was almost seven o'clock and the workmen had begun to arrive at the canning factory. The boss of the clam diggers was very much interested in the tractor, and asked me what sort of a trip we had had. I had to admit that it was not so good.

"We saw you starting out last night," he said. "We yelled at you to tell you the tide would soon be in. When you paid no attention, we decided you probably knew what you were doing. We decided your machine was probably fast enough to get you across ahead of the tide."

"It wasn't," I said. "Would it be possible," I went on, "for me to hire some of your clam diggers to help unload that lumber, put the wheel back, then reload the wagon?"

"I'm afraid not," he said. "We only have about an hour before the tide comes in, and I will have to keep all hands busy to get out enough clams to keep the factory going until this afternoon."

"Maybe," I said, "we could speed up the clam digging a little with our tractor."

"You could try," said the boss clam digger.

"Come, Andy," I said. "Let's see what we can do."

We ran the tractor out to the disabled wagon, and hitched onto the big road plow. Then we drove back and forth across the mud flats, plowing big deep furrows, and in about ten minutes we had turned out more clams—according to what the boss clam digger told us—than twenty men could dig in a whole morning.

The boss clam digger was very much pleased and he let us have a dozen men to unload the lumber, put on the wheel, and re-load the lumber. Meanwhile, three men with baskets picked up the clams.

When the tide began to come in, a little after eight o'clock, we had our lumber loaded and the wagon and tractor parked beside the canning factory all ready to go. And the canning factory had about three times as many clams as they could have dug in the same length of time by hand. It was a very satisfactory arrangement all around.

The boss clam digger told me that the tide would go out again at about four in the afternoon and that the sand flats would be free from water from then until about eight. As I felt that this information was reliable I decided to start out for the Seaside Inn at four o'clock. In the meantime I have been sitting around the office of the canning factory writing this report, and eating great quantities of excellent steamed clams which the boss clam digger was kind enough to offer me.

It is now noon, and the tide is almost at its highest point. But before long it will be running out, and as soon as it gets off the flats we will be on our way. The boss clam digger will mail this report when he goes home to Hubbardston this evening. And tomorrow I expect to send you another report stating that I have successfully demonstrated that it is possible to haul freight across Sandy Inlet. I also hope that either tomorrow or some time within the next few days I may be able to get hold of Mr. Hubbard and talk him around into a reasonable frame of mind.

Very truly yours,
ALEXANDER BOTTS.

FARMERS' FRIEND TRACTOR COMPANY
SALESMAN'S DAILY REPORT
Date: Saturday, July 4, 1925.
Written from: Hubbardston, Maine.
Written by: Alexander Botts, Salesman.

My report today will be a short one. A whole lot of things have happened, but it will not take long to tell about them.

Yesterday afternoon at about one o'clock, soon after I had finished my yesterday's report, an airplane went by over the canning factory. It was coming from the direction of Hubbardston and it headed out over Sandy Inlet toward the Seaside Inn, so I knew that it must be the airplane salesman taking Mr. Hubbard for a hop. As the machine went over, I noticed that the motor was missing and spluttering a good deal. But it flew right on until it got more than half way across the inlet. Then it seemed to hesitate. And finally it glided down gently into the water.

Everybody around the canning factory immediately became very much excited. Because this plane was not a seaplane. It was only a small land machine with wheels on the bottom. The boss clam digger got out a couple of pairs of big field glasses and we stood on the shore and trained the glasses on the plane. It seemed to be about three miles away. Its nose was completely under water, while the tail and the rear edges of the upper wings stuck up into the air. As we looked we saw two men climb up on top of the wings and start waving their arms.

"They're not killed anyway," said the boss clam digger, "and I hope they're not hurt, because we can't rescue them till the tide goes out."

"Haven't you got a boat?" I asked.

"We have an old dory with a motor in it," he said, "but it can't make any speed. And if we went out there now, we'd only get washed out to sea by the tide."

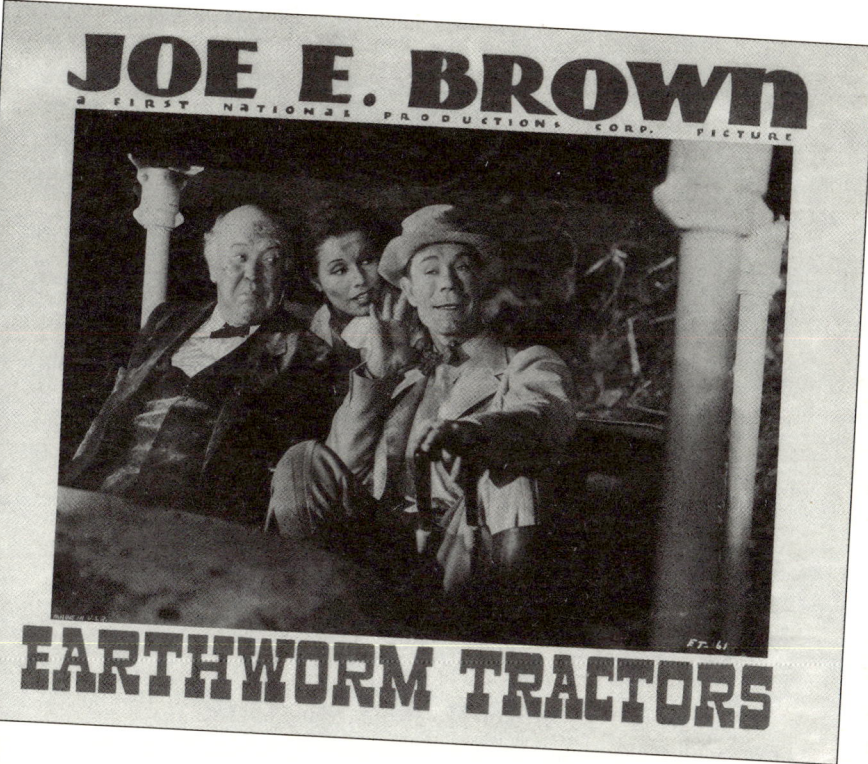

From the driver's seat of an Earthworm tractor, Alexander Botts works his salesman magic on cantankerous lumberman Sam Johnson and his sympathetic daughter Mabel in this vintage Earthworm Tractors *lobby card.*

We watched the wrecked plane for about ten minutes. The two men kept up their frantic waving. Then we noticed a motor boat coming in from the sea. It was full of people.

"Good," said the boss clam digger. "That boat has seen their signals. And it seems to be fast enough to buck the tide."

We watched the boat. The tide was evidently pretty strong, but the boat came along steadily. It had almost reached the plane when it suddenly stopped. We stared at it through our glasses until our eyes were tired, but we couldn't see that it moved an inch. It seemed to be stuck.

Two o'clock came. Then three o'clock. All this time, of course, the tide was running out. And a little before four o'clock the sand flats began to emerge.

"All right," I said, "it's time for us to be moving."

Andy and I got into the tractor, and with the load of lumber rolling along behind we started out across the inlet. Everything went fine. And about an hour later we had reached the stranded plane. The propeller had been broken, and the wings slightly damaged when they hit the water, but otherwise it seemed to be all right. Mr. Hubbard and the pilot came walking across the sand to meet us. Neither one of them was hurt.

The last time I had seen Mr. Hubbard he had told me that if I ever spoke to him again he would knock my block off. But for some reason or other he had, by this time, apparently changed his mind. When I asked him if he would like a ride for himself and his friend, and a tow for his machine, he replied most politely and with many thanks that he most certainly would. He and the pilot, at once climbed upon the lumber wagon.

"The motor went dead on us," explained the pilot. "We smashed things up a little when we came down. But we can fix her up if only we can get her moved out of here before the tide comes back in."

"I'll get her ashore for you all right," I said. "But first I want to see these other people."

I drove over to the motor boat, which was several hundred yards away, high and dry on top of a small rock. It had apparently hit this rock rather hard, and there was a good sized hole knocked in the bottom of the boat. As we drove up I heard a female voice. It was Mabel, the young niece of the gentlemen from New York.

"Well! Well!" she said. "If it isn't old Captain Botts himself with his sea-going tractor!"

"Right you are," I said. "This seems to be a regular reunion." And it was. For there in the boat sat the gentleman from New York, the four aunts, the dog, the canary bird, the four trunks, the eighteen suit cases, all the various bundles, blankets, sweaters, and umbrellas. And in the stern sat old Captain Dobbs.

I at once jumped down from the tractor and advanced upon Captain Dobbs, scowling in a very threatening manner.

"Captain Dobbs," I said, in a voice that resembled as closely as possible the tone of my old first sergeant in the Army, "you are the guy who gave me a lot of phoney dope about the tides in this inlet. And you have gotten me in very wrong with Mr. Hubbard. If you will own up like a man, I will forgive you and I will salvage your boat. If not, I will leave it here where the next high tide will wash it around over these rocks and probably knock it all to pieces. What do you say?"

At first the poor old captain was very evasive. But I was completely hard-boiled. And finally he admitted that he had lied to me about the tides. He had all kinds of excuses. He was a poor man. He had a wife and children to support. His motor boat was his only source of income: And if Mr. Hubbard got a tractor he would lose his job of carrying stuff to the Seaside Inn, and he and his family would probably starve to death. I really began to feel rather sorry for the old bird.

Mr. Hubbard listened to all these explanations in silence. Then he merely said, "This is very interesting indeed," and suggested that we move out of there before the tide came back.

Accordingly we loaded the four aunts, the gentleman from New York, the four trunks, the eighteen suit cases, the dog, the canary bird, the blankets and sweaters, Captain Dobbs, Mr. Hubbard, and the airplane pilot on to the wagon. Mabel took her accustomed place on the seat of the tractor. We dragged the motor boat carefully and gently off the rocks and hitched it on behind the lumber wagon with a piece of heavy rope. After this we drove over to the plane and hitched it on behind the boat. And then we started across the sands toward the Seaside Inn.

As we moved along we looked like a regular circus parade: And I am pleased to report I had ample power to handle the four tons of lumber, the heavy-weight passengers, the motor boat, and the airplane. We arrived at the inn all safe and sound and just in time for a splendid supper.

After I had finished eating I got ready to launch forth on one of my best selling talks. But I didn't need to. Mr. Hubbard signed up for a ten ton tractor without any urging at all. His order is enclosed with this report.

Early this morning, when I started back across the sands in the tractor with Andy, everybody was on hand to wish me good-bye and good luck. Mr. Hubbard thanked me, the gentleman from New York and the airplane pilot shook me cordially by the hand, and the four aunts actually thawed out sufficiently to smile pleasantly. The dog barked and the canary bird chirped. Poor old Captain Dobbs waved to me from the shore, where he was hard at work repairing his boat. And Mabel thanked me for having given her the most thrilling, adventurous, and enjoyable time she had had for a long while.

As Andy and I drove out over the sand I reflected sadly that one of the most, melancholy things about a travelling salesman's life is the fact that he is continually making beautiful friendships which are tragically broken when he has to move to the next town.

I was considerably cheered up, however, when we arrived at the canning factory. The boss clam digger came out, greeted me most affectionately, and at once signed up for a five ton Earthworm to be used in digging clams. His order is enclosed.

I am leaving for Boston tonight. And in conclusion I wish to state that I think I have done rather well. I have caused two tractors to be bought where most salesmen could not have sold even one. And I have done far more. I have opened up new markets. And it is my fond hope that in the future we may sell many more Earthworm tractors for the four new uses which I have discovered: —first, transporting passengers and freight to inaccessible summer hotels; second, rescuing shipwrecked mariners; third, salvaging disabled airplanes; and fourth, adding to the health and nourishment of the nation by digging vast quantities of clams.

Faithfully yours,
ALEXANDER BOTTS.

More Trouble with the Expense Account

EARTHWORM TRACTOR COMPANY
EARTHWORM CITY, ILLINOIS
OFFICE OF THE SALES MANAGER

January 2, 1932.

Mr. Alexander Botts,
Vice President in Charge of Tractor Sales,
Deane Supply Company,
Mercedillo, California.

DEAR BOTTS: Your letter of recent date is received, and we are very glad that you are accepting our offer to reenter the sales department of the Earthworm Tractor Company.

As I have indicated in a former letter, you are to act as a traveling sales-promotion agent. I inclose a list of Earthworm tractor dealers whom we want you to visit, set down in the order in which we wish you to visit them. The first is Mr. George Grubb, Rio Pedro, California. We are writing Mr. Grubb that you will call on him in the near future.

We want you to spend a week or two with each dealer, analyzing his problems, helping him with suggestions and advice, and teaching him the various sales methods which you used in the old days as a salesman for this company, and which you have recently employed so successfully, in spite of the depression, in selling tractors for the Deane Supply Company.

We will pay you four hundred dollars a month, which represents your old salary of five hundred minus the 20 per cent cut which we have been forced to make throughout our organization. We will also allow traveling expenses; and in this connection I feel that I should remind you that the good old days of extravagant expense accounts are gone. Our slogan for 1932 is: "Net profits are more important than gross volume." We are insisting that all our traveling representatives practice the most rigid economy. I inclose five hundred dollars advance expense money, and suggest that you use it sparingly.

Kindly start as soon as possible, and send us frequent reports of your progress. We have every confidence in you, and wish you the best of luck.

Most sincerely,
GILBERT HENDERSON,
Sales Manager.

ALEXANDER BOTTS
SALES PROMOTION REPRESENTATIVE
EARTHWORM TRACTOR COMPANY
RIO PEDRO, CALIFORNIA,

Wednesday, January 6, 1932.

Mr. Gilbert Henderson,
Sales Manager,
Earthworm Tractor Company,
Earthworm City, Illinois.
Via Air Mail.

DEAR HENDERSON: Well, here I am. I have started in with a rush. You will note that I already have a supply of swell official embossed stationery, which I ordered in advance, and which I am using in this, my first report, to let you know that I arrived in Rio Pedro this morning, that I called on Mr. George Grubb, and that I have already got things moving so satisfactorily that I will need a thousand dollars additional expense money right away. I want you to wire me the money as soon as you receive this letter—otherwise I may be held up in the very important undertakings which I am initiating in this region.

It certainly seems wonderful to be working once more for the good old Earthworm Tractor Company. Of course, it would be even better if I had my wife along, the way I did on the great European trip. But Gadget is pretty busy these days. Alexander Botts, Junior, and Gadget the Second are now almost three years old, and they are the finest pair of twins in the San Joaquin Valley. They are, however, a lot of work, so Mrs. Botts felt she had to stay at home.

But don't get the idea that being alone will cramp my style. I still have just as much brains and ability as ever, and I have a feeling that this new enterprise is going to be the real climax of my career. The fact that I am spending more money than you expected is a most hopeful sign, because it indicates that I am promoting far more activities than you ever dreamed of; although part of the extra expense is due to the fact that our dealer here is a pathetically moribund specimen, who does not know the meaning of the word "cooperate."

When I introduced myself to Mr. George Grubb this morning, he at once told me that I was simply wasting my time. He said that the tractor business in this region was completely shot, that he hadn't sold a single machine for six months, and that he had no sales in prospect.

"And if I can't sell tractors around here," he said, "nobody can. So you might as well take the next train out of town. I don't want to waste my time listening to a lot of ignorant suggestions from an outsider like you who doesn't understand the conditions here, and probably doesn't know anything about selling tractors anyway."

These ungracious remarks, naturally, pleased me very much. I saw at once that in working with Mr. Grubb I would run into various difficulties. And difficulties always stimulate me, because I can look forward with so much pleasure to the warm glow of satisfaction which is sure to envelop me when I have overcome them.

I proceeded to handle Mr. Grubb with all my old-time tact and adroitness. An ordinary sales representative might have been discouraged at the old guys opening remarks, or he might have lost his temper and told him—truthfully enough—that he was an egregious ass to turn down in this loutish way a perfectly friendly and well-meant offer of assistance. But I made neither of these mistakes.

"Mr. Grubb," I said, with a pleasant smile, "your remarks are partially true. As yet, I know nothing of conditions in your territory. But I can learn. Accordingly, I plan to take a room at the hotel, stay around a few days and see if I can stir up something of interest. I might even locate a prospect for you. But whatever happens, I will not call on you or bother you in any way until I have something definite to tell you."

"You'd better not," said Mr. Grubb. "And I warn you again that you are just wasting your time. There isn't anybody around here that wants to buy an Earthworm tractor. And even if they did, they haven't got the money to pay for it. There just is no business any more at all."

"Well, I guess I'll look around, anyway," I said. "Good morning, Mr. Grubb."

"Good-by," he said.

Leaving this poor idiot sitting gloomily in his office, I walked briskly down town and began nosing about asking questions. Everybody was most pessimistic. Having noticed that business was slightly sick, they had decided it was on its deathbed. Times were terrible, they told me, and nothing was going on at all. Even the new post office, which the Government was just starting to build, was held up because the contractor had been unable to get the proper kind of stone.

When I heard this last bit of information I began to prick up my ears. My subtle intuition told me that here there might possibly be some business for tractors. And I was right. Before long I located a rather sad and disagreeable old party by the name of Ira Button who owns a sandstone quarry about ten miles away up in the mountains, and who had contracted, for a very pleasing sum of money, to supply the stone for the monumental new post office. He had worked the quarry for several months, taking the stone out and getting it ready. Then, last week, just as he was going to start shipping it to town by motor trucks, the highway bridge over the Rio Pedro Canyon was washed out and the only road from his quarry was completely cut off. He said the state highway department would probably build a new bridge, but it would take many months to complete it. And, as the stone had to be delivered within four weeks, it looked as if poor old Mr. Ira Button was completely blown up. So there he sat in his office, drawing little pictures on the blotter, thinking about his troubles and doing nothing at all to remedy them.

"What sort of a place is that canyon?" I asked. "Are the sides straight up and down or sloping?"

"They're sloping," said Mr. Button. "But they're a pretty steep slope."

"Is it possible for a man to climb down into this canyon and up the other side?" I asked.

"Yes."

"Very good," I said. "What you need is an Earthworm tractor. With one of these mechanical marvels you can pull loads over the roughest country. You can put your stone in a wagon, take it down into the canyon, ford the stream and drag it up the other side."

"I thought of that," said Mr. Button, "and I asked Mr. Grubb, the Earthworm tractor dealer, if it could be done."

"What did he say?"

"He said I was crazy. He said the tractor would get smashed to pieces the first trip. And he didn't want to do business with me anyway, because I have no money to pay for a tractor. I've sunk everything I own in the quarry."

"That's too bad," I said. "But you'll have plenty of money, won't you, when you deliver that stone?"

"Yes, if I deliver it."

"Did old Grubb go out and look over the ground with you?"

"No, he said he didn't have time to bother with it."

"All right," I said, "you and I are going to inspect that canyon, Mr. Button. Is that your flivver out in front?"

"Yes."

"Very good. Let's go."

We went. A drive of about ten miles brought us to the edge of the Rio Pedro Canyon—two hundred feet deep, a quarter of a mile wide, with a rapid stream in the bottom, rushing past the wreckage of the old highway bridge.

"The quarry," said Mr. Button, "is right over there on the other side, less than half a mile away. So near, and yet so far."

"All right," I said. "Let's investigate."

After spending several hours scrambling around over the rocks, I located what looked like a perfectly practicable tractor route, and made up my mind to put on a demonstration.

The banks near the old bridge are too steep even for an Earthworm, but by driving about a mile up-stream we can make a crossing just above the great Rio Pedro Falls, where the canyon is not more than a hundred feet deep, and where the banks don't have much more than a forty-five-degree slope. After crossing the canyon we will bring the stone to the end of the present road, and it will then be taken to town in motor trucks.

While we were tramping around we met another man who

was looking over the canyon. He was particularly interested in the waterfall, which is about a hundred feet high, and very beautiful. He said he was coming up next Saturday with a group of people who are going to take some moving pictures of the place.

This at once gave me another splendid idea. I told the gentleman I expected to be up there myself in a few days with a tractor, and I said I would pay him any reasonable price up to five hundred dollars for a series of shots showing the tractor and the wagon negotiating this difficult and rocky country. The moving-picture man refused to commit himself in advance, but I feel certain he will fall in with my plans.

And my demonstrations will thus kill two birds with one stone. It will sell a tractor to Mr. Button, and it will provide our advertising department with a remarkabe picture which it can send all over the country to show the skeptics exactly what an Earthworm tractor is capable of when handled by a man who really understands it.

Upon our return to town, I discovered that Mr. Ira Button has no wagon adequate for the rough work I am planning, so I ordered one to be specially made by the local blacksmith and wheelwright. It will be of unusual size and strength, but the cost will be only three hundred dollars, and the maker has promised to rush the work and have it ready by Saturday morning.

After arranging for the wagon, I called on Mr. George Grubb, our dealer, and laid the whole beautiful scheme before him; suggesting that he lend me one of his tractors and stand the expense of the wagon. But, as I had feared, he failed to become enthusiastic.

"The country around that canyon is entirely too rough for tractors, Earthworms or any other kind," he said. "And I certainly won't let you use one of my stock machines to put on any such demonstration. You would just knock the thing all to pieces. And I have no intention of paying for that fool wagon you say you have ordered. The whole plan is idiotic. This man Button can't buy a tractor. He hasn't got the money to pay for it."

"He'll have the money," I said, "as soon as he delivers that stone."

At this Mr. Button laughed in what I can only describe as a jeering manner. "If he had the faintest chance of getting that stone down here," he said, "I might trust him. But he hasn't. So, if he wants to buy a tractor from me, he'll have to pay cash—which he can't. So that's the end of it."

"Not at all," I replied. "I have been sent to help you, and I am going to help you in spite of yourself. You have some Earthworm tractors on hand here in your warehouse?"

"I have just one—a sixty-horsepower model."

"Exactly what I want," I said. "Here is my offer: I will rent this machine from you for one or more days, starting next Saturday, at twenty-five dollars a day. I will pay for the wagon I have ordered. I will haul out enough stone for Mr. Button so that he can get a first payment from the people who are building the post office. This will enable him to offer you a first payment on the tractor, and when you see how things are going, I am sure you will be only too glad to sell him the machine. In the remote contingency that he doesn't buy the tractor, the Earthworm Tractor Company agrees—through me, its representative—to return the tractor to you in perfect condition or pay you for it in full. Nothing could be more generous than that. You can't lose. What do you say? Will you rent me the tractor?"

"Well," he said, "if you want to make a fool of yourself, and if the Earthworm Tractor Company is willing to pay for your foolishness, it is all right with me."

"Very good, Mr. Grubb," I said. "I'll call for the tractor on Saturday. Good afternoon."

As it was then almost six o'clock, I came back to the hotel and ate supper. I have been spending the evening writing this report. Tomorrow and Friday I will superintend the construction of the wagon and do some more general investigating. And on Saturday the real excitement will start.

I have given you a very full account of my activities, so that you may see that my extra expenses are really a form of enlightened economy. I may not have to spend all of the thousand dollars, but I am having you send it to me anyway, just to be on the safe side. And even if I do use it all, the expenditure of these few paltry dollars will be completely overbalanced by the benefits derived from the moving picture and from the revival of the tractor business which my demonstration will accomplish.

Most sincerely,
ALEXANDER BOTTS.

GEORGE GRUBB
EARTHWORM TRACTOR DEALER
RIO PEDRO, CALIFORNIA

January 6, 1932.

Mr. Gilbert Henderson,
Sales Manager,
Earthworm Tractor Company,
Earthworm City, Illinois.
Via Air Mail.

DEAR MR. HENDERSON: Your representative, Mr. Alexander Botts, has arrived. And as long as you have sent out this man to offer me unsolicited and gratuitous advice on how to run my own business, I am going to take it upon myself to give you a little advice on how to run yours.

Of all the crazy ideas ever evolved by the Earthworm Tractor Company—and there have been many—this latest scheme is the most cockeyed. It wouldn't be so bad if times were good. But you pick out the very moment when business is at its worst and I am already worried to death, and proceed to annoy me further by sending a lunatic who wants to make a disgusting exhibition of himself by performing a lot of monkeyshines all over my territory.

Mr. Botts blew in here this morning, and already has arranged to give a demonstration hauling stone over a section of mountain country which is so rough that he is sure to smash up the tractor before he can accomplish anything at all. And the purpose of this demonstration is to sell a tractor to a man who has absolutely no money to pay for it. Mr. Botts further tells me that he is going to hire a man to take moving pictures of his demonstration for advertising purposes. A sweet advertisement that will be—a picture showing an Earthworm tractor attempting to drive over a lot of rocks and bowlders, and knocking itself to pieces in the attempt.

I always try to be fair with you people, and I am cooperating with Mr. Botts as much as I reasonably can. Upon his assurance that the Earthworm Company would pay all expenses and make good any damages that might ensue, I have told him that he can use for his demonstration a sixty-horse-power Earthworm tractor which I have in stock here.

But I hate to do it. I hate to risk a four-thousand-dollar machine in this way, even if I don't have to stand the loss myself.

And I'm afraid the whole procedure will make the Earthworm tractor ridiculous in the eyes of the public. It is bad business. Instead of wasting your money on wild schemes like this, you might better reduce the price of the tractor and give your hard-working dealers a bigger discount. Think it over.

Very truly,
GEORGE GRUBB.

TELEGRAM

EARTHWORM CITY ILL JAN 9 1932

GEORGE GRUBB
RIO PEDRO CAL
AM WIRING BOTTS TO CANCEL THE DEMONSTRATION OF
WHICH YOU DISAPPROVE AND TO CONFINE HIS ACTIVITIES
TO GIVING YOU SUCH ADVICE AND SUGGESTIONS AS YOU
DESIRE STOP OUR ONE THOUGHT IN SENDING MR BOTTS
WAS THAT HE MIGHT HELP YOU AND WE STILL HOPE AND
BELIEVE THAT HE MAY BE ABLE TO DO SO
GILBERT HENDERSON

Botts' tractor "demonstrations" might be tough on the riders but never seem to phase the Earthworm!

TELEGRAM

EARTHWORM CITY ILL JAN 9 1932

ALEXANDER BOTTS
CARE GEORGE GRUBB
RIO PEDRO CAL
YOUR LETTER RECEIVED BUT AM NOT SENDING THE FUNDS
YOU REQUEST STOP REFER TO MY LETTER OF JANUARY
SECOND NET PROFITS RATHER THAN GROSS SALES THE
WATCHWORD FOR NINETEEN THIRTY TWO STOP EXPENSES
MUST BE KEPT DOWN STOP YOU HAVE NO AUTHORITY TO
FINANCE DEMONSTRATIONS STOP THAT IS THE DEALERS
BUSINESS STOP YOU WILL AT ONCE CANCEL PLANS FOR THE
DEMONSTRATION DESCRIBED IN YOUR LETTER UNLESS
GRUBB WILL STAND ALL EXPENSE STOP YOUR JOB IS TO
ASSIST DEALER WITH ADVICE AND TACTFUL SUGGESTIONS
STOP LETTER FROM GRUBB INDICATES YOU HAVE FAILED TO
USE TACT AND HAVE GIVEN NO SUGGESTIONS WHICH HE
CONSIDERS WORTH ACTING UPON STOP WAKE UP AND TRY
TO MAKE YOURSELF A HELP RATHER THAN A HINDRANCE TO
MR GRUBB STOP WATCH THAT EXPENSE ACCOUNT
　　　　　GILBERT HENDERSON

TELEGRAM

RIO PEDRO CAL JAN 9 1932

GILBERT HENDERSON
SALES MANAGER
EARTHWORM TRACTOR CO
EARTHWORM CITY ILL
YOUR WIRE RECEIVED STOP AM MUCH DISAPPOINTED IN
YOUR ATTITUDE STOP HOW DO YOU EXPECT ME TO ACCOM-
PLISH ANYTHING WHEN YOU WONT BACK ME UP WITH THE
NECESSARY FUNDS QUESTION MARK AND HOW DO YOU

EXPECT ME TO HELP THIS GUY WITH ADVICE AND SUGGES-
TIONS WHEN HE WONT LISTEN TO ANYTHING I SAY ANOTHER
QUESTION MARK AM GOING AHEAD WITH DEMONSTRATION
ANYWAY AND WILL SEND YOU FULL REPORT AS SOON AS I
HAVE TIME STOP IN HASTE

        ALEXANDER BOTTS

GEORGE GRUBB
EARTHWORM TRACTOR DEALER
RIO PEDRO, CALIFORNIA

        Saturday evening, January 9, 1932.

Mr. Gilbert Henderson,
Sales Manager,
Earthworm Tractor Company,
Earthworm City, Illinois.

DEAR MR. HENDERSON: I inclose my bill for $3521.64, which
you owe me for one sixty-horse-power Earthworm tractor. The
amount represents the list price of $4000, plus freight, and
minus my dealer's commission. Things have turned out exactly
as I told you they would—only worse. I had expected this wild
representative of yours to damage my tractor to some extent.
But I had not supposed he would be able to convert it into a
total loss.

In case Mr. Botts has not written you of his exploits this
afternoon, or in case he has attempted to excuse himself by sending you some highly adorned cock-and-bull story, I will give you
a brief account of the facts as I observed them.

Owing to various outside matters of business, I did not reach
my office today until two o'clock in the afternoon. When I arrived, my secretary handed me the telegram which you had sent
in answer to my letter. My secretary also stated that there had

been a telegram for Mr. Botts, which she had given him when he came into the office toward the end of the morning.

"Did Mr. Botts," I asked, "make any remarks after he read his telegram?"

"Yes," she replied. "He said the message gave him a big laugh. He said that his boss at the factory didn't want him to put on this demonstration, but he was going to anyway. He said he had already agreed to buy a special wagon from the blacksmith, and he had promised Mr. Button to haul some stone for him, and he had arranged with a moving-picture man for the taking of a picture. He told me he just didn't have the heart to disappoint all these people, so he took the tractor and drove away."

Upon hearing this, I was, naturally, much displeased. I didn't want Mr. Botts using my tractor to put on a demonstration against your orders. So I at once got into my car and drove out the Rio Pedro Canyon road with the intention of stopping him. Unfortunately, I was too late.

When I reached the broken highway bridge, I stopped the car. Somewhere in the distance I heard the roar of a tractor motor. As the noise seemed to come from somewhere in the canyon, I climbed down the steep bank to the edge of the river. Then, following the direction of the noise, I walked upstream for almost a mile. Finally I rounded a bend and came in sight of the great Rio Pedro Falls. On the bank of the stream at the top of the falls, I observed Mr. Alexander Botts and my Earthworm tractor. He was evidently preparing to drive across the stream at the very brink of the cataract.

Two motion-picture cameras, with their operators, were perched in advantageous positions on the rocky canyon wall. There appeared to be a number of people present, but I could not tell how many, as my view was limited by the fact that I was looking up from the bottom of the falls.

At once I shouted to Mr. Botts to stop, but the roar of the

motor and the thundering of the waters completely drowned out my voice. I waved frantically, but no one noticed me. The walls of the canyon for some distance below the falls are sheer rock. In order to reach the top of the falls I would have had to follow the stream for almost a mile down to the neighborhood of the ruined bridge, then climb out of the canyon and return along the rim. There was no time for this.

As I watched, I saw Mr. Botts step down from the tractor, and, with the assistance of another man, place a very lifelike-looking dummy in the driver's seat. This procedure certainly showed up Mr. Botts in his true colors. He was perfectly willing to risk my tractor for the sake of his half-witted advertising motion picture, but he was not willing to risk his own worthless neck. Once more I yelled "Stop" at the top of my voice. But no one heard me. I saw Mr. Botts throw in the clutch. Slowly and steadily, with no one to guide it but the dummy driver, that tractor started moving straight across the rushing stream not more than three feet from the edge of the waterfall. The men with the moving-picture cameras seemed to be working feverishly.

At first, I thought the machine would get across all right. It held its direction straight enough, but it had been aimed a little bit wrong, so that its course, instead of carrying it parallel to the edge, brought it gradually nearer and nearer. Finally, about two-thirds of the way across, it toppled over, and with a sickening plunge disappeared into the depths of the pool at the bottom.

As the disaster was so complete, and as there was, obviously, nothing more I could do, I retraced my steps, climbed out of the canyon and drove back to town.

Mr. Botts has not yet dared to show up here at the office. If he does, I shall simply have him thrown out at once. And in the future I must insist that all business between myself and the Earthworm Tractor Company be handled direct, and not through any such outlandish emissaries as this Botts person.

In conclusion, I draw your attention once more to the inclosed bill. I shall expect your check in full payment by return mail.

Very truly,
GEORGE GRUBB.

EARTHWORM TRACTOR COMPANY
EARTHWORM CITY, ILLINOIS
OFFICE OF THE SALES MANAGER

Monday, January 11, 1932.

Mr. Alexander Botts,
Care Mr. George Grubb,
Rio Pedro, California.
Via Air Mail.

DEAR BOTTS: Your telegram, stating that you were about to put on a demonstration in spite of my direct orders to the contrary, arrived on Saturday.

Today I have received a letter from Mr. George Grubb, telling of the disastrous consequences of that demonstration, and stating that he expects the Earthworm Company to pay for the tractor which was destroyed in the course of your highly reckless activities.

As we have not yet heard from you, we do not know exactly how many more heavy expenses you have incurred. It is obvious, however, that you have deliberately and completely disregarded my instructions to the effect that your expense account must be kept down to a minimum, and have completely failed to accomplish anything in the way of assisting our dealer, Mr. George Grubb.

In these circumstances, it is necessary for us to advise you that your services will no longer be required by this company. If you care to submit an itemized statement of your expenses, the same will be considered by our accounting department.

Very truly,
GILBERT HENDERSON,
Sales Manager.

ALEXANDER BOTTS
SALES PROMOTION REPRESENTATIVE
EARTHWORM TRACTOR COMPANY
RIO PEDRO, CALIFORNIA,

Wednesday, January 13, 1932.

Mr. Gilbert Henderson,
Sales Manager,
Earthworm Tractor Company,
Earthworm City, Illinois.
Via Air Mail.

DEAR HENDERSON: I meant to write you before, but I have been very busy. And it is just as well I waited, because now I can answer your snappy little letter, which has just arrived. It certainly seems like the good old days to have you bawling me out so thoroughly and so completely. I sure got to hand it to you, Mr. Henderson. You may be getting old, but you're not losing any of your vitality or any of your command of the English language.

When I got to the end of the letter, and saw that you were actually pulling the old bluff of pretending to fire me, it just made me feel good all over.

It also seemed just like the dear old days to have you giving me definite instructions as to what I should do, in spite of the fact that you are so far away that you, naturally, are completely ignorant of conditions here. And I see you are still making the same old error of concentrating your attention too strongly on the size of the expense account. "Net profits rather than gross sales" is a good slogan, but you should always remember that increasing the profits may be accomplished just as well by adding to the receipts as by cutting down the expenses.

In my recent activities here in Rio Pedro, it is true that I ran up a good many expenses. But these expenses were necessary in order that we might receive even greater advantages. When I wrote you my former letter, I had everything organized on a perfectly sound basis. I had every reason to expect that, at an outlay of a few paltry hundreds of dollars, I would sell a tractor, and, by so doing, teach the opinionated and obstinate Mr. Grubb a much-needed lesson in salesmanship, and inspire him to go ahead and make further sales on his own account. In addition, I expected to get a magnificent motion picture for the use of the advertising department. Either one of these achievements would have justified the expense. So, even if no other factors had been involved, I should have probably disregarded your telegram and gone ahead with my demonstration.

But by the time that telegram arrived, I had discovered and taken advantage of certain new factors which were so favorable to my enterprise that it would have been idiotic to hold back. The discovery and utilization of these new factors was due entirely to my own energy and resourcefulness. Early last Saturday morning the blacksmith informed me that the big three-hundred-dollar wagon would be completed a little before noon. So, instead of loafing around town for several hours until it should be ready, I persuaded Mr. Button to drive me out to the canyon for a final inspection of the ground. Incidentally, we had heard that the moving-picture people were already there, and I wanted to talk to them and make definite arrangements for our picture.

When we arrived at the canyon, we discovered a very curious situation. The whole landscape was swarming with humanity. Instead of a small group taking shots of the scenery, as I had expected, there was a large outfit from one of the big studios in Hollywood, engaged in the production of a stupendous and spectacular drama of the great open spaces. Besides the producing and executive staff, there were a lot of stars and featured players, and an appalling mob of extras, including several dozen cowboys and at least five hundred wild Indians.

Leaving Mr. Button sitting in the car, I began walking around looking for the advance agent I had talked with a few days previously. But I could not find him. Either he was not there or he was lost in this great crowd. I therefore approached a gentleman who was standing beside a camera and told him I wish to have a few private movies taken. He let out a loud laugh. "You'll have to see the director about that," he said, "and from the way the old guy is carrying on this morning, there isn't one chance in a thousand he'll do anything for anybody. Boy, that lad is sore."

"Has there been some trouble?" I asked.

"I'll say there has. According to the plot of this picture, the hero and heroine escape across the canyon. The villain tries to follow them in a big tractor, and he gets swept over the falls. That's the big scene, and it looks now as if it has gone hay-wire."

"It has?"

"Yes. The director didn't want to smash up a new tractor by sending it over the falls, so he brought along an old secondhand piece of junk. And now this old tractor has broken down completely, and they can't even drive it up to the top of the falls, let alone run it over."

"Ah, ha!" I said at once. "This is a lucky break for me."

It was, indeed, a most unusual and unexpected piece of good fortune. But I wish to point out, for the benefit of certain people in the Earthworm Tractor Company who may be inclined to think that my success as a salesman is due entirely to what they call fool luck, that I never would have discovered this situation unless I had been up on my toes and chasing about the country with my eyes wide open and my mind on the alert. And I never would have been able to exploit the opportunity to its fullest extent, had I not had the skill and finesse to nurse the situation along until the time was ripe to take definite action.

Most people would have rushed to the director at once, and tried to sell him a tractor. But I decided to make a careful and cautious approach. My first move was to walk over to where the director was standing and listen unobtrusively to what was going on.

The director was a large man with a red face, and he seemed in a state of great agitation. "This is a mess," he said. "Just look at all these people standing around, drawing their salaries and doing nothing. We've got to finish up here today, and we can't do it unless we get a tractor."

Various assistants began fluttering about and explaining that it would take two days to repair the tractor, and just as long to get another one up from Los Angeles.

"There must be tractors somewhere in this God-forsaken country," he said. "And it's up to some of you guys to locate one."

"If you are looking for a tractor," I said, stepping forward, "I have one down at Rio Pedro. If you want to use it, I can bring it up here."

"How long will it take?" he asked.

"About two hours," I said.

"All right," he said. "How much do you want for it?"

"We'll discuss that when I arrive. Good-by."

I hurried back to the road and had Mr. Button drive me to town as fast as possible. When I reached Mr. Grubb's office, his secretary handed me your telegram directing me to cancel the demonstration. Naturally, I paid no attention to these instructions, and, after sending you a brief wire in reply, I took the tractor, hooked onto the big wagon which the blacksmith had just finished, and drove as rapidly as possible to the canyon; arriving about three hours after I had left.

During this time, the director—just as I expected—had worked himself up into a state of far greater anxiety and impatience than ever. Besides, I now had the tractor on hand where he could look at it and realize that it was exactly the machine he needed. All this made it possible for me to bargain with him more successfully than when I first talked to him.

In fact, I now had him where I could make him eat right out of my hand. During my absence he had sent several of his assistants down to scour the farming country around Rio Pedro, and report whether they could find a tractor. Fortunately, he had as yet heard nothing from these people. He had also tried to make the five hundred wild Indians drag the old broken-down tractor by main strength up to the top of the falls. But after an hour's work, they had moved it only a hundred yards, and gave it up as a bad job.

I was now his only hope, and he was willing to buy the tractor at two or three times the list price. I told him, however, that I did not care to sell, and I proposed an arrangement that I had thought out very carefully. First of all, I insisted that he let me haul one load of stone from the quarry around to the road, in order to show Mr. Button, the quarry man, that it could be done. I also insisted that moving pictures be taken of this trip. At first, the director kicked like a steer, because this would delay everything for about an hour. But I remained firm, and at last he agreed. The trip was entirely successful. We got several thou-

sand feet of wonderful pictures, and the moving-picture company will send you the films, free of charge, as soon as they are
developed.

After the trip with the stone was over, I took the tractor up
the canyon again. And in consideration of a payment of six thousand dollars in cash, he ran the old baby over the big waterfall.
Perhaps I was a fool to do it so cheap. The poor director would
have willingly paid more. However, I am not the man to take a
mean advantage of someone else's misfortunes, and I am
pleased to report that the director thanked me warmly, and
stated that he was entirely satisfied with the deal.

I am even more pleased to report an additional achievement.
After the moving-picture people departed, I went down to the
foot of the waterfall to see what was left of the tractor, and I
was delighted to discover that instead of descending upon a heap
of bowlders, as at Niagara, the waters of this cataract plunge
directly into a very deep pool. This at once gave me an idea. And,
by working all day Sunday with several of Mr. Grubb's mechanics and a long cable and a winch from Mr. Button's quarry, we
were able to hook onto the tractor and drag it up on the bank. A
thorough examination showed, just as I had expected, that it
takes more than a drop of one hundred feet into a pool of water
to destroy a sturdy Earthworm tractor. The radiator, part of the
hood, and various minor widgets were smashed up. But a couple
of day's work and a few hundred dollars' worth of parts purchased from Mr. Grubb have sufficed to put the machine back
in running order, apparently just as good as new.

So everything has worked out even better than I expected. I
have paid old man Grubb the full list price of four thousand
dollars for his tractor, plus freight, so you don't have to bother
about the bill which he sent you. And I have sold the machine
and the big wagon to Mr. Button, who will use them to haul out
his stone. I have chosen to regard the tractor as secondhand,
placing the price, including the wagon, at three thousand dollars cash. This money was advanced by the contractor who is

building the post office, as soon as he found out that the tractor was actually able to bring out the stone which he needed.

Mr. Grubb seems to be the most surprised man in all Southern California. The poor sap actually didn't know, until I showed him, that an Earthworm tractor is built strong enough to negotiate this rough mountain country around here. He tells me that as soon as he can get in another machine, he will put on a demonstration for a man in the western part of the county who is engaged in a big logging operation and will probably take several machines as soon as he is shown how well they get over the hills and rocks.

Having disregarded your telegram instructing me to cancel my demonstration, I will now disregard your letter telling me I am fired, and proceed to the next job, with the feeling that I have made a reasonably auspicious start. And I think you ought to agree with me. Possibly you will not have the imagination or the artistic sensibilities necessary to appreciate the remarkable movie I have made. Possibly you may not be much impressed by the sale of the tractor to Mr. Button or by the way I have waked up Mr. Grubb. But certainly, in view of the interminable manner in which you have been harping upon the subject, you cannot fail to appreciate my expense account, which may be summed up as follows:

RECEIVED FROM MOVING-PICTURE DIRECTOR. $6,000.00
RECEIVED FROM IRA BUTTON FOR TRACTOR AND WAGON. 3,000.00

    TOTAL RECEIPTS. $9,000.00

PAID TO MR. GEORGE GRUBB, FOR TRACTOR, GAS, OIL, SPARE PARTS,
    LABOR, AND SO ON. $4,571.29
PAID TO BLACKSMITH, FOR WAGON. 300.00
PAID TO MYSELF (TRAVELING AND MISCELLANEOUS EXPENSE). . . . 246.37
PAID TO MYSELF, FOR THIS MONTH'S SALARY (I THOUGHT I MIGHT AS

WELL HOLD THIS OUT, SO AS TO SAVE YOU THE TROUBLE OF SENDING
ME A CHECK LATER. YOU WILL NOTE THAT I HAVE DECIDED TO RAISE
MY PAY TO AN AMOUNT MORE NEARLY CORRESPONDING TO WHAT I AM
WORTH)... 500.00

TOTAL EXPENSES...................................... $5,617.66
TOTAL RECEIPTS...................................... $9,000.00
TOTAL EXPENSES...................................... 5,617.66

NET PROFIT (WHICH YOU HAVE BEEN TALKING ABOUT SO
    CONTINUALLY).................................... $3,382.34

I inclose a draft for this last amount, and in conclusion I
wish to suggest that if you would only hire a few more men like
me, you wouldn't have to worry about whether you sold any tractors or not. You could run the whole company on the profits from
the salesmen's expense accounts.

        Very truly,
        ALEXANDER BOTTS.

Good News

EARTHWORM TRACTOR COMPANY
EARTHWORM CITY, ILLINOIS
INTEROFFICE COMMUNICATION
Date: Wednesday, September 5, 1934.
To: GILBERT HENDERSON, PRESIDENT.
From: ALEXANDER BOTTS, SALES MANAGER.
Subject: Good news.

This is just a brief note to let you know that I am planning to be out of town for a while, and that I want you to look after my office work while I am away.

The cause of my sudden departure is a telegram just received from Mr. Sam Blatz, studio manager of Zadok Pictures, Inc., Hollywood, California. Mr. Blatz states that he is about to produce a motion picture called The Tractor Man Comes Through, with that well-known star, Buster Connolly, in the title role. The picture calls for twelve large tractors and twelve elevating graders. Mr. Blatz would like to use Earthworm machines. But they must be delivered in Hollywood within a week; otherwise he will have to employ equipment furnished by the Behemoth Tractor Company.

Naturally, I am getting after this business with all the energy I possess. It means not only a big sale but also a chance for us to get a truly stupendous amount of swell publicity. Imagine having our tractors and graders appearing in a motion picture which will be seen by millions of people all over the country, and throughout the world as well!

I am having shipped, this afternoon, twelve eighty-horse-power Earthworm tractors and twelve elevating graders on a special through-freight train which should reach California by next Monday. And, as this deal is too important to trust to our Los Angeles dealer, I am starting for the Coast tonight by plane.

You may rest assured that I am embarking on this venture with the greatest enthusiasm. After more than a month of dull office routine, I find myself with an irresistible yearning for action and excitement. And there ought to be plenty of both in Hollywood.

Don't forget to look after my job while I am gone. As it is only a little more than a month since I took your place as sales manager, on the occasion of your elevation to the presidency, you ought to remember enough about the sales work to get by all right.

As ever,

ALEXANDER BOTTS.

P. S.: I wanted to tell you personally about this great opportunity. But when I called at your office a few minutes ago, your secretary informed me that, in spite of the fact that this is Wednesday, not Saturday, you had departed for an afternoon on the golf links. So I am forced to give you the glad news in this written communication, which you will probably read sometime tomorrow—provided you should happen to drift into the office.

A. BOTTS.

EARTHWORM TRACTOR COMPANY
EARTHWORM CITY, ILLINOIS
OFFICE OF GILBERT HENDERSON, PRESIDENT
Air mail.

Thursday, September 6, 1934.

Mr. Alexander Botts,
Care Zadok Pictures, Inc.
Hollywood, California.

DEAR BOTTS: On my arrival at the office this morning, I found your communication of yesterday awaiting me. I wish you the best of luck in your attempts to make this important sale. And I will look after your work during your absence.

However, I wish to point out, for your guidance in future, that your place, as sales manager, is here. Actual selling work in the field should be left to our dealers and salesmen. Furthermore, I wish to remind you that it is not the policy of this company to go to the heavy expense of shipping large orders way across the country until a sale has actually gone through. And unless you have previously consulted me, I do not want you ever again to rush off this way on the assumption that I will handle your office work for you.

Please hurry back as soon as possible.

Very sincerely,

GILBERT HENDERSON.

HOLLYWOOD-PLAZA HOTEL
HOLLYWOOD, CALIFORNIA
Air Mail.

Saturday afternoon, September 8, 1934.

Mr. Gilbert Henderson,
President,
Earthworm Tractor Company,
Earthworm City, Illinois.

DEAR HENDERSON: Your letter is received. I want you to know that I appreciate your doubts as to the wisdom of my procedure in shipping the tractors and graders ahead of time and in coming out here myself. Also, I can understand your reluctance to take over the work of my office in addition to your own heavy duties as president of the Earthworm Tractor Company. But when I explain what I have already accomplished out here, and what I am planning to accomplish in the future, you will see that my course has been entirely justified, and you will be very glad to do your part by carrying on my work during my absence— even though it may interfere to some extent with your afternoons on the golf links.

I arrived at the Glendale Airport on Thursday morning, and at once took a taxi to the studio of Zadok Pictures, Inc., which is several miles southwest of Hollywood. My first reaction, quite naturally, was a tremendous thrill of excitement at finding myself suddenly set down right in the midst of the glamorous activities of the motion-picture business. The Zadok Studio is truly amazing—an enormous lot, half a mile square, covered with tremendous sound stages, elaborate outdoor sets, huge administrative buildings and other structures, and swarming with

Alexander Botts' faith in his Earthworm tractor is unsurpassed. In this Earthworm Tractors *movie still, Botts hooks his machine to an entire house. (Wisconsin Center for Film and Theater Research)*

carpenters, electricians, various miscellaneous helpers, actors, and actresses—the latter being, in some ways, the most intersting. The whole place is possessed of a quality which I can only describe as enthralling.

Even the surroundings of the studio are full of interest. The adjoining boulevard is lined with handsome filling stations, gay and colorful signboards, and a lot of refreshment stands that are truly astounding—one of them, for instance, being in the form of an old mill, and another built to represent a gigantic ice-cream freezer. A short distance away is a huge alligator farm, where—for some reason which I have not as yet discovered—they are engaged in raising literally hundreds of these curious reptiles. At one side of the studio is a low hill with a complete oil field—scores of big derricks and dozens of storage tanks. And scattered all over the landscape are countless thriving real-estate developments with clusters of little plastered bungalows sprouting up like mushrooms.

When I called at the office of Mr. Sam Blatz, the studio manager, his secretary informed me he was so busy that he could not see me until the following afternoon. This caused a certain amount of delay. But, as it turned out, it was all for the best, because it gave me a chance to roam about the studio and pick up a whole lot of firsthand information about the motion-picture business.

And when I finally saw Mr. Blatz, yesterday afternoon, I was able to speak to him in his own language, and put over a sales talk that was a real wow. Even so, I had a hard time. Mr. Blatz had already seen the Behemoth tractor people, and they had offered him unusually generous terms. However, when I explained that our machines were vastly superior, that we would agree to terms just as generous as the Behemoth, and that we could make delivery early next week, his resistance broke down completely, and in less than ten minutes he closed the deal for twelve Earthworm tractors and twelve graders.

And this is not all. After thanking me most effusively for everything I had done for him, Mr. Blatz gave me a cordial invitation to remain at the studio as long as I desired. He pointed out that I could be a great help in handling the unloading of the tractors, in teaching the mechanics to operate them, and, later on, in acting as technical expert on tractors during the filming of the picture. He said that he would put a studio car at my disposal, and that I would be considered a guest of the company for as long a period as I cared to remain.

This hospitable offer I promptly accepted—not, as you might suppose, because of the selfish pleasure I would derive from hanging around this fascinating studio, but rather because of the very real service I can render the Earthworm Tractor Company by remaining on the job our here a little longer. How important this service is you will realize as soon as I describe the interesting project on which I am now engaged.

After thanking Mr. Blatz, and congratulating him for his good judgment in inviting me to remain at the studio, I asked him to give me a copy of the screen play, The Tractor Man Comes Through. As soon as this was in my hands, I wished Mr. Blatz a very cordial good afternoon and hurried back to the hotel in my luxurious studio car. Last night I read the play, and as soon as I had finished it, I decided that it was all wrong. Not only was it weak in a dramatic sense but it did not have anywhere near enough tractor stuff in it. What it needed was a complete revision by a real tractor expert.

Accordingly, bright and early this morning, I set to work. And I am getting along so well that I expect to have an entirely new version all ready to present to Mr. Blatz on Monday morning. The changes I am making will improve the quality of the picture so much that Mr. Blatz is almost certain to adopt all of them. And the wealth of tractor stuff which I am introducing will provide publicity of incalculable value to the Earthworm Tractor Company. A brief resume of what I am doing will make this clear.

The original play is a rather uninspiring drama of love and hate in the swamps along the lower Mississippi River. The hero—played by Buster Connolly—is a more or less inconsequential young man in charge of a fleet of tractors which are being used in the construction of a levee. And the love interest is a girl who lives in the swamps. This is not a bad set-up, but the author has spoiled it by paying too much attention to the girl and not enough attention to the tractors.

I am changing this in two ways. In the first place, I am cutting out most of the silly love passages. And in the second place, I am improving the levee-building sequences by expanding them into an exhaustive pictorial study of tractor dirt-moving operations—including not only the work of the elevating graders but also a lot of activities with dump wagons, blade graders, sheep's-foot tampers, bulldozers, scarifiers, land levelers, fresnos, and a lot of miscellaneous scrapers, packers, rollers, winches, and other forms of equipment too numerous to mention.

In addition to this I am building up the character of the hero. Instead of having him a mere second-rate straw boss on the levee, I am presenting him as a person of real consequence in the community. Besides his levee work, he is a road contractor, which gives me a chance to introduce a lot of scenes of tractors working on the roads. Also, he owns a large cotton plantation and a lumber camp, which provides an excuse for showing Earthworm tractors engaged in plowing, harrowing, cultivating and skidding logs. And, before I get through, I may even give the hero a trip up north, so we can run in some snowplow work.

Another improvement which I am making is in the method of killing off the villain. Instead of letting him drown in a very uninteresting way in the Mississippi River, I am going to have all twelve tractors run over him, one after the other. This ought to be a scene that will cause a real shudder of horror to sweep through the audience.

But my greatest and most sensational contribution is the grand climax. In the original play, when a big flood comes down the river and breaks through the levee, the hero rescues the girl from her house in the lowlands and carries her off on horseback to the safety of the hills. In my version, all this horseback foolishness is cut out, and the hero arrives in a tractor. He finds that the rescue is apparently impossible, because the girl is suffering from pneumonia or pellagra or something, and cannot be moved from her bed. In this desperate extremity, the hero hitches his tractor to the house, and drags the whole thing, with the girl in it, through miles of deadly swamps, swarming with alligators—which they can rent from the alligator farm down the road—and, after many bloodcurdling adventures, he finally reaches the safety of the hills. The hero's followers, with other tractors, haul away the barn, with the cows in it, and the various corncribs, hen houses and pigpens, with their respective contents. Not only is the girl rescued but all her property is saved. And it is just in the nick of time, because, right on the heels of this spectacular and astounding moving operation, comes the awe-inspiring influx of the swirling waters of the flood.

As you see, my improvements are going to be the making of this play, both as an artistic production and as a colossal advertisement for Earthworm tractors. So it is very fortunate that I came out here.

I must now get back to my literary labors. Good luck to you, and don't work too hard.

As ever,
ALEXANDER BOTTS.

TELEGRAM

EARTHWORM CITY ILL SEP 10 1934

ALEXANDER BOTTS
HOLLYWOOD PLAZA HOTEL
HOLLYWOOD CALIF
DELIGHTED THAT YOU PUT OVER SALE BUT I AM WORRIED BY
YOUR STATEMENT THAT YOU AGREED TO VERY GENEROUS
TERMS STOP PLEASE WRITE ME FULL DETAILS AT ONCE AND
INCLOSE COPY OF SALES ORDER STOP I DO NOT FEEL THAT
THE PUBLICITY VALUE OF THIS PICTURE WILL BE SUFFI-
CIENT TO WARRANT YOUR WASTING ANY MORE TIME ON IT
STOP THE IMPORTANT THING IS THE SALE OF THE TWELVE
TRACTORS AND THE TWELVE GRADERS STOP THIS HAS NOW
BEEN ACCOMPLISHED SO THERE IS NO REASON FOR YOUR
REMAINING IN CALIFORNIA STOP I AM TOO BUSY TO LOOK
AFTER YOUR JOB MUCH LONGER STOP YOU WILL RETURN TO
EARTHWORM CITY AS SOON AS POSSIBLE
EARTHWORM TRACTOR COMPANY
GILBERT HENDERSON PRESIDENT

HOLLYWOOD-PLAZA HOTEL
HOLLYWOOD, CALIFORNIA
Air Mail.

Monday evening, September 10, 1934.

Mr. Gilbert Henderson,
President,
Earthworm Tractor Company,
Earthworm City, Illinois.

DEAR HENDERSON: Your telegram is here, and I am somewhat disappointed in it.

I believe you are making a mistake in feeling that the publicity this picture is going to give us is only one of the minor advantages of the deal which I have put through. I regret that you are placing undue importance on the mere selling of the twelve tractors and the twelve graders. Also, it is a bit unfortunate that you are in such a hurry to know the exact nature of the somewhat generous terms which I granted Mr. Blatz. And it is kind of too bad that you want me to send you a copy of the sales order.

As a matter of fact, the publicity is not only the most important, it is the only advantage we get out of this deal. The sale is of no consequence at all, because the terms of my agreement with Mr. Blatz provide that we lend him the tractors and graders free of charge. Hence, there has been no sale, and I can't send you a copy of the sales order because there is no sales order.

I fear that this news may be somewhat of a shock to you, because the wording of your telegram seems to indicate that you read my former letter so carelessly that you jumped to the totally unwarranted conclusion that I had actually sold something out here. I never said anything of the kind. If you will read over my letter, you will see that I merely said I had closed a deal with Mr. Blatz. So it is not my fault if there was any misunderstanding.

However, there is nothing to worry about, because my arrangement with Mr. Blatz is perfectly fair to everyone concerned, and the terms are the best that we could get, under the circumstances. Naturally, I would have enjoyed selling all this stuff, but before I arrived, the Behemoth Tractor Company had already offered to supply, absolutely free of charge, twelve of their tractors and twelve of their elevating graders. And Mr. Blatz, although he preferred Earthworms, did not want them badly enough to actually pay any money for them. So there was only one thing to do. As a sale was clearly impossible, I abandoned all thought of making it, and concentrated my efforts on this wonderful opportunity for motion-picture publicity. And I have succeeded admirably. All I had to do, in addition to lending them a mere hundred thousand dollars' worth of tractors and graders, was to sign a simple agreement releasing the motion-picture company from liability in case there is any damage to this property while it is in their possession. And in return for this, we get a chance to put over at least a million dollars' worth of splendid publicity. So, you see, the advantages are all on our side.

However, if we are going to exploit this magnificent opportunity to the fullest possible extent, it will be necessary for me to stay out here long enough to make sure that the picture is loaded with as much Earthworm-tractor propaganda as it can possibly hold. In a former letter I explained how I was revising the screen play so that the picture will do right by our tractors. The revision was completed yesterday, and the next step is to submit it to Mr. Blatz. But I cannot do this right away, because the guy is out of town. He left unexpectedly last night by airplane for New York, where he is to confer with Colonel Zadok, the head of the company, and with various bankers who seem to have acquired, in some mysterious and insidious manner, a considerable influence in the business. Mr. Blatz expects to be back on Wednesday, and he left word that he hoped I would be able to attend a story conference which he will hold on that day for the purpose of discussing the tractor picture. Obviously, there is only one course for me to pursue. I will have to stick around here until Wednesday, at least.

In the meantime, I am finding plenty to occupy me. This morning with the help of a large force of expert mechanics from the production department, I unloaded the tractors and graders, which had arrived on a nearby siding, and brought them over to the lot.

This afternoon I visited a number of people who are to be connected with the forthcoming tractor picture, and tried to sell them my ideas for revising the script. I wanted to get them on my side, so that they would back me up when I present my plans to Mr. Sam Blatz at the story conference on Wednesday. My efforts, however, were not very successful.

The first person I interviewed was Mr. Buster Connolly, the star of the picture. I found him a short distance outside the lot, looking at a large and elaborate bungalow which belongs to him and which was in the process of being moved to the Zadok studio from another studio where he had previously worked. It appears that every motion-picture star that amounts to anything has to have a bungalow where he can loll around at such times as he is not actually working. When I arrived upon the scene, Mr. Connolly's bungalow was coming past the oil derricks on the shoulder of the hill at one side of the Zadok lot. It was being dragged along very slowly and painfully by means of an antique and clumsy arrangement of cables, pulleys and winches.

This gave me a wonderful opening. After explaining the changes I wanted to make in the forthcoming picture, I offered to bring up my tractors and put on a real demonstration. I told Mr. Connolly that I would move his bungalow down to the lot so fast that it would make his hair stand on end, and would also give him an idea of the sensational effect we would produce with the spectacular house-moving climax which I had decided to put into the picture. But Mr. Connolly was not impressed.

"I won't let you touch my bungalow," he said. "And, further-more, I don't like your machines. When Sam Blatz gets back I'm going to see him and have practically all the tractor scenes taken out of the picture."

"But, Mr. Connolly," I said, "the tractors will be the making of the picture. They'll be the most interesting thing in it."

"That's just the trouble," he retorted angrily. "The audience will be looking at the tractors all the time, and they won't pay any attention to my acting. Thus, the picture will be ruined."

"Oh, I see," I said. And, indeed, I began to see only too well what was on his mind. He knew the tractors would be splendid picture material. He was afraid they would steal the show from him. And he was so stubborn that I found it impossible to argue with him. Consequently, after a very disappointing interview, I left him and went around to see the director of the picture.

The director sprung an idea that was exactly the opposite of Mr. Connolly's, but just as bad from my point of view. He said he was in favor of cutting out practically all the scenes involv-ing tractors, because tractors, in his opinion, are "slow-moving props," without any picture value whatever. I offered to disprove this assertion by giving him a demonstration. He refused. Then I tried to describe the thrilling effects which could be obtained by showing our Earthworms plowing majestically across hor-rible swamps, through dense forests and over rugged moun-tains. But he would not listen. He had seen the tractors coming into the lot that morning. They moved slowly. Hence, they were slow-moving props, entirely devoid of interest. And nothing I could say had any effect. So, finally, I had to abandon my efforts, and leave him in the same state of besotted ignorance in which I had found him.

My next, and final, call was on the production manager, who has charge of the studio equipment. This guy promptly announced that he was going to advise Mr. Blatz to cut out all the tractor scenes, on the ground that they would necessitate very expensive sets, or even more expensive trips to outside locations. And he was just as opinionated as Mr. Connolly and the director, so I soon gave up all thought of reasoning with him, and walked away in disgust.

But don't get the idea that I am discouraged. Mr. Sam Blatz is the boss around here. He has already shown his intelligence, and his appreciation of tractors, by arranging with me for the use of our machines. Consequently, I am able to contemplate the future with the greatest of confidence. When I see Mr. Blatz at the story conference on Wednesday, I will be prepared to present my ideas in such a clear, forceful and convincing manner that he is almost certain to follow my advice. Hence, the ignorant opposition of such unimportant underlings as the star, the director and the production manager will count for nothing at all. And the picture will be produced in such a way that it will be not only a credit to Zadok Pictures, Inc., but also an invaluable piece of propaganda for the Earthworm Tractor Company.

Yours enthusiastically,

ALEXANDER BOTTS.

TELEGRAM

EARTHWORM CITY ILL SEP 13 1934

ALEXANDER BOTTS
HOLLYWOOD PLAZA HOTEL
HOLLYWOOD CALIF
OUR ATTORNEY BELIEVES THAT YOUR LENDING TRACTORS
TO MOTION PICTURE COMPANY IS VIOLATION OF NRA CODE
ALTHOUGH AS USUAL HE IS NOT QUITE SURE STOP IN ANY
EVENT IT IS ABSOLUTELY CONTRARY TO OUR POLICY STOP

YOU WILL NOTIFY MR. BLATZ THAT HE MUST BUY THE
TRACTORS AND GRADERS AND PAY FOR THEM STOP IF HE
REFUSES YOU WILL REMOVE ALL OF THIS MACHINERY AND
TURN IT OVER ON CONSIGNMENT TO OUR LOS ANGELES
DEALER IN HOPES OF FUTURE SALE ELSEWHERE STOP YOU
WILL RETURN TO EARTHWORM CITY AS SOON AS POSSIBLE
AS WORK IN YOUR OFFICE HERE IS PILING UP
　　　　　EARTHWORM TRACTOR COMPANY
　　　　　GILBERT HENDERSON PRESIDENT

HOLLYWOOD RECEIVING HOSPITAL
HOLLYWOOD, CALIFORNIA
Air mail.

　　　　　　　　　　Thursday evening, September 13, 1934.

Mr. Gilbert Henderson,
President,
Earthworm Tractor Company,
Earthworm City, Illinois.

DEAR HENDERSON: It is my painful duty to report to you that I
have been suddenly overwhelmed by a series of crushing and
incredible disasters. Your telegram has been forwarded to me
here at my new address, but, in the present situation, it does
not mean anything at all to me. I cannot do any of the things
you want me to do. And I cannot even do any of the things I want
to do myself. I cannot stay out here to help with the tractor picture, because there is not going to be any tractor picture. I cannot hurry back to Earthworm City, because I am laid up in the
hospital with a broken ankle. And I cannot repossess the tractors and graders, because there are no tractors and graders any
more. They have, in fact, ceased to exist as such. So, about the

only thing I can do is sit up in bed and write you an account of the unbelievable combination of catastrophes which have defeated all my best-laid plans.

The first blow descended upon me early yesterday evening at the story conference held in Mr. Blatz's office at the studio. All the people concerned in the tractor picture were there, and each one was prepared to present his own ideas on the subject. But the wind was immediately taken out of all our sails by Mr. Blatz himself, who had just arrived from New York full of a whole set of new and outlandish ideas.

Mr. Blatz told us that the financial powers had decided that what the company needs at the present time is something that will ring the cash register in a big way. And they had concluded that the best means of accomplishing this was to produce a picture which would cost more than any other picture heretofore produced in the entire history of the industry. The idea, if you can call it that, seems to be that, instead of making several ordinary pictures which would cost two or three hundred thousand dollars apiece and bring in perhaps a half a million apiece, they will concentrate all their efforts on one production which will cost over a million dollars, and will bring in—they hope—several millions at the box office.

In accordance with this plan, they are going to junk the tractor drama and three or four others that had been scheduled for early production, and put everything they have into a stupendous, monumental, sensational, magnificent, and overpowering epic superspectacle based on Milton's Paradise Lost.

Mr. Blatz admitted, quite frankly, that, from a picture point of view, Mr. Milton's stuff is not so hot, but he was fairly goggle-eyed with enthusiasm over the commercial possibilities. He pointed out that this man Milton has been built up and advertised so long and so extensively by all the college professors and all the high-school teachers of English throughout the entire country that his name has become a household word, synonymous with culture and the higher things of life. This situation is just naturally made to order for the publicity department, which will rush about the country organizing John Milton Booster Clubs in every city, town, hamlet and crossroads. Indorsements will be sought, and doubtless received, from women's clubs, parent-teacher associations, literary societies, and all the rest of the innumerable organizations which are interested in improving the mind and raising the standard of good taste and artistic appreciation in America. Fathers, mothers, clergymen, school teachers, college professors and civic leaders generally will be so thoroughly sold on the high value of the picture that they will urge every man, woman and child throughout the length and breadth of the land to see it.

As director of the picture, they are hiring a world-renowned Russian theatrical producer. This bird knows nothing about motion pictures, and he cannot even speak English, so he will be completely useless around the studio. But the real work can be done by an American assistant director who really knows his business, and the name of the famous Russian will tend to pull in that large and influential group of Americans who believe that nothing can be truly worth while in an artistic way unless it comes out of Europe.

And this is not all. It is realized that there exists in America a considerable substratum of ignorant dumbbells who have a deep suspicion of anything they think is highbrow. To attract this element, they will use, in the cast, a whole group of stars who have a known appeal to the lower classes. Besides Buster Connolly, who has a great following among lovers of thrills and Western melodrama, there will be four popular comedians, three lady stars of the hot-mamma type, and various handsome juvenile men, to say nothing of acrobats, adagio dancers, circus performers, stunt men, and an enormous corps de ballet. The sets and the costumes will be the most elaborate ever seen—they have already ordered one thousand harps and one thousand pairs of wings, with real feathers, for the angels—and the dance ensembles will be lavish beyond description. In fact, there is only one place where they will economize—they won't have to pay anything to the original author.

As soon as Mr. Blatz had completed a description of his ambitious plans, the entire group at the conference—with one notable exception—gave voice to their admiration and approval. The only sour note was sounded by myself, in the form of a plaintive protest at the way they were letting the Earthworm Tractor Company down with nothing to show for all the expense we had incurred in bringing the tractors to California at Mr. Blatz's express request. But my objections were completely drowned out in the great flood of enthusiasm for Mr. John Milton.

And then, while I was still reeling from the effects of this first blow, there descended upon my unfortunate head a second disaster of even greater magnitude. The building was suddenly shaken by the shock of a distant explosion, and soon after we began to hear cries of "Fire!" We all rushed outside, and followed a crowd of excited studio employees to the western boundary of the lot. And here a truly appalling sight met our eyes.

One of the oil-storage tanks up among the derricks on the near-by hill had caught fire. Apparently this tank was only partly filled with oil; it must have contained a certain amount of air mixed with oil vapor in deadly proportions. At any rate, it had exploded, and spread the fire all over the hill. The flames were roaring up from dozens of derricks and tanks. And, as we watched, another tank blew up with a tremendous report, and a great river of burning oil started down the hill toward the studio of Zadok Pictures.

Much to our relief, the flow of this fiery river was arrested, high up on the hill, by a long, low bank of earth, which had presumably been thrown up as a protection for the studio in case of just such an emergency as this. But our relief was short-lived, for it soon appeared that this embankment was not high enough. A small quantity of the burning oil came over the top, and it was evident that if a few more tanks let loose, the blazing fluid would come pouring down the hill and engulf the studio. Fire engines were already on the way from Culver City, Los Angeles, Hollywood, Beverly Hills and Santa Monica. But it was obvious that they would be of little use.

There was only one thing to do. I rushed over to the shed where my tractors and graders were stored. And, as I went, I called loudly for my mechanics to man the machines. Fortunately, several companies were on the lot, taking night scenes. So most of my mechanics were present. And they—gallant and intelligent fellows that they are—had already conceived the same idea which had come to me.

In less than five minutes I had men on every tractor and every grader. And in less than ten minutes, we came charging out through the big side gate of the lot, and advanced up the hill toward the fire.

By this time, the electrical department had mounted hundreds of enormous kleig lights at various vantage points. And these, in conjunction with the light from the fire, made the entire scene as bright as day.

Directly in front of us on the slope of the hill stood Buster Connolly's expensive but silly-looking bungalow. We promptly hooked onto it with three tractors and hauled it down into the lot. Then I started running the twelve tractors, each one pulling a grader, back and forth across the face of the hill so as to throw up a really effective barrier about halfway between the studio and the small dam which was temporarily holding the burning oil in check.

It began to look as if the studio might be saved. The tractors were roaring on their way, and the elevating graders were plowing up the earth and casting it onto the new embankment so fast that victory would be assured in fifteen or twenty minutes.

At this juncture, however, my own participation in the fight was abruptly terminated. As I was rushing to and fro, and hither and yon, shouting orders and encouragement to my trusty followers, I inadvertently tripped over a large plant of the variety known as prickly pear. This unfortunate accident not only filled me up with a lot of spines, in a most annoying way, but also caused me to sustain, as I landed on the hard ground, a broken ankle. It was the same ankle which I injured once before down in Mississippi. A number of husky lads promptly picked me up and carried me down to the highway. And before I knew exactly what was happening to me, I had been loaded into an ambulance and dragged away to this hospital, where the doctors proceeded to give me ether, so they could properly set the broken bones.

When I finally regained the full use of my mental faculties, several hours later, I insisted that the nurse call up the studio and find out how things were going. The news that she brought me was partly good but mostly bad. When the inevitable break in the upper embankment occurred, the lower one, so hastily constructed by our tractors and graders, had reached a height sufficient to stem the tide of the burning oil. So the entire Zadok Studio had been saved. But at the time of the break, our tractors and graders were on the upper side of the new earthwork. The brave mechanics had time to leap to safety over the barrier, but the twelve tractors and the twelve graders were all left behind, and were completely destroyed.

Thus ends the magnificent enterprise upon which I embarked, last week, with so much hope and enthusiasm. At the moment, I am feeling too wretched and miserable to make any definite plans for the future. But, probably, as soon as I am well enough, I shall come creeping piteously back to Earthworm City, hoping and praying that my job has not been taken away from me.

Yours with deep sorrow,
ALEXANDER BOTTS.

HOLLYWOOD RECEIVING HOSPITAL
HOLLYWOOD, CALIFORNIA
Air Mail.

Friday afternoon, September 14, 1934.

Mr. Gilbert Henderson,
President,
Earthworm Tractor Company,
Earthworm City, Illinois.

DEAR HENDERSON: I have a little news for you. My ankle is getting along very well, and I am feeling quite comfortable.

This morning I got in touch with the local adjuster for the Illinois Eureka Fire Insurance Company, which, as you know, handles our business. The adjuster has inspected the remains of our tractors and graders, and is reporting them as a total loss. So, under the terms of our policy, we are to receive the full value, plus freight. This means that the fire wasn't such a bad idea after all; we get paid for these machines just the same as if we had actually sold them.

And here is more news. Mr. Sam Blatz called on me this morning to thank me for my part in saving the studio and thus making it possible for them to go ahead, without any delay, in the production of their great superspectacle. When I asked if he was referring to the Paradise Lost picture, he replied that he was, except that their plans had been slightly changed and they were not going to use the great Milton epic after all. It appears they had hired some guy to read the book for them, so they could find out what it is all about. And they had also consulted with the Hays office. Most of the authorities had then agreed that it would be pretty difficult to get Paradise Lost past the censors and the various purity organizations. Apparently, one of the main characters in the book is Satan himself, and this puts entirely too much emphasis on sin. So they have decided to do John

Bunyan's Pilgrim's Progress instead. This book—which apparently has nothing to do with Paul Bunyan, owner of the famous blue ox—contains a number of objectionable passages, but they can be eliminated without much trouble.

Mr. Blatz pointed out that the switch to the Bunyan opus was in reality only a minor change in their plans. The really essential features—such as the elaborate production and the publicity aimed at the culture groups—will go through just the same. The only real difference would be that, instead of forming Milton societies all over the country, the publicity department would bend its energies toward the formation of bigger and better Bunyan clubs.

"And in this new setup," Mr. Blatz explained, "we find we won't need Buster Connolly, so we are going to have him make the tractor picture after all—only there will be a lot of changes in that too."

"I suppose you're going to leave out all the tractors?" I asked suspiciously.

"I'm afraid we can't," said Mr. Blatz. "You see, the most spectacular part of the picture has been made already."

"I don't understand."

"It's like this, Mr. Botts. When that fire started, we had four separate companies working on the lot. And the entire production force was present, all ready to take advantage of this great opportunity. The electricians set up their lights, and the directors and the cameramen went into action. And the results are really extraordinary. Never before has a fire of this size been covered by so many expert cameramen with such a wealth of high-grade equipment. And never before have I seen such beautifully taken fire pictures. We have the whole thing—blazing oil derricks, exploding tanks, the moving of that bungalow from out of the very jaws of death, the building of the embankment, the escape of the tractor operators in front of the blazing river of oil, and the final destruction of the tractors and the graders. We even have a delightful bit of comedy relief—where some jackass tripped and did a beautiful high-gruesome into a prickly pear. It is all so astounding, so magnificent, so colossal, that we are going to use it as the climax of our tractor picture. To do this, we shall have to shift the scene of our story from the Mississippi swamps to California, and have the hero rescue the girl and her house from an oil fire. We want to make this a real tractor picture, with lots of tractor stuff all through it, so we are hoping that you will be able to lend us twelve more tractors and twelve more graders to be used in the earlier sequences."

"Nothing would please me more!" I said. And then my warm enthusiasm was suddenly chilled by the icy fingers of a cold doubt. "I am afraid, however," I said sadly, "that it can't be done. Look at this."

I handed him your telegram. He read it and glanced at me inquiringly.

"We must face the facts," I said. "You will have to buy these tractors and graders, and pay real money for them, or else you'll have to use Behemoth machines."

"We can't use Behemoths," said Mr. Blatz, "because the most important part of the picture has already been made with Earthworms." He pondered the matter for some time. "Oh, well," he said at length. "It's only a hundred thousand dollars—a mere drop in the bucket as compared to what we ought to take in on this picture. Do you want me to sign an order or something for these things?"

"As a matter of form, you might as well," I said nonchalantly. "And you might make me out a check also."

So he did, and I am enclosing the order and the check herewith. Please ship the stuff at once. And I'm afraid you'll have to handle my office work a little longer, because the state of my ankle makes it necessary for me to leave tomorrow for several weeks' vacation, as the guest of Mr. Sam Blatz at his luxurious ranch in Hidden Valley up in Ventura County.

Yours respectfully,

ALEXANDER BOTTS.

Grand Canyon Brain Storm

EARTHWORM TRACTOR COMPANY
SAN FRANCISCO BRANCH
SAN FRANCISCO, CALIFORNIA

Thursday, January 18, 1940

Mr. Alexander Botts,
Sales Manager,
Earthworm Tractor Company,
Earthworm City, Illinois

DEAR BOTTS: You might be interested in the enclosed photograph of a curious accident to one of our Number D77 two-yard Diesel Earthworm shovels. The owner of the machine, Mr. George Markland, has been using it on a bridge-construction job on the highway along the rim of the Grand Canyon near Navaho Butte, Arizona. This highway is now being improved to serve a recently discovered tungsten mine, which is important in the present defense program.

One night last week Mr. Markland left the shovel on ground which sloped gently toward the canyon. Apparently the brake was not properly set, for in the morning he found that the machine had rolled down the slope and over the edge—landing on an inaccessible rock shelf or terrace about three hundred feet straight down.

The photograph, taken by Mr. Markland, shows that the shovel has suffered very little damage, and I thought you might be able to use this in your sales work to prove the remarkable sturdiness of our construction.

There seems to be no hope of salvaging the machine. The only possible method would be to lower workmen on ropes, take it apart, and haul it up the three-hundred-foot sheer cliff piece by piece. Any such attempt, however, might easily dislodge it from its precarious perch on the narrow rock shelf, and permit it to plunge several thousand feet into the very depths of the canyon. Furthermore, the only machinery in the region capable of hauling up the disassembled parts is owned by a rival contractor, Mr. Oscar Sneed, who is so hostile to Mr. Markland that there is no chance of getting his co-operation.

This unfortunate accident may be the end of Mr. Markland's career as a contractor. He has no money to pay for another shovel. And if he can't get another shovel, he can't complete his contract. This, in turn, will make him liable for a heavy penalty payment, and will throw him into bankruptcy.

He arrived in San Francisco this morning and pleaded with us to sell him another shovel for nothing down, and the rest when, as, and if he completes his contract. But after consulting our credit man out here, I was forced to refuse. I should like to help him out, as he is a good man and completely honest. But he still owes half the purchase price on the shovel he has lost. He also owes a lot of other bills. And it seems better for us to take our loss on the present debt rather than to send good money after bad. Please remember this in case Mr. Markland appeals direct to you at the home office.

I expect to be here several weeks longer checking over the present somewhat uncertain condition of our export business to the Orient.

Most sincerely,
GILBERT HENDERSON,
President,
Earthworm Tractor Company

OFFICE OF ALEXANDER BOTTS
SALES MANAGER
EARTHWORM TRACTOR COMPANY
EARTHWORM CITY, ILLINOIS

Saturday, January 20, 1940

Mr. Gilbert Henderson,
Earthworm Tractor Company,
San Francisco Branch
San Francisco, California

DEAR HENDERSON: Thanks for the picture. I am sorry to hear of Mr. Markland's troubles. But I am happy to announce that I am planning to take vigorous action in this matter at once.

As you know, it is part of my religion to give the customers Real Service. I always make it a point to see that every purchaser of Earthworm equipment receives all the help we can give him in operating his machinery so efficiently that he makes the greatest possible profit out of his operations and is thus constrained to act as an enthusiastic booster for our products. This policy, important at all times, is practically mandatory in the case of Mr. Markland—first, because I have met him and he is a friend of mine and a swell guy; second, because he has not yet paid for his shovel; and, third, because he is working on a project essential to the national defense.

I have decided, therefore, to fly out to Arizona this afternoon and take personal charge of Mr. Markland's affairs. Naturally, I cannot be sure of my exact course of action until I arrive in Navaho Butte and look over the ground. But if the shovel has fallen only a few hundred feet, and is still in good condition, it ought to be fairly easy to salvage it—in spite of Mr. Markland's pessimism.

And if I need the equipment owned by this guy Oscar Sneed, I am sure I can get it. I realize Mr. Sneed is difficult to deal with. During the past year he has written me a whole series of insulting letters demanding free repairs on two DG90 tractors, one D77 shovel, and four WS2 scrapers—all of which machinery broke down because of his own failure to maintain and lubricate it properly. As I have refused all of his absurd demands, there is at the moment a certain coolness between us. But when I meet him personally, I am practically certain that I can smooth him down and warm him up with the genial power of my friendly personality, and thus enlist his willing co-operation.

In any event, with me on the job, Mr. Markland's troubles will soon be overcome. And I know you will agree that the long journey to Arizona will be justified.

Besides, I am so completely worn down by the weary monotony of office routine—always a great trial to anyone of my active temperament—that I feel a little trip somewhere is necessary to restore me to my natural state of mental and physical vigor.

If Mr. Markland is still in San Francisco, please tell him that I have turned his picture over to the advertising department, and that they will send him a check for ten dollars in payment thereof. It is my hope that this small but nevertheless tangible honorarium may lift him, if only slightly, out of the low state of mind which your letter indicates he is now in.

If there are any new developments in Mr. Markland's affairs, please let me know. I will be staying at whatever turns out to be the best hotel in Navaho Butte.

Most sincerely,
ALEXANDER BOTTS

P. S. Tell Mr. Markland that, on second thought, I am applying the ten dollars to his unpaid balance on the shovel.

EARTHWORM TRACTOR COMPANY
SAN FRANCISCO BRANCH
SAN FRANCISCO, CALIFORNIA

Monday, January 22, 1940

Mr. Alexander Botts,
Earthworm Tractor Sales Manager,
Try All Hotels,
Navaho Butte, Arizona

DEAR BOTTS: When I sent you that photograph, I merely thought you might use it to show some of your prospects the sturdy construction of our machinery. I never even dreamed it would start you off on one of your impulsive trips halfway across the country.

Please remember that, as Sales Manager of the company, you are an executive. As such, it is perfectly proper for you to make occasional trips to confer with our dealers and representatives in various parts of the country. But, in general, your proper place is at the home office. An ordinary routine salvage job is something that should obviously be delegated to others. In no case should you do it yourself.

Besides, this particular enterprise is nothing but a wild goose chase. Mr. Markland and I have discussed the matter in great detail, and we agree that, on the basis of all commonly accepted engineering practices, the salvage of his shovel is entirely impractical.

I shall be awaiting your assurances that you are abandoning this ill-advised enterprise and returning at once to Earthworm City.

Very sincerely,
GILBERT HENDERSON

NAVAHO HOTEL
NAVAHO BUTTE
ARIZONA

Tuesday, January 23, 1940

Mr. Gilbert Henderson,
Earthworm Tractor Company,
San Francisco Branch,
San Francisco, California

DEAR HENDERSON: Your letter has just arrived, and I agree with you that a man of my position should, whenever possible, delegate to others all routine jobs. But the job which brought me to Arizona was not routine. An esteemed customer was in danger of going broke. And there was no one else to whom I could have delegated the job—for the very good reason which you yourself set forth: the salvaging of Mr. Markland's shovel was, on the basis of all commonly accepted engineering principles, entirely impractical.

That is why I came myself. And already I have good reason to be glad that I did. Not being limited or hampered by any of these same commonly accepted engineering practices, I have been able, since my arrival here early yesterday morning, not only to work out a practical plan of operation, but to carry it through to a triumphant conclusion.

In other words, while you and Mr. Markland have been merely talking and figuring out reasons why this job could not be done, I have done it. Mr. Markland's shovel, I am happy to announce, is now back where it belongs on the bridge site. It is in perfect running condition, and all ready to go to work.

If Mr. Markland is incredulous regarding my quick salvaging operation, you may give him the following simple and straightforward explanation: I merely let myself down on a three-hundred-foot rope to the rock shelf on which the shovel rested. Having ascertained that the sturdily constructed machine was in good running condition, I unfastened the boom-end of the hoist cable, pulled it out of the sheaves, fastened it to the end of the rope, climbed up the rope to the rim of the canyon, and pulled the cable up after me. My next move was to secure the end of the cable around a jutting ledge of rock that happened to be nearby. After this I slid down the cable, started the motor of the shovel, and threw in the hoist clutch. This, of course, started the hoist-drum revolving—thus reeling in the cable, and causing the shovel to pull itself straight up the three-hundred-foot cliff, and over the edge onto the more or less level ground at the top.

Having accomplished this seemingly difficult feat with so little trouble, I threaded the cable back through the sheaves, and gave the machinery a brief work-out to prove that it was all in good order.

As there is nothing more to be done, I am leaving for Earthworm City this evening. And I would suggest that Mr. Markland hurry back to Navaho Butte and resume operations—bearing in mind that it might be well, in the future, to park his shovel for the night at a reasonable distance from the canyon, on ground which slopes away from, rather than toward, the rim.

Yours proudly, if I do say it myself,
ALEXANDER BOTTS

P. S. I forgot to say that I am much impressed with the Grand Canyon. It is without doubt the most magnificent and awe-inspiring abyss I have ever known any of our machinery to fall into.

TELEGRAM

SAN FRANCISCO, CALIF. JAN. 25, 1940

ALEXANDER BOTTS,
EARTHWORM CITY, ILL.
MARKLAND DOES NOT BELIEVE YOUR STORY OF SALVAGING
SHOVEL. REFUSES TO HURRY BACK TO NAVAHO BUTTE. HE
SAYS EASTERN TOURISTS, WHEN CONTEMPLATING THE
"MAGNIFICENT AND AWE-INSPIRING ABYSS" OF THE GRAND
CANYON, OFTEN BECOME EMOTIONALLY OVER-WROUGHT
AND SUBJECT TO MILD HALLUCINATIONS AND DELUSIONS.
HE THINKS YOUR ACCOUNT OF CLIMBING LIKE A MONKEY UP
AND DOWN THAT ROPE, AND USING THE HOIST CABLE,
WHICH IS ONE INCH THICK AND EIGHTY FEET LONG, TO LIFT
HIS ENTIRE SEVENTY-TON SHOVEL STRAIGHT UP A 300-FOOT
CLIFF IS "JUST ANOTHER GRAND CANYON BRAIN-STORM." I
AM INCLINED TO AGREE WITH HIM, AND WOULD SUGGEST
THAT YOU TRY TO PULL YOURSELF TOGETHER AND WIRE ME
A PROMPT AND RATIONAL EXPLANATION.
      GILBERT HENDERSON

TELEGRAM

EARTHWORM CITY, ILL. JAN. 26, 1940

GILBERT HENDERSON,
EARTHWORM TRACTOR BRANCH,
SAN FRANCISCO, CALIF.
KINDLY REFER TO MY LETTER OF JANUARY 24. THAT IS MY
STORY AND I ADHERE THERETO—FOR THE PRESENT AT
LEAST. LET ME KNOW WHEN MARKLAND STARTS BACK FOR
NAVAHO BUTTE.
      ALEXANDER BOTTS

EARTHWORM TRACTOR COMPANY
SAN FRANCISCO BRANCH
SAN FRANCISCO, CALIFORNIA

Monday, January 29, 1940

Mr. Alexander Botts,
Sales Manager,
Earthworm Tractor Company,
Earthworm City, Illinois

DEAR BOTTS: Your telegram arrived last Friday. On Saturday, Mr. Markland—having failed to get any additional credit—left sorrowfully for Arizona to wind up his affairs. And this morning—Monday—he wired me from Navaho Butte: "My profound apologies and heartfelt thanks to Mr. Botts. He really did salvage the shovel, and it is in perfect working condition. I expect to finish job in about two weeks, and will then have enough money to pay off bills on shovel and everything else, with handsome profit besides. Again, many thanks."

All of which sounds very fine indeed—but somehow I don't know whether to believe it or not. Last week Mr. Markland convinced me that this shovel could not be salvaged. Then you almost convinced me that you *had* salvaged it. Then Mr. Markland found such glaring flaws in your story that I was sure you had *not* salvaged it. And now Mr. Markland claims you have done it after all.

It just doesn't make sense. Can it be that both you and Mr. Markland are suffering from these Grand Canyon brain storms? Or am I the one that is crazy?

If you have any possible explanation, or any additional facts, which might permit me to achieve even a faint comprehension of what has been going on at Navaho Butte, I hope you will write me before they arrive with the wagon and roll me off to some institution.

Yours expectantly,
GILBERT HENDERSON

OFFICE OF ALEXANDER BOTTS
SALES MANAGER
EARTHWORM TRACTOR COMPANY
EARTHWORM CITY, ILLINOIS

Wednesday, January 31, 1940

Mr. Gilbert Henderson,
Earthworm Tractor Company,
San Francisco Branch,
San Francisco, California

DEAR HENDERSON: Needless to say, your letter handed me a hearty laugh. At the same time I can sympathize with your mental confusion.

This confusion, of course, is not in any way my fault.

Nor is it the fault of the Grand Canyon. I will admit that my emotions were a bit overstimulated by the contemplation of the Canyon's dizzy depths, and by the thought that Nature has here produced an excavation far more extensive than anything that could be achieved even by our peerless dirt-moving machinery.

And I will also admit that at one point in the proceedings I had a real brain storm. But its only effect was to inspire an unusually clear and effective bit of thinking—as I will explain later on.

Any misunderstanding that may have occurred was the natural result of the following factors:

1.   To salvage the shovel, I had to make a very unusual deal with the local contractor, Mr. Oscar Sneed.
2.   To put over this deal, I had to agree to keep it a secret from Mr. Markland, and from everybody else at Navaho Butte.
3.   This secrecy was—and is—necessary, because, if the details should leak out, Mr. Sneed might be in serious difficulties with the police.
4.   As long as Mr. Markland was in San Francisco, I could not be completely frank with you, for fear you might spill the beans.

In my letter, I tried to give you a hint of this. I stated flatly—and truthfully—that I had managed to get the shovel back where it belonged. But I prefaced my account of the actual salvage methods by saying it was merely something you might tell Mr. Markland—thus implying that you did not have to believe it yourself. Unfortunately, this delicate subtlety completely escaped you.

But now that Mr. Markland has left San Francisco, I can tell all—on the understanding that you keep it confidential. And, in order that you may understand exactly what happened, I will start at the beginning.

I arrived at Navaho Butte late on the evening of Sunday, January 21. After a good night's rest at the Navaho Hotel, I arose at crack of dawn, hired a drive-it-yourself car, and started for

Mr. Markland's bridge job on the highway which runs along the rim of the Grand Canyon. This highway is being realigned and paved, and the work necessitates the construction of three bridges across small side canyons.

Mr. Markland has a contract for one of these bridges. Mr. Sneed has contracts for two.

I arrived first at one of Mr. Sneed's jobs. Mr. Sneed himself was not present, but a gang of men were busily pouring concrete for one of the piers. At once it occurred to me that I might as well get a little advance dope on Mr. Sneed, and thus be in a better position to approach him in case I should need his help.

I therefore handed the foreman a cigar, and engaged him in conversation. Having noted that the cement-mixer was in a truly horrible state of repair, I promptly complimented the foreman for his skill in doing such a fine job with such poor equipment. This clever move on my part at once established me in his mind as a person of rare discernment—which indeed I am—and brought out some very useful information.

To begin with, the foreman made it clear that he did not like his boss, and was planning to quit as soon as he could locate another job. "If I was to call old man Sneed a skunk," he said, "I would be insulting a noble animal."

"Could you be more specific?" I asked. "Exactly what is it that you dislike about Mr. Sneed?"

"He's a low-down dirty crook," said the foreman. "All he knows is making big profits by driving his men like slaves, and double-crossing everybody he meets. Besides, he's drunk half the time. He's always raising hell on the job. He won't give anybody enough time to take care of the equipment properly. He won't spend any money for repairs. And when anything breaks down he blames somebody else—like last week when the shovel went phut"

"Oh," I said. "The shovel went phut?"

"Yes. The crowd clutches—on account of the linings being pretty near worn out—got chattering and slipping till the operator was half crazy. So he shut down, and tried to help them a little by tightening them up a bit and washing them out with gasoline. And just then Mr. Sneed came along, drunk as usual, and bawled him out for loafing on the job. For punishment, he told him he would have to work most of the night—on his own time and with no extra pay—driving the shovel to the next job."

"What next job?"

"This other bridge that he's putting in. It's about sixteen miles farther out on this same road. He had some dirt up there that he had to dig out in a hurry, and he thought it would be a smart idea to bamboozle the operator into moving the shovel free. But the operator wouldn't do it. He quit."

"I can't say I blame him"

"Me neither," said the foreman. "So then Mr. Sneed said, 'All right, I used to be a shovel-runner in the old days; I'll drive it up there myself.' So he did. And that's not all—" Here the foreman drew me to one side, and began speaking in a mysterious whisper. "Don't tell Mr. Sneed I told you this," he said. "I don't want him to fire me till I'm ready to quit."

"You may have complete confidence in my discretion," I said.

"All right," he replied, still whispering mysteriously. "When Mr. Sneed drove the shovel to the other job, he had to pass right by Mr. Markland's bridge job. And that was the night Mr. Markland's shovel fell into the canyon"

"You don't mean you're accusing Mr. Sneed—"

"I ain't accusing nobody," said the foreman. "I don't know what happened that night. But I do know that Mr. Sneed wanted all three of these bridge contracts, and he was plenty sore at Mr. Markland for underbidding him on one of them. I also know that when Mr. Sneed is sore—and drunk besides, like he was that night—he is apt to do almost anything. And that is all I've got to say."

"Thank you very much," I said. "You have said plenty." I then complimented him once more on the efficient handling of his job, handed him five cigars, and resumed my journey—meditating deeply.

It occurred to me that if the depraved Mr. Sneed had really pushed Mr. Markland's shovel into the canyon, and if I could prove it, I might possibly be able to saddle the criminal with the responsibility of salvaging the machine—thus saving myself a great deal of tedious labor.

With this pleasing thought in mind, I drove happily onward, enjoying the pleasant weather, and glancing sidewise from time to time to admire the beauties of the Grand Canyon, which, I am free to admit, is certainly some gully.

After about eight miles, I reached the site of Mr. Markland's bridge, and found the scene to be very much as I had anticipated. A single glance over the rim of the canyon at the unfortunate shovel, lodged on its narrow shelf of rock a few hundred feet down in those awe-inspiring depths, made me think that perhaps Mr. Markland had been right after all in his belief that any attempt at salvaging the machine would be impractical. Instead of discouraging me, however, this thought only served to reinforce my feeling that it would be very nice indeed if I could wish the job off onto somebody else as, for instance, Mr. Oscar Sneed.

Accordingly, I continued on my way. And after about eight miles more I came to Mr. Sneed's second bridge job. Here I learned from some of the workmen that Mr. Sneed had just fired one of his tractor drivers, and had temporarily abandoned the shovel to drive the tractor. At the moment he was up the line about half a mile after a load of gravel, but he was expected back very soon.

While awaiting his return, I improved my time by looking over the big shovel, which was parked nearby. As I think I told you in a former letter, Mr. Sneed's shovel was one of our Number D77 two-yard Diesels—the same model as Mr. Markland's. In view of all the complaints in Mr. Sneed's recent letters, I had expected to find this piece of equipment in very bad condition. Much to my surprise, however, I found that it was apparently in very good shape. Then my quick eye detected something very peculiar—the name plate bearing the number of the chassis had been removed. I climbed into the cab. I looked for the motor number, which, as you know, is stamped on the rear of the crankcase. And I found that this number had been filed off—apparently quite recently.

About this time I heard the noise of a motor, accompanied by a lot of creaking and clanking. Looking out the door of the cab, I saw arriving a Number DC90 Earthworm tractor pulling a trailer-load of gravel. The tractor was obviously in very bad repair—reminding me of that ancient wise-crack which I first heard about the year 1909: every nut on the machine was loose, except the driver, and he was tight.

The tractor stopped. I jumped down, and walked over beside it.

And, in the few seconds which this action required, I experienced something which Mr. Markland would doubtless call a Grand Canyon brainstorm, but which might better be termed a flash of pure inspiration. In the twinkling of an eye, all the vague and disjointed questions and suspicions which had been building up in my mind fitted themselves together like the pieces of a puzzle. A great wave of comprehension swept over me. At last I understood what had been going on around here. And I realized that I was master of the situation; the Lord had delivered Mr. Sneed into my hands.

I looked up at the driver of the tractor. "Are you Mr. Sneed?" I asked.

"Yes," he said, roughly. "Who are you? What do you want?"

I introduced myself, and said I had come to see about the repairs on the shovel which he had asked for in his letters.

"I've changed my mind," he said sourly. "I don't want any repairs. And I want you to keep away from that shovel."

"Afraid I might find out something?"

"If you want to keep out of trouble," he said, "you'll get to hell out of here right now. You'll make tracks down that road. And you won't come back—see?"

"I can see a lot more than you think," I said. "So, if you want to keep out of trouble, and also out of jail, you'll listen to what I have to say. To begin with, I happen to know that you have been just itching to get even with Mr. Markland for taking one of these bridge contracts away from you?"

"So what?"

"So I can make a pretty good guess as to what happened that night last week when you started to drive your shovel up here. You were about half-drunk—like you are now. You couldn't think very well, but you could still think a little—like you can now. So, when you reached Mr. Markland's bridge job, and noticed that his shovel was parked on ground that sloped toward the canyon, you got to thinking that it would serve him right if you released the brake and let the old baby roll over the edge."

"I never did any such thing!"

"No. You thought some more. And you hit on a better plan. It occurred to you that your shovel was a worn-out wreck. Mr. Markland's was in swell shape. But they were the same model. They looked alike. And nobody would ever know if you made a switch. So what you finally did was dump your own machine into the canyon, and drive away with Mr. Markland's"

"You're crazy. I never even thought of any such thing."

"Sure you did. And it wasn't such a bad idea at that—for a guy like you. If Mr. Markland lost his shovel, he couldn't complete his bridge. That would give you a chance to take over, and finish the job—using Mr. Markland's own shovel. And it would be perfectly safe. Everybody would think it was a simple accident—Mr. Markland forgot to set his brake, and his poor old shovel just rolled away."

Mr. Sneed glared down at me from the seat of the tractor. "The whole thing is a damn lie," he said. "If you don't take it back, I'll come down there and knock your words right back down your throat. I mean it, too. I've killed men for less than what you've just said to me"

"Take it easy," I said. "There are a lot of workmen around here that would like nothing better than to testify against you in court. So any attempt at murder would just get you a longer term in the pen. The only way you can save your skin is to do what I tell you. And my demands are very reasonable"

"What do you mean—reasonable?"

"There are three requirements. First, you drive this shovel—which belongs to Mr. Markland—back where it belongs. Second, you give me an order—with certified check attached—for a new shovel for yourself, to replace the one you dumped into the canyon. And, third, you promise to behave yourself in the future. If you do all this by tomorrow noon, I'll keep the whole matter dark."

"Suppose I refuse?"

"Then I call in the sheriff."

Mr. Sneed smiled in a sort of forced way. "It's a nice bluff," he said, "but it won't work. You got a smooth story, but it's all guesswork. You can't prove I ever put any shovel in any canyon."

"I don't have to," I said. "All I need is to prove that this shovel here belongs to Mr. Markland. And I can do it"

"How?"

"As a matter of fact, I've done it already. I've checked the motor number, and it agrees with the number on the machine we sold Mr. Markland."

At this point, Mr. Sneed's smile became a bit more spontaneous. "Now I know you're lying," he said. "There ain't no number on this motor. I filed it off."

"You filed off the regular number," I said. "But you missed the secret number"

"What secret number?"

"All motor manufacturers," I explained patiently, "put secret numbers inside their products."

"What for?"

"Mainly," I said, "to circumvent the devious activities of just such people as you."

"And there's a secret number inside this machine?"

"Certainly"

"Where inside?"

"That," I said, "is part of the secret. If I told you, you would soon get rid of the secret number too. And now," I went on, "I must be getting back to town. You have until tomorrow noon to carry out my instructions—"

"Wait a minute," said Mr. Sneed. "Even if it was true that I stole this shovel—which I don't admit—it would only get me in worse trouble if I returned it"

"How so?"

"Taking it back would be just the same as admitting I stole it in the first place. When people found out about it, they would have the cops after me in no time."

"You can move the shovel at night—secretly," I said. "And I've already promised that I won't squeal on you."

"But people would notice that my shovel was gone."

"Tell them you took it to a new job at some mine off across the desert. That would explain it all right"

"Maybe so, but how could anybody explain two shovels at Mr. Markland's bridge job—one in the canyon and one on top? People would get suspicious, and pretty soon they would begin to suspect me."

"Maybe," I said, "you could let down a box of dynamite on a long wire, and blow that other shovel off its perch. It looks to me as if it would fall into a part of the canyon that is invisible from the rim, and completely inaccessible."

"I guess that's true."

"All right," I said. "If you'll do everything I've told you, I'll do the rest. I'll spread the story around town that I hauled the shovel up out of the canyon myself—using special secret methods known only to the engineers of the Earthworm Tractor Company."

"Will anybody believe that?"

"Sure. People will swallow almost anything if it is fed them by an expert from out of town like me. And, even if they doubt me, I'm the one that's a liar—not you. So you'll be completely protected—provided, of course, you get everything attended to by tomorrow noon."

Leaving Mr. Sneed to think this over, I returned to town. Late that night I heard a distant explosion. Early next morning I drove out and found a perfectly good D77 Earthworm shovel parked beside Mr. Markland's bridge, and no shovel at all on the ledge three hundred feet below the rim.

A few hours later, back at the hotel, a very subdued Mr. Sneed handed me an order for a new shovel, with certified check attached. "You're certainly a good guesser," he said, with grudging admiration. "You had the whole story just about right. But, even so, I would have got by with it if it hadn't been for that damn secret number"

"Even the most perfect crime," I reminded him, "always had a flaw somewhere. So let this be a lesson to you; crime never pays."

I then made him promise to behave himself in the future, wished him goodbye, and sallied forth to spread my salvage story. Later in the day, I wrote the same tale to you, adding a few graphic details to make it more convincing. And, when I finally departed for Earthworm City that night, I felt that my trip to Arizona had been well worth while.

Trusting that you will agree, I am,

Most sincerely,

ALEXANDER BOTTS

P. S. Don't start worrying about that secret number. It was located inside my own head—not the motor—and was composed almost entirely of hot air generated by the Grand Canyon brain storm.

The Cockroach Cavalry

OFFICE OF ALEXANDER BOTTS
SALES MANAGER
EARTHWORM TRACTOR COMPANY
EARTHWORM CITY, ILLINOIS

Thursday, May 1, 1941

Mr. Gilbert Henderson,
President,
Earthworm Tractor Company,
Earthworm Branch Office,
Washington, D. C.

DEAR HENDERSON: This is to let you know that I have decided to resign my position as Sales Manager of the Earthworm Tractor Company and join the army. My reasons are as follows:

I have just heard that the army has canceled their contract for five hundred of our recently developed "fighting cockroaches" or one-man midget tanks—and this at the very moment when we are getting into actual production. As you, in spite of all your efforts at Washington, have been unable to prevent this disaster, I feel that it is up to me to do something about it.

Instead, however, of attacking this and other related problems in my present capacity as a representative of the company, I have decided that I can accomplish more by getting a commission as an officer, and working inside the army—which is where most of our difficulties seem to originate.

Another reason for my action is that I am getting sick of my job as Sales Manager. Ever since the national defense program began to create a demand for more tractors than we can produce, I have had to spend all my time persuading customers not to buy tractors—a job which would drive any good salesman crazy.

In view of the above considerations, I am today forwarding to the War Department my application for a commission as a tractor expert in the Specialist Reserve of the United States Army. And I want you to use any influence you may have with the brass hats down there to see that this application goes through at once.

As I was only a private in the last war, I do not expect too high a rank. On the other hand, as I am probably the leading tractor expert in the country, I should think a commission as colonel would be about right.

Yours patriotically,

ALEXANDER BOTTS

Alexander Botts, played by the inimitable Joe E. Brown, matches up an Earthworm tractor against old-fashioned horsepower in the film Earthworm Tractors.

EARTHWORM BRANCH OFFICE
WASHINGTON, D. C.

Wednesday, May 7, 1941

DEAR BOTTS: Your letter of resignation was a distinct surprise. After thinking it over, however, I am inclined to believe that your decision to join the army is a wise one. In the past, the principal flaw in your otherwise sterling character has been an unfortunate tendency toward insubordination and lack of respect for authority. For this reason, I feel that a period of service under the strict discipline of the army will do you a lot of good.

As we shall want you back after the emergency, I am granting you a leave of absence rather than accept your resignation. And it is my earnest hope that when you return you will have seen the error of your ways, and that you will agree with my feeling that efficiency in any organization can be achieved only when all orders are obeyed cheerfully and promptly, with no monkey-business or back talk.

I am happy to inform you that I have taken up your case with a number of my friends in the War Department, with the result that you have been commissioned a captain in the Specialist Reserve assigned to the mechanized cavalry. You will receive orders to report for duty in a few days.

Wishing you the greatest possible success in your new career,

Cordially yours,
GILBERT HENDERSON

To: Mr. Gilbert Henderson, Washington, D. C.
From: Captain Alexander Botts, Fort Clemens, Missouri.
Date: Monday, May 12, 1941
Subject: A Hideous Mistake Has Been Made.

This is to inform you, Henderson, that your well-meant efforts to start me on my army career have resulted in getting me launched completely upside down, backward and in the wrong direction. When my commission and orders arrived last week, I was naturally disappointed to find that I was only a captain, and that, instead of receiving an important post in Washington I had been assigned to a regiment stationed in Missouri. But that was not the worst. It was not until this morning, when I arrived to report for duty here at Camp Clemens, that I became aware of the horrible fate that was in store for me.

As I entered the camp gate—attired in my new uniform and riding in a taxi which I had hired at the nearby railroad station—I began craning my neck in an attempt to see what sort of tanks and other mechanical equipment this regiment employed. At once a cold chill came over me. A feeling of ominous foreboding gripped my vitals. There were no tanks. There was no mechanical equipment. Instead, my horrified gaze rested upon rows and rows of horses, tied to picket lines. In every direction they cluttered the landscape—horses, horses, horses, horses—swishing flies with their silly tails, gnawing at bunches of hay, or just gazing about in a vacant manner.

We stopped in front of the tent of the regimental commander, Colonel H. H. McKenzie-Morton. I entered, introduced myself, and presented my orders. The Colonel—an elderly gentleman, perhaps sixty years old—was unusually stiff and military. Right away I knew I didn't like the guy. And I have reason to suspect that he felt somewhat the same about me.

"Listen, Colonel," I said. "I thought I was coming to a tank outfit. What is the meaning of all these horses I see outside?"

"This is a cavalry regiment," said the Colonel, with a touch of austere pride. "A real live cavalry regiment. Thank the Lord, we have not yet been forced to adopt this modern craze for vile inanimate machinery."

"In that case," I said, "the sooner I get out of here the better."

"What do you mean?"

"When you gaze on me," I explained, "you are gazing on a man who is probably the greatest authority on tractors and crawler equipment the world has ever known. Up until last week I was the Sales Manager of the great Earthworm Tractor Company. My commission is supposed to be in the mechanized force. But apparently some half-wit at the War Department has ignorantly assigned me here. So there is only one thing to do, Colonel. I want you to put through an order in a hurry sending me back where I belong."

"Do I understand," asked the Colonel, "that you are presuming to issue orders to me your superior officer?"

"Don't be silly, Colonel," I said affably, "I am a business man. You won't get anywhere trying to pull this hard-boiled military stuff on me. All I'm trying to do is to correct a foolish mistake."

Unfortunately my attempt to smooth matters down only seemed to goad the Colonel into a deplorable exhibition of military unreasonableness.

"Captain Botts," he said, "you are now in the army. You have been ordered to duty with my regiment. You will obey this order."

As he spoke, Colonel McKenzie-Morton glared at me so fiercely that I almost laughed in his face.

"Come on, Colonel," I said. "Be yourself. Be reasonable. You may not have a great deal of sense, but you must have enough to realize that there is no point in having me hang around this dump with all these silly horses. If you won't give me permission to go, I'll just have to leave without permission."

At this the Colonel rose to his feet. "Captain Botts," he said, speaking quietly but with suppressed passion. "No subordinate can come into my post of command and speak to me as you have spoken—and expect to get by with it. Ordinarily I should be only too glad to dispense with the services of an officer who is nothing but a mechanic. But in your case I feel that I have a certain duty to perform. Quite obviously, you have not the slightest conception of the meaning of military discipline. For your own good, therefore, and for the good of the Service, I must take it upon myself to knock a little sense into you. Your request for a transfer is hereby refused, and you will remain in this organization until such time as you get over your insubordinate attitude and give evidence that you are fit to perform the duties of an officer in the United States Army."

About this time it gradually began to come over me that Colonel McKenzie-Morton meant business, and that very likely the big bum had the necessary authority to carry out his idiotic ideas. As I stood there in front of him, getting more and more uneasy, my mind began turning back to the far off days of 1918 when I had been a private in the first World War. I began to recall various half-forgotten occasions when I had collided with certain obnoxious persons who at that time had held authority over me. On every one of these occasions, the higher authorities—to the best of my memory—had always won out. Can it be, I asked myself, that history is about to repeat itself? The answer was not long in arriving.

"I will have an orderly show you to your tent," said the Colonel. "You will remain there to await further orders. And let there be no mistake. When I say that you will remain there, that is exactly what I mean. If there is any attempt on your part to leave this camp without my permission, you will be placed under immediate arrest. Have I made myself clear?"

"Yes, sir," I said.

That terminated our little conference, and I have been spending the rest of the morning sitting here in my tent writing this letter. Now that you understand the situation, you will realize, I hope, that the next move is up to you. There seems to be nothing I can do by myself. If you have read this far, you will realize that the army system of discipline—far from improving me, as you apparently hoped—has merely made it possible for this colonel to practically kidnap me, and thus sabotage all the good I might have done toward improving the mechanization of the army.

The next move is therefore up to you. You must rush around to the War Department at once, see all your influential friends, and insist that I be rescued from this wretched livery-stable outfit at once.

Yours,

ALEXANDER BOTTS

———————

TELEGRAM

NEW YORK, N. Y. MAY 14, 1941

TO CAPTAIN ALEXANDER BOTTS,
FORT CLEMENS, MO.
YOUR LETTER FORWARDED TO ME HERE. I WILL TAKE UP
YOUR CASE WITH WAR DEPARTMENT WHEN I RETURN TO
WASHINGTON IN ABOUT TWO WEEKS. IN THE MEANTIME, I
AM SURE YOUR EXPERIENCE WITH REAL ARMY DISCIPLINE
WILL DO YOU A LOT OF GOOD.

GILBERT HENDERSON

FORT CLEMENS, MISSOURI,

Thursday, May 15, 1941

DEAR HENDERSON: Your callous indifference to my fate, evidenced by your statement that you won't do anything for me for about two weeks, does not bother me as much as might be supposed. As a matter of fact, I am now getting along so well here that I want to stay a little longer. This does not mean that I am weakly submitting myself to the absurd army system of discipline. Quite the contrary. What I am doing is giving the system a much-needed cleaning up and de-lousing—commencing with old Colonel McKenzie-Morton as Louse Number One.

The opportunity for opening my campaign came on the afternoon of the day I arrived, when the Colonel summoned me to his tent and spoke about as follows: "Captain Botts, your ignorance of horses and military matters makes it impossible for me to assign you to any duty with this regiment in keeping with your rank. I have therefore decided to give you a pick-and-shovel job. Unfortunately, as you are an officer, I do not feel justified in requiring you to swing a pick personally—much as I should like to. So I am putting you in charge of a small detail of enlisted men—most of them unruly characters who are being given extra fatigue duty as punishment for insubordination. They are to dig a ditch for a water main. My adjutant will take you out at once and explain the nature of the operation. You will start work tomorrow morning. Tomorrow afternoon I shall inspect what you have been doing. And I shall expect to find that you have, made satisfactory progress. That is all."

When the adjutant showed me the ditch-digging project, I saw at once that it was a real honey. A half mile of four-inch water main had to be buried four feet deep. And only twelve men with picks and shovels had been assigned for the entire job.

The adjutant—a good egg—gave me some helpful information. "I think the Colonel is trying to ride you," he said. "These men he is giving you are a mean bunch. They are all mechanics who enlisted in the cavalry on the understanding that they would be placed in mechanized units. When, through some mistake, they were sent here, they became sullen and rebellious. So you'll have to be plenty tough if you expect to get anything out of them"

"It seems to be a custom in this army," I said, "to put square pistons in round cylinders. But thanks for the tip. I think I can handle these birds all right."

I promptly went to the camp telephone exchange and called our St. Louis Earthworm Tractor dealer. Appealing to his sense of patriotism, I asked for help. And I am happy to say that he rallied around at once—not, like some people, after about two weeks.

The next morning, when I marched my little pick-and-shovel brigade out to the diggings, I had a pleasant surprise in store for them. Our St. Louis dealer, after traveling all night, had arrived with a fleet of large trucks, loaded down with no less than three ditch-digging machines, several small tractors with bulldozers, and a lot of miscellaneous equipment. As soon as the eyes of my mechanics lit on all this beautiful machinery, their bitterness vanished like a bug sucked into a tractor radiator. With lusty good will, they unloaded the equipment, and in almost no time at all the dirt began to fly.

By noon the ditch was completed. By three P.M. the pipe was laid in the bottom, and the ditch had been backfilled. After we had thanked the dealer, he disappeared with his machinery in the direction of St. Louis. I then gathered my crew in the shade of a large pine tree, and served them with refreshments from an ice cream wagon which I had sent for from one of the neighboring towns.

About this time Colonel McKenzie-Morton came trotting up on a handsome steed. When he saw that the entire detail—instead of being hard at work as he had probably expected—was in reality lolling about on the greensward lapping up ice cream cones, he practically went off his nut.

"Captain Botts," he yelled, glaring down from his high horse, "I gave you a definite order to perform a certain definite task. And what do I find? You permit your men to loaf about as if they had nothing to do. What do you think this is, a Sunday-school picnic? Have you any explanation as to why you have deliberately disobeyed my orders?"

While this harangue was going on, I had called my men to attention—a procedure which, according to my vague memories of 1918, seemed the proper thing under the circumstances. I advanced to a point directly beside the Colonel's horse, saluted as snappily as I could, and glared up at the old guy. I then got off a little speech whose effect I was able to heighten by using that obsolescent third person form of discourse occasionally affected by old-fashioned and superannuated military men.

"Sir," I said, "as long as the Colonel has seen fit to reprimand Captain Botts in the presence of his men, Captain Botts requests the privilege of answering this reprimand at once and in the presence of these same men."

"If you've got anything to say for yourself, you'd better say it and say it quick, without all this beating around the bush."

"The Colonel's charges reveal that he does not know what he is talking about," I said. "Therefore, Captain Botts demands a trial by court-martial—at which he will be prepared to prove that he has carried out the Colonel's orders in toto—"

"Don't be a damn fool," said the Colonel.

"And, at which Captain Botts will also be prepared to prove that the Colonel has used profane language unbecoming an officer and a gentleman—"

"All right," snarled the Colonel, "you'll get your court martial."

"Easy now, Colonel," I said, relapsing into ordinary English. "The only orders I got were to dig a ditch, lay a water main, and fill up the ditch again. Okay—the job is done."

"Are you trying to tell me that with only twelve men working less than a day, you have buried a half mile of pipe four feet deep? It's impossible!"

"That's what you think," I said. "And, in the horse and buggy age in which you exist, it would be. But to a modern mechanic like me, it is as simple"—I snapped my fingers—"as that."

I then took the old Colonel over to the scene of our labors and showed him the freshly turned earth. I explained in great detail how I had very sensibly borrowed the necessary equipment, and exactly how the job had been accomplished. And, in the end, he had to believe me. He was convinced—but far from licked.

"Captain Botts," he said, "you seem to be a very bright young man, but you are not quite bright enough. I'm going to let you off this time, but you will soon find that in the army, this smart aleck attitude of yours will get you into very serious trouble. That is all." He turned his horse and trotted back to camp. The rest of us followed on foot.

That was day before yesterday. Since then, the Colonel has been using me and my twelve-man detail on various odd jobs cleaning up around the camp. I have told my men that if they will play ball with me now, I will do everything I can to get them into a mechanized outfit later on. They are therefore working for me very dutifully, and everything is going smoothly.

I have thus completed the first part of my army-improvement campaign. The Colonel has been shown that my up-to-date system of intelligent leadership plus machinery works much better on a ditch-digging job than his antiquated system of bull-headed discipline and horse-and-buggy technique. Although he is still sore, and probably laying for me, he has undoubtedly lost much of his previous feeling of infallibility. And he is therefore ripe for the next phase—in which I plan to demonstrate how mechanical cavalry, when intelligently led, can just naturally skin the pants off of his quaint medieval horse outfit.

In preparation for this event, I have wired the factory to ship me—at one of the nearby towns—a half dozen of our recently-perfected small cockroach tanks. These machines I will keep in hiding until next week, when there is to be a war game—or sham battle—between this cavalry outfit and an infantry regiment from Fort Leonard Wood. Then, as soon as old Colonel McKenzie-Morton gets into trouble—as he is sure to do with all these fool horses to cope with—I will offer the services of my tanks. As the Colonel will want to win the battle, and as he must have at least a faint substratum of common-sense in his otherwise heavily hossified intellect, he will have to accept, I will then put over a real mechanized attack which will win the battle.

In gratitude, the Colonel will be constrained to listen to my request for a transfer, and to put in a good word for our tanks with the War Department—thus making it easier for me to get our contract reinstated. If everything goes as I expect, it will be unnecessary for you to take up my case with the big shots at Washington. I have a feeling that I am going to work everything out by my own efforts.

> Yours,
>
> ALEXANDER BOTTS

TELEGRAM

NEW YORK, MONDAY, MAY 19, 1941

TO CAPTAIN ALEXANDER BOTTS
FT. CLEMENS, MO.
AS YOU ARE NOW ON LEAVE OF ABSENCE FROM THE EARTH-
WORM COMPANY, YOUR ACTION IN ORDERING SHIPMENT OF
THOSE SIX TANKS IS ENTIRELY UNWARRANTED—ESPECIALLY
AS YOU HAVE NO AUTHORITY TO ACCEPT THEM ON BEHALF
OF THE ARMY. YOU WILL SHIP THEM BACK AT ONCE. I WOULD
FURTHER SUGGEST THAT YOU ABANDON YOUR FUTILE
EFFORTS TO IMPROVE THE ARMY AND CONDUCT YOURSELF
IN SUCH A WAY THAT THE ARMY MAY HAVE A CHANCE TO
IMPROVE YOU.
GILBERT HENDERSON

To: Mr. Gilbert Henderson, Earthworm Branch Office, Graybar
Building, New York City.
From: Captain Alexander Botts, Camp Clemens, Missouri.
Date: Wednesday, May 21, 1941
Subject: Trouble with the Army System of Discipline.

I beg to report that the army system of discipline is still doing
me no good. As a matter of fact, it has now got me under arrest
and confined to quarters, so I am utterly unable to ship back
those tanks as you request. Furthermore, I am facing court-
martial charges which the Colonel may be able, this time, to
make stick.

I must therefore renew my request that you get down to
Washington in a hurry, pull all the wires in sight, and try to get
me out of this mess. And, in order that you may appreciate the

seriousness of the situation, I will give you a brief and snappy account of what has occurred.

Night before last, Colonel McKenzie-Morton called in all of the officers of the regiment and explained the two-day sham-battle which was to start the following morning. It seemed that an infantry regiment, supported by several batteries of field artillery, was to advance from the south up the narrow Ozark valley in which our camp is located, and try to capture a small town ten miles behind us. Our job was to prevent this—not by shooting, of course, but by outmaneuvering the enemy. The issue would be decided by umpires—army officers with white hat-bands—who were supposed to swarm all over the field, and decide who had got there first with the most fire-power.

"Our mission is defensive," said the Colonel. "But a real cav-alryman—" here he swelled out his chest—"thinks only of attack. Our defense will therefore be dynamic. Holding the lines in the valley here with half our force, we shall send the other half through the mountains on our right to fall upon the enemy's flank, and annihilate him. And I wish to point out," he contin-ued, fixing his gaze directly on me, "that for work such as this the horse is still supreme. As both our flanks rest on mountain-ous country devoid of good roads, we have no use whatever for mechanical innovations such as portées."

Note: Portèes are motor trucks used for transporting cav-alry horses when they have to get some place in a hurry. Mod-ern cavalry, of course, fights on foot. But a good cavalryman is so dependent on the companionship of his horse that he always has to take him along, even when he has to drag him in a truck to a battle where he won't be any use after he gets there. This procedure is obviously so cumbersome that I could well under-stand Colonel McKenzie-Morton's doubts on the matter.

When the Colonel had concluded his remarks, I arose and

attempted to make a little speech of my own. "Colonel," I said, "I am just as skeptical of portée cavalry as you are. But that does not mean that all motorized equipment is no good. If you want to put on a real flank movement tomorrow, the ideal equipment is the Earthworm Tractor Company's cockroach cavalry—"

"Captain Botts," interrupted the Colonel severely. "No one has asked for any comments from you on this or any other matter."

"All right," I said to myself, "if you won't listen to me, I will have to show you."

Next morning, after the bulk of the regiment moved out, I marched five of my twelve mechanics to the freight station where our six little one-man cockroach tanks had arrived several days previously. The boys at the factory had done a remarkably thorough job on the equipment—each tank being supplied with a machine gun, plenty of blank ammunition, lights, winch, cable, tools, and everything else that could be desired. When my men saw these mechanical masterpieces, their enthusiasm knew no bounds. And after a brief period of instruction they were raring to go. We climbed aboard, and started forth on a flanking movement which for sheer speed and scope was designed to make the horse cavalry look like a bunch of paleological snails.

The horses had started around our right flank, so I chose the left and, on account of my superior speed, I decided to move in a very wide arc, sweeping so far out beyond the enemy's right flank that the possibility of meeting hostile patrols was practically eliminated.

The hardest part was getting over the first ridge. We followed trails so narrow that no tank bigger than our three-foot wide midgets could have gotten through. We crossed mountain swamps which would have mired down any man or horse. And at one place we had to use the winches and cables to pull the machines up over an almost vertical thirty-foot cliff. By this time I began to realize that Colonel McKenzie-Morton had probably been very wise in not attempting this particular terrain with his horses. Even with our splendid little mechanical cockroaches the going was very slow indeed. By sunset we had covered—according to a map I had mooched from the adjutant—only ten miles. But we were over the ridge, and had reached a good gravel road in the valley beyond.

From here on it was easier. Speeding along country roads at thirty to forty miles an hour, we zigzagged our way—east, then south, then west, and finally north—over a gigantic sweep of over two hundred miles which brought us directly behind the center of the enemy's lines. This I hoped would be the one place they would not be expecting us.

And I am happy to report that I was right. Our first contact with the enemy came shortly after dawn when we rounded a blind curve in the road and found ourselves directly behind a battery of field artillery. Swinging into line, we almost scared the cannoneers to death with a mighty burst of blank ammunition from our machine guns. At once an umpire popped up and demanded an explanation. I opened the shutter of the turret. I explained that I had just annihilated the battery. He seemed puzzled. He said he had not been informed that the opposing forces had any tanks. I assured him that we did. And, as I had the machines right there to prove it, he finally admitted that his information must have been faulty, and ruled that the battery was out of action for the balance of the maneuvers.

Encouraged by this success, I led my fighting cockroaches down the road for another mile, where we had the rare privilege of shooting up a squad of military police, but got no credit for it because there was no umpire around. After that we did not bother with enemy forces unless we saw the white hat-band of an umpire near by. We roared up one road and down another.

We caught one whole infantry company in a field, and an umpire ruled that half of them were out of action. After a couple of hours, we got another battery of field artillery.

Later in the morning we grabbed a messenger on a motorcycle and read the messages he was carrying. From these we learned that two batteries, consisting of eight seventy-five millimeter field pieces, had been withdrawn from the lines and concealed at various cross roads throughout the area as a defense against our little roving fleet of tanks. I realized that if we got in range of one of these seventy-fives, the umpires would at once rule us out of action. So I decided that it might be wise for us to get out of there and head for home. On the way back, however, I resolved to attempt a final exploit which, if successful, would be far more brilliant than any of our previous successes. What I planned was nothing less than the capture of the commander-in-chief of the enemy.

We had heard that this gentleman, an infantry colonel, had his headquarters in a camp behind the left flank of his regiment. As the terrain between us and this camp was by this time presumably infested with seventy-five millimeter cannon, we decided on another grand sweep.

We drove thirty miles south until we were well out of the battle area, then straight west into a group of mountains, then north, and finally east so as to take the camp on the opposite side from where they would probably be looking for us.

This maneuver took longer than we expected. We got lost several times. But about two o'clock in the afternoon we finally emerged from the wooded mountains, and saw the camp directly ahead of us. Roaring down the dusty road at forty miles per hour we shot full speed into the camp gate—discharging bursts of blank machine gun fire as we went. In front of me I saw a tent with two flags in front of it. Straight for that tent I headed. At the last minute I slammed on the brakes, cut the machine gun and skidded to a stop with the front end of my tank just inside the door. Peering into the gloom of the interior I saw an officer with what looked like silver eagles on his shoulders. Beside him was a man with the white hat-band of an umpire. I flung open the shutter of the turret.

For a moment I considered the possibility of getting off a real historic wisecrack, something like "Surrender in the name of the Earthworm Tractor Company and the Cockroach Cavalry!" but, somehow, this seemed a little fantastic. So I merely said, "Sir, you are my prisoner."

It was my moment of triumph. As I clambered out of the tank, I said to myself, "If only that suspicious and skeptical old Colonel McKenzie-Morton could see me now!"

This wish, I regret to say, was granted with startling suddenness.

"Captain Botts," said Colonel McKenzie-Morton—for it was indeed he—"what is the meaning of this outrageous conduct?"

I gazed at him with speechless astonishment. Slowly I began to realize what had happened. While lost in the mountains, we had traveled farther than I had supposed. We had turned the flanks of both armies. We were once more behind our own lines. And I had just captured my own commanding officer.

But he would not stay captured. With a burst of military language which almost blew the sides out of the tent, he informed me that I was the one who was a prisoner. I was under arrest. I would be confined to my tent. I was guilty of insubordination, disobedience of orders, lack of respect for my superiors, and many other things.

"Last week," he said, "you made a smart aleck request for a court-martial. All right—this time you are going to have it. And now you can get out of here, and take your filthy machinery with you. And don't try to give me any back talk."

As I could think of nothing better to do, I backed the tank

out of the tent, had my men park our machines at the rear of the camp, and retired to my tent—where I have been writing this letter.

So now, Henderson, you can see how the army system of discipline—which you have so fatuously affected to admire—has permitted this equimaniac Colonel to halt all my efforts toward modernizing the army. This halt, however, will be only temporary—provided you do your part. You must hurry to Washington. You must explain the situation to the highest authorities in the War Department. You must persuade them to order the court-martial charges dropped, to transfer me out of this livery stable outfit, and to put me in the Ordnance Corps where I can be of real service in the defense of my country. Do not fail me. I am counting on you.

Yours hopefully,
ALEXANDER BOTTS

P.S. Next Morning. May 22, 1941

This is to report that Colonel McKenzie-Morton came in about an hour ago to announce that my punishment would be even worse than he had previously intended.

"Captain Botts," he said. "I have just received from the umpires a complete account of your activities yesterday and the day before. It appears that you accomplished a very remarkable flanking maneuver—going completely around the enemy, and causing a degree of confusion behind their lines which was an important factor in this regiment's successful defense of its position. All this, however, in no way excuses your gross insubordination in acting without any authority from me. I have decided, therefore, that I cannot let you off with a mere trial by a military court."

"But listen, Colonel—"

"I have decided," he continued, "that your complete lack of any sense of military discipline will make it impossible for you ever to become a successful cavalry officer. I am, therefore, throwing you out of this magnificent arm of the service and—at the request of a couple of Ordnance officers who have been acting as observers at the maneuvers—I am demoting you to the Ordnance Corps. You are, therefore, released from arrest. You will report at once to the two Ordnance officers whom I mentioned, and you will be prepared to leave with them this afternoon. Good-bye."

The two Ordnance officers turned out to be splendid fellows. They had been so impressed by the performance of the cockroach tanks that they are going to recommend the reinstatement of our contract. And they rank so high that their recommendation is certain to be followed. They have arranged to transfer my twelve mechanics into a mechanized outfit. And they are going to appoint me as chief inspector at the factory in Earthworm City during the production of the tanks.

In view of all this, I am happy to inform you that I will not need your influence at the War Department after all. And I also wish to inform you that I have seen the error of my ways and come around to your way of thinking on the subject of discipline. I am now prepared to admit that obedience is necessary for the proper conduct of any enterprise. And whenever I have occasion, in my future career as inspector at the factory, to issue any orders to you, Henderson, I shall expect them to be obeyed promptly and cheerfully, without any back talk or monkey-business.

Yours,

ALEXANDER BOTTS

Alexander Botts
Obeys Orders

EARTHWORM TRACTOR COMPANY
BRANCH OFFICE
WASHINGTON, D. C.

Thursday, May 13, 1943

Capt. Alexander Botts,
Fort Kane, Florida

DEAR BOTTS: A friend in the War Department informs me that you will soon complete your work in Florida, and that you will have a leave of absence before reporting for your next assignment on the Alaska Highway.

As you will undoubtedly be passing through Earthworm City, I would like you to spend three or four days helping us out on a very important project. The recently organized Scully Scraper Company, at their new factory just across the river from our Earthworm City plant, has completed a pilot model of a new type of self-propelled scraper, which is powered by one of our motors, and which the U. S. Army engineers are considering using for the construction and maintenance of military roads and airfields.

In adapting our motor to this novel machine, certain difficulties have arisen which will probably make necessary a complete rebuilding job. This will require the advice of someone thoroughly familiar with construction work in the field.

Because of your wide experience in our Earthworm sales department and, more recently, in the Army, I feel that your counsel in this matter will be invaluable. I have already discussed the matter with the authorities here in Washington, and I shall be hopefully awaiting your acceptance of my suggestion.

Most sincerely,

GILBERT HENDERSON
President Earthworm Tractor
Company

FORT KANE, FLORIDA

Saturday, May 15, 1943

DEAR HENDERSON: Your suggestion is hereby turned down flat. My leave, exclusive of travel time, is for only four days. It is the first leave I have had since I entered the Army two years ago. And I refuse to spend it picking the bugs out of some newfangled scraper. I have other plans.

Although, in my business correspondence with you, I have not had occasion for a long time to mention my family, you must not forget that I have an unusually high-grade wife and two very remarkable children. It is with them, in our modest but attractive home on Earthworm Heights, that I intend to spend every minute of my pitifully short period of freedom.

So you can take your old scraper and do anything you want with it, provided you do not bother

Your former sales manager,

ALEXANDER BOTTS

EARTHWORM TRACTOR COMPANY
BRANCH OFFICE
WASHINGTON, D. C.

Monday, May 17, 1943

Capt. Alexander Botts,
Fort Kane, Florida

DEAR BOTTS: When I showed your somewhat discourteous letter to the Army authorities here, they at once informed me that
they consider your assistance in this scraper project a military
necessity. And I understand that an order has been issued can-
celing your leave and directing you to report to Maj. Henry W.
Hooper, who is the Army representative at the plant of the Scully
Company.

I am sorry to disrupt your plans, but you must remember
that with the nation at war your personal desires cannot be considered. And I am glad that the matter is now settled. Even
though you may be so unpatriotic as to turn down a request from
me, I feel sure you will bear in mind that the first duty of a soldier is to obey, and that it would be unthinkable for you to disregard a direct military order.

Very sincerely,

GILBERT HENDERSON

———————————

EARTHWORM CITY, ILLINOIS

Saturday evening, May 22, 1943

DEAR HENDERSON: All right. You win. The Army order arrived
in Florida at the same time as your letter. And I know you will
be delighted to hear that I am carrying it out to the fullest extent of my ability. Even though I have grave doubts about the
way things are going, the habit of obedience has become so much

a part of my character during my two years in the military service that I am no longer capable of insubordination.

Since my arrival in Earthworm City yesterday morning, my time has been so completely taken up in carrying out the orders of Major Hooper at the Scully Scraper Company that I have had no time even to see my family—which, I suppose, will give you a certain cheap and temporary satisfaction.

As soon, however, as I explain what goes on out here, and describe the truly remarkable project which your interference has compelled me to undertake, it is very possible that you may not be quite so pleased with yourself. In order that you may have a full understanding of the affair, it will be necessary for me to start out by describing my arrival in Earthworm City yesterday morning, and then work up gradually to the unfortunate situation which now exists.

As I gazed from the window of the train which brought me down the valley toward this great tractor metropolis, I noticed that it was raining hard and that the river seemed unusually high. The conductor claimed it was the biggest flood ever known in these parts, with the gauge on the Earthworm Avenue Bridge at 26.5 feet, and the water still rising.

When we reached Earthworm City, it was clear that the business section and residence districts, being on high ground, were in no danger. But I was worried about the Earthworm Tractor plant, which, as you know, is located on the flats along the river at the edge of town. I hurried over, and ran into a situation that was at once tense and encouraging.

Confronted by the sudden danger that the plant might be inundated, the entire organization of the great Earthworm Tractor Company had gone into action in a way that brought a thrill to my heart. All production in the shops had ceased and thirteen thousand men, ably led by their own foremen and superintendents, had marched forth to defend the crumbling levee which extends for some ten miles along the river bank and protects not only the Earthworm factory but the large farm area to the south and east. Trucks were arriving from all directions laden with bags. Hundreds of willing workers were filling these bags with sand at the dump outside the foundry, and loading them back in the trucks. Great fleets of tractors with bulldozers and scrapers were laying up roads across the bottom lands so the trucks could take the filled bags to various points on the levee. And all along the levee, as far as I could see, were great swarms of men, working like ants in the mud and the rain.

As the levee was a mere bank of ordinary earth—good old Illinois farm land—it was not completely leakproof. From time to time, at the weakest places, the water would seep through and suddenly come boiling up at the bottom of the inside slope. At once hundreds of men would swing into action—piling on thousands of sandbags if necessary—until the leak was stopped. At other places, where the levee was low, ramparts of sandbags were laid up to keep the muddy waters of the river from spilling over the top.

Some of the men had boots and raincoats. Some did not. But everyone, no matter how wet and dirty and tired, was working. There is nothing like a good flood to bring out the fighting spirit in a man. And the coordination and management were as remarkable as the fighting spirit. Orders from the foremen were transmitted through a system of loud-speakers set up by the electrical department. Field offices, first-aid stations, food stations and comfort stations had been set up in tents and portable shacks. At the factory, girls in the cafeteria slapped together tons of sandwiches which were transported to the workers along with a deluge of soup that almost rivaled the flooded river.

The boys in the purchasing department were keeping the telephone wires hot ordering rubber boots, raincoats, ponchos, shovels, wheelbarrows, hundreds of miscellaneous articles, and especially bags. They called up bag manufacturers, cement companies, seed merchants, grain elevators, fertilizer manufacturers, junk dealers, and everybody they could think of in the entire Midwest who might have bags. And they kept great fleets of bag-laden trucks rolling in. At the time of my arrival they had already received more than a million bags, with more to come.

One of the engineers, who had been talking with the Government flood expert, said that by tomorrow afternoon the crest was expected to reach twenty-nine feet. This would flood our shops five feet deep—if the levee broke. "But none of us are worried," he continued. "With everybody working the way we are, we've got this thing licked already."

"I agree with you," I said. And, heaving a somewhat premature sigh of relief, I prepared to depart, buoyed up by a feeling of confidence, which, I regret to say, has turned out to be completely unjustified.

Before leaving, I made a few discreet inquiries about my new boss, Major Hooper. I learned that he had visited the Earthworm plant several times to get advice about the Earthworm motor which had been installed on the new scraper. It was reported that he had received his Army commission largely on the recommendation of his father-in-law, Mr. Mark Scully, who lives in New York, and who is the founder and principal owner of the Scully Scraper Company. It was further reported that this Major Hooper is generally considered to be an inconsequential nincompoop.

It was with definite misgivings, therefore, that I started across the Earthworm Avenue Bridge. From this high-level structure I got a good view of the river—higher, swifter and muddier than I had ever seen it. Here and there I noticed trees and fragments of houses floating along. The old abandoned railroad bridge, a half mile downstream, seemed almost level with the water. Masses of wreckage were piled against it and the current was flowing through the open draw at high speed.

As I approached the opposite shore, I saw at once that the small factory of the Scully Scraper Company is on much lower ground than the Earthworm plant—being nestled in a hollow between the river and the bluffs, and protected by a curving levee not more than a half mile long. This levee was being strengthened by several hundred men—presumably from the scraper plant. They were working earnestly enough, but they lacked our superb Earthworm organization. They did not have enough sandbags. And the levee did not look any too good.

Entering the factory, I found Maj. Henry W. Hooper pacing his office in a state of considerable agitation. He was a disagreeable-looking shrimp in a new and very expensive uniform, with well-polished gold leaves on his shoulders. His face betokened a man who is both weak and stubborn, timid and conceited.

"The situation is terrible," he said. "If the levee breaks, the factory will be under twenty feet of water. Drastic action is required. And I won't let anybody argue me out of it."

"My name," I said, "is Botts."

"Never heard of you," he snapped. "What do you want?"

Note: At first I thought the major was joking. But no. Preposterous as it may seem, this man—who had been assigned as my superior officer in a job involving the use of tractor motors—was so ignorant of his subject that he had never even heard of one of the best-known tractor authorities in the whole country. It just goes to show that mistakes will occur even in such a splendid organization as the United States Army.

I started to explain. "I have been sent from Florida," I said, "to help you with your new scraper—"

"Oh, yes," he interrupted. "I remember now; I was notified that you were coming. Naturally, we have no time now for rebuilding the new scraper. This flood business is too urgent. But I think I can use you." An evil and crafty look came into his face.

"I am ready," I said.

"Good. Are you capable of obeying orders, literally and unquestioningly? And can you keep your mouth shut?"

"Certainly."

"Then I think you will do. I don't want you to say a word to anyone else about what I am now going to tell you. I have a plan for licking this flood. And I shall need your help."

"Good. What is the plan?"

"I am going to blow up the Earthworm Tractor Company's levee."

For a moment I was speechless. Then I said, "I don't think I quite understand, sir."

"It is very simple. Our present methods of flood control are all wrong. By building levees all along both sides of the river we merely confine the water and cause it to rise higher than ever. The only natural and sensible way to keep down the crest is to let the river spread out over the lowlands."

"Well," I said, "there might be something in that."

"Of course there is. Take the present case. As long as we and the Earthworm people keep building up our levees, the river, held in the narrow channel between, will get higher and higher, until both levees break. But if—"

"I think I get you," I said. "If either one of the levees were blown up, the other would be saved."

"Not at all," he said. "Breaking our levee would flood less than a square mile. The effect on the river would be negligible. But breaking the Earthworm Company's levee would flood almost a hundred square miles—which ought to lower the crest of the river very materially. It is obvious, therefore, that the Earthworm levee is the one that must go—especially when you consider that a flood over here would be far more disastrous than on the other side."

The major paused to let his argument sink in. And the more it sank in, the less I liked it.

"How so?"

"The Earthworm shops are on higher ground. A broken levee would flood them to a depth of scarcely five feet—nothing at all as compared to the twenty feet we would get here. Then, too, the Earthworm Company has plenty of money and resources to repair damage. The Scully Company, on the other hand, has already absorbed practically all the fortune of my wife's family. With us, a flood would be a real disaster."

"How did you happen to choose me to help you?" I asked.

"I have already mentioned my plan to several of the company executives here. But they would not listen to me."

"Why not?"

"They are hopelessly prejudiced. They all live in Earthworm City. They have friends in the Earthworm Company. And they seem to be afraid that these friends might not approve of my plan."

"Yes, I see what you mean."

"But with you it is different," said the major. "You are from Florida. You have no connections here. You can look at this thing in an impersonal, objective way."

Note: For a moment I debated whether I should enlighten Major Hooper on this point. But, just in time, I remembered that I am a soldier, and that in the Army it is not considered good form for a subordinate to contradict his superior and tell him he does not know what he is talking about. I therefore kept quiet.

"Another advantage in using you is that you are under my command. You are subject to my orders." The major swelled his little chest and tried to look important.

"Just what do you want me to do?" I asked.

"Can you drive a truck?"

"Yes."

"Good. I want you to drive me, in one of the company trucks, to a quarry about ten miles out in the country, where I have arranged to buy a thousand pounds of dynamite. I was very fortunate in locating it. And the only way I could get it was by certifying it is needed for Army purposes."

"I see"

"We will load this dynamite in our truck," Major Hooper continued, "bring it back here and put it into bags. And tonight, under cover of darkness, we will take it over and place it at a strategic point on the Earthworm Company's levee."

"Why put it in bags? And why under cover of darkness?"

"If we arrive in broad daylight with a lot of boxes labeled 'dynamite' we would attract attention, and people might try to stop us. This way, everybody will think we are merely strengthening the levee with sandbags"

"And after the dynamite is in place?"

"We will return here to the factory. If, as and when our levee shows signs of giving way, we can rush over at an instant's notice and shoot the works. If our levee holds, we need do nothing. You see, I feel that it would be morally wrong for us to flood the Earthworm factory unnecessarily"

"It is a feeling," I said, "which does you credit."

"Thank you," he said. "And now, let's get going."

Note: At this point I will admit that I experienced a momentary weakening of my high resolve to be a good soldier and obey the orders of my superior officer. Having spent so many years as a member of the Earthworm organization, it was almost beyond my powers even to consider committing an act which would bring disaster and distress upon my erstwhile friends and associates. My courage, however, was restored when I suddenly remembered the wise counsel expressed in your recent letter. "I feel sure," you had said, "you will bear in mind that the first duty of a soldier is to obey, and that it would be unthinkable for you to disregard a direct military order." This, as far as I was concerned, settled the matter.

Reluctantly, but with a feeling that I was doing my duty, I drove Major Hooper to the quarry. We loaded the truck with twenty boxes of dynamite and returned to the Scully plant. The major opened the door of a small storage building at the rear of the lot, and I drove the truck inside. The only other piece of equipment in the building was the pilot model of the new self-propelled scraper—which I had been sent here to work on, but which

I had not up to this time even had a chance to look at.

While the major went out to get some bags, I gave it a brief inspection. It looked all right to me. Later on, if I have an opportunity to try it out, I will send you a report on how it works.

Before long, the major returned with twenty-five empty bags of a brilliant red color and bearing the name of some sort of patent poultry feed.

"These are an odd lot," said the major. "They came from a near-by chicken farm, and they are probably the only ones around. The unusual color will make it easy for us to recognize them when the time comes to set off our blast"

We got busy at once. After closing the door of the building, we opened the boxes, took the paper off the sticks, crumbled the dynamite into the bags and lifted them gently into the truck. The job was a delicate one—especially as this was what is known as 60-per-cent dynamite, which is much juicier and richer in vitamins than the more usual 40-per-cent variety. After a couple of hours, we had our truck neatly loaded with what anybody along the levee would naturally suppose to be twenty-five bags of sand. We then concealed the empty dynamite boxes in the pan of the scraper, closed the door of the building, got ourselves a bite of lunch, and returned to Major Hooper's office.

The major had saved out two sticks of dynamite. He inserted a cap and a short length of fuse in each.

"These," he explained, as he put them in his desk drawer, "are to set off the explosion. I have fixed up two of them, so if one should fail, we'll still have the other. And remember," he continued, "you are not to say a word about this business to anyone"

"Yes, sir," I said.

Note: As he did not forbid writing about it, I feel that this letter is not in any way a violation of his order. Later in the afternoon, the major went out to inspect the levee, which has given me a chance to write to you. I have described the situation in great detail, so that you may be familiar with all the facts. It is possible that before long you may receive, from the executives at the Earthworm factory, sensational and garbled reports of dire disaster. And if my part in the proceedings becomes known, it may be that unjust accusations will be leveled at me. If so, I want you to know that I am innocent of all blame. All I have bean doing is following your advice and obeying orders.

It is now evening. The major has returned with the news that the levee is perfectly safe until tomorrow at least. He has therefore stretched out and gone to sleep on a cot which has been installed in the office; setting an alarm clock for midnight, at which time he plans to place the dynamite.

As for myself, I am too overwrought for sleep. From the window I can see the dark flow of the river—silent, ominous, sinister. On the near side, the men from the Scully factory are working on their pathetic little levee by the light of lanterns. Across the river, the more enterprising Earthworm boys have set up thousands of electric lights. Beyond looms the great Earthworm plant—the finest tractor factory in the world, now threatened by the greatest disaster in its history.

Far away in the night, a group of levee workers are singing the melancholy strains of River, Stay Way From My Door—a song which I never really appreciated till tonight. It almost makes me want to cry. But I must pull myself together. After all, I am doing my duty as a soldier. So I will sign myself,

Yours proudly,

ALEXANDER BOTTS

P.S.: 3 A.M. Sunday. Just back after placing those twenty-five red bags directly against one of the weakest places on the Earthworm levee. I will rush this letter to the airport, so it can catch the morning plane and be waiting for you when you reach your office Monday morning.

Yours hurriedly,

A. BOTTS

EARTHWORM TRACTOR COMPANY
BRANCH OFFICE
WASHINGTON, D. C.

Monday, May 24, 1943

DEAR BOTTS: Immediately upon receipt of your incredible letter, I got in touch with the Army authorities here. As telephone communication with Earthworm City has been disrupted by the flood, they promptly sent telegraphic orders to both Major Hooper and yourself, forbidding you to blow up our levee, and directing you to remove the dynamite at once. It is hoped these orders may get through in time. Meanwhile, as we have no word from Earthworm City, we can only hope for the best.

I may say that I am totally at a loss to understand your outrageous conduct in this affair. Even partial flooding of the great Earthworm plant would do infinitely more damage to our war effort than total loss of the insignificant fly-by-night Scully Scraper establishment. This Major Hooper, therefore, is obviously either a madman or a criminal.

Such being the case, it was—and is—your duty to use every means at your command to prevent him from carrying out his destructive plans. Nothing in my previous letter and nothing in the Army Regulations can fairly be construed as obligating you to give aid and assistance—as you admit you have done—to a dangerous maniac.

Kindly take notice, therefore, that you will be held strictly responsible for anything that may happen.

Yours,

GILBERT HENDERSON

EARTHWORM CITY, ILLINOIS

Wednesday, May 26, 1943

DEAR HENDERSON: The telegraphic orders arrived this morning, at the same time as your letter—too late to have any effect.
Acting like a good soldier and obeying the orders of my superior, Major Hooper, I had already set off the dynamite, thus opening an enormous gap for the river to pour through, and, incidentally, completely wrecking the self-propelled scraper, landing
Major Hooper in jail and myself in the hospital. Nevertheless,
and in spite of the remarks in your letter, my conscience is clear.
I have obeyed orders. And in case you have received no adequate
news of the recent momentous events out here, I will now give
you a brief account of same.

On Sunday afternoon, the river, as had been predicted,
reached a crest of twenty-nine feet, and then slowly began to go
down. Both the Earthworm and Scully levees, by Herculean efforts, had been strengthened so that they held. The rain had
stopped. The sky was clear. By Sunday night the water was down
several inches. We began to think the battle was won—without
using the dynamite. Lulled into false security, I went to sleep on
one of the cots in Major Hooper's office.

A little after dawn on Monday morning, I was rudely awak-
ened. The major was shaking me. "Get up!" he yelled. "The river
is rising again! It's now at twenty-nine and a half. Another few
inches and we are lost! We've got to blow up that Earthworm
levee! And we've got to do it right now!"

I sprang to my feet. Fortunately, I was fully dressed. I had
slept in my uniform. The major handed me one of the sticks of
dynamite which he had equipped with cap and fuse. I put it in

the pocket of my blouse. He put the other in his own pocket. We ran outside, jumped into the major's car and started across the high-level Earthworm Avenue Bridge.

"I don't understand this," I said suspiciously. "I thought the river was going down."

"It was. But not any more. It's all on account of that old abandoned railway bridge."

He pointed. I looked. The bridge along its entire length was completely jammed with floating wreckage—trees, timbers and flotsam of all kinds. Even the open draw, which had been clear the day before, was now choked with a great mass of debris.

"That junk has been accumulating down there for days," said the major. "It didn't matter as long as the draw was open, but last night a big barn came floating along and got stuck in the opening. A lot more stuff has piled up against it and formed a regular dam. The water is backing up fast."

"Then somebody ought to blow up the bridge."

"I hear that's just what the Earthworm people want to do. But they can't locate any dynamite. Apparently we got the last that's available."

By this time we were across the river, and the major had parked the car beside the Earthworm levee. A couple of hundred feet away I could see our bright red "sandbags," nestling against the side of the embankment.

"Why can't we use our dynamite to blow up the railroad bridge?" I asked.

"We haven't got time," said the major. "The water is already at the very top of our levee. It's still rising fast. We've got to relieve the pressure right now. And shooting this levee will do it just as well as shooting the bridge. Let's go!"

He leaped from the car. I followed.

"Wait," I said. "You don't understand. It won't take any longer to—"

"Keep quiet!" he said, whispering excitedly in my ear. "These workmen around here will hear you."

"But listen—"

"Not another word. I am giving the orders around here. And you will do as you are told."

"Yes, sir."

"You will walk down the levee here. You will place your stick of dynamite in the middle of those red bags. You will light the fuse. You will then run back here, shouting a warning for everybody else to run. If they don't run, and get hurt, it's their own fault."

"Yes, sir."

Very reluctantly—because I did not like the idea of setting off even one stick of dynamite on the Earthworm flood defenses—I started to walk along the levee. But almost at once a peculiar accident occurred. Some power stronger than myself—and for which I take no responsibility—seemed to impel me to place my foot on the slipperiest sandbag in sight. Naturally, I slipped. And the next moment I had tumbled—taking care, however, not to bump my pocket—to the bottom of the embankment, where the same mysterious impulse caused me to let out a cry of anguish.

"Ouch!" I yelled. "Help! I have broken my leg!"

Several of the men who had been working on the levee rushed to my assistance. Realizing that circumstances outside my control had now made it physically impossible for me to carry out my orders, I looked up to see what the major was doing. After a moment's hesitation, he walked along the levee. He reached the red bags. He pulled the stick of dynamite from his pocket. He inserted it between two of the bags. A number of workmen were placing sandbags near by, but they were too busy to notice what was going on. The major lit the fuse. I could see it sputtering. The major started back toward the car.

"Run for your lives!" he yelled. "The levee is going to blow up! Run for your lives!"

The nearby workmen sprang to action with sudden and terrific energy. And what they did will always live in my memory as a splendid example of the high spirit that pervades the splendid Earthworm Tractor organization.

One of the men grabbed the sputtering fuse and hurled it into the river. Another sent the stick of dynamite into the water after it. And a half dozen of them leaped upon the scurrying little major, flattened him in the mud, and then sat down on him. Others came running from all directions.

There were cries of "Kill him! Lynch the dirty Nazi!" But as the danger seemed to be over, calmer counsel prevailed. Somebody yelled, "Turn him over to the cops!" He was lifted to his feet and dragged roughly along the levee toward the road.

By this time I had discovered that, strangely enough, my leg was not broken after all. I was not hurt in any way. I climbed to the top of the levee.

The men who had grabbed the major were still dragging him along. When they reached the point where I was standing, they paused for breath, and this gave the major a chance to whisper to me.

"Don't let them know you were with me," he said. "Just watch your chance and shoot off that dynamite as soon as you can."

"Yes, sir," I replied.

As this was the first order from Major Hooper that I could obey with real enthusiasm, I promptly rushed off to carry it out. I ran to the car, drove back to the Scully plant, cranked up the pilot-model self-propelled scraper, and headed the big machine for the railway bridge.

Note: In that postscript to my previous letter, I was so rushed, because of my desire to get the letter into the mail, that I did not have time to explain how I had sneaked out while the major was asleep, emptied all the dynamite into the boxes hidden in the pan of the scraper, and filled up with real sand the red bags which we later placed on the Earthworm levee. This action on my part not only insured the Earthworm levee against all danger of being blown up; it also preserved the dynamite for a better use; and it involved no disobedience of orders, as the major had never told me not to do it.

When I reached the abandoned railroad bridge, I put the gears in low, headed the big scraper out over the ties, jumped out, lit the fuse on my stick of dynamite and threw it into the pan of the scraper. Running back along the road, I looked over my shoulder and saw the machine crash into the wreckage in the draw. A moment later there was a tremendous explosion. Fragments were hurled high in the air. They came raining down all around. Something hit me on the head. And when I woke up, I was here in the hospital.

They tell me the blast cleared the draw. The water rushed through. The level of the river fell. Both levees were saved. And by this time all danger is past. The scraper was a total loss, but another one will be ready in ten days—at which time I will report to work on it.

The major is still in jail, awaiting instructions from Washington. But that does not worry me. In his absence, I seem to be in command of myself. And, as I have now completely recovered from my trifling scalp wound, I have issued myself an order to take a ten-day leave in the bosom of my family. Needless to say, I will obey this order like the true soldier that I am.

Yours,

ALEXANDER BOTTS

I Want Out

FORT QUINAULT, WASH. SEPT. 24, 1945.

TO GILBERT HENDERSON, PRESIDENT,
EARTHWORM TRACTOR COMPANY,
EARTHWORM CITY, ILLINOIS.
BIG EMERGENCY. JUST RETURNED FROM PACIFIC EXPECTING
DISCHARGE. FIND MYSELF ASSIGNED HERE TO TRACTOR
BATTALION APPARENTLY SLATED FOR EARLY SHIPMENT
BACK TO HONOLULU. HAVE ADVISED COLONEL DAGGETT,
COMMANDING OFFICER, THAT THE EARTHWORM TRACTOR
COMPANY'S RECONVERSION PLANS ABSOLUTELY DEMAND
MY IMMEDIATE DISCHARGE SO I CAN RESUME MY OLD JOB
AS SALES MANAGER. DAGGETT, WHO SEEMS TO BE CRAZY,
ABSOLUTELY REFUSES CO-OPERATION. NOTHING MORE I CAN
DO HERE. IF YOU HAVE ANY INFLUENCE WITH THE WAR
DEPARTMENT, PLEASE PULL ALL POSSIBLE WIRES AS HARD
AND AS QUICK AS YOU CAN. THE WAR IS OVER. I DON'T WANT
TO STAY IN THE ARMY. I WANT TO GET OUT. HELP. HURRY.
URGENT. RUSH.
ALEXANDER BOTTS, MAJOR, AUS.

EARTHWORM BRANCH OFFICE
SEATTLE, WASHINGTON

Tuesday, September 25, 1945

Maj. Alexander Botts,
Fort Quinault, Washington.

DEAR BOTTS: Your telegram has been forwarded to me here, and I hasten to assure you that you have no cause for worry. Your many friends in the Earthworm Company have not forgotten you. We want you back. You are perfectly right in assuming that our reconversion plans absolutely demand your immediate discharge so you can resume your old job as sales manager. We need you so badly that we have been continuously hounding the authorities in Washington. And I am glad to report that they have promised us you will be discharged at the earliest possible moment.

I can also reassure you regarding the Fort Quinault tractor battalion. As it is equipped with a hundred of our Earthworm tractors, I have kept in close touch with it. The order sending it to Honolulu was issued away back on July fifteenth, but held up because of lack of shipping. On August third the battalion was ordered to Manila, but again there were no ships available.

After the Japanese surrender, it was decided that this tractor outfit would not be needed overseas, and I was able to negotiate an agreement, in connection with the cancellation of our war contracts, by which the hundred tractors in the Fort Quinault battalion—which are badly needed by our customers— are to revert to us.

The order of August third was therefore killed. And I have come to Seattle to investigate sales outlets for these very machines.

You can see, therefore, that you need not worry about your discharge—which will be along very soon. And you need not worry now—in September—about being sent overseas under an order of July fifteenth, which was superseded by an order of August third, which has since been canceled.

Most sincerely,

> GILBERT HENDERSON.
> President, Earthworm Tractor
> Company.

PORT QUINAULT, WASHINGTON.

Wednesday evening, September 26, 1945.

DEAR HENDERSON: Your incredibly complacent letter is here, and this is to let you know you are all wet, and if you really feel that you are going to need me as much as you claim in the coming reconversion program of the Earthworm Tractor Company, you will snap out of your dreams and do something. I would have telegraphed or telephoned you, only you are the kind of person who never seems to grasp an idea until it is explained at great length and in tedious detail, so I will give you the story in full, and send it by air mail, which should reach you sometime tomorrow.

To begin with, I want you to try to get through your head the following basic points: 1. I am still in the Army. 2. I want to get out. 3. I am assigned to an outfit that has orders to proceed to Honolulu on the next available ship. 4. Regardless of anything they tell you in Washington, nobody here has been informed of any change in these orders, so they still stand. 5. If I once get started for Honolulu, I may be in the Army for months to come. 6. I don't want to be in the Army for months to come. 7. I want to get out.

Maybe you are wondering why I don't handle this myself. The answer is that in the Army everything has to be taken up through channels—which, in this case, means that I have to work through my immediate superior, Colonel Daggett, who is not easy to work through—as you will understand when I explain the sort of mug he is.

My first contact with him was several days ago when I first arrived in this dump. The colonel was making a speech to a company of tractor drivers who had apparently just joined his outfit. They looked like a highly competent bunch, and most of them had many service ribbons and overseas stripes. The colonel had them lined up at attention, and he was sounding off like a bass horn.

"I'm going to give you men some plain talk straight from the shoulder," he said. "I will mince no words. Never in my life have I seen a more unmilitary group. Just because you have been overseas doesn't mean that you are soldiers. Far from it. In fact, the discipline in combat areas in this war has, in general, been so lax that the longer you have been overseas the, sloppier you have become.

"But now that you are members of my command there is going to be a change. I'm going to make real soldiers out of you. From now on, you're going to stand up straight, shave every day, rub those grease spots off your pants. When you meet an officer, you're going to salute, and salute properly. When you get an order, you're going to obey, with no back talk or monkey business. Starting tomorrow, you're going to have four hours of close-order drill every day, and you're going to watch yourselves and behave like soldiers . . . or else. That is all. . . . Sergeant, you may dismiss the company."

After hearing this oration, I decided to get a little information before reporting to the colonel. I approached a lieutenant who looked reasonably civilized.

"What," I asked, "is the matter with this Colonel Daggett? Is he the guy that won the war or something?"

"Nerts," said the lieutenant, urbanely. "He has never even been out of the United States. And that, if you ask me, is the main trouble with him."

"What do you mean?"

"Colonel Daggett," said the lieutenant, "is an old-timer with a one-track mind. All his life he has been wrapped up in the Army. He never relaxes. He has no social life. He reads practically nothing but the Maxims of Napoleon and the works of Clausewitz. He never thinks of anything but discipline and military etiquette."

"And why wasn't he sent overseas?"

"How do I know? Maybe they thought he was too narrow-minded. Anyway, while many of his fellow old-timers were fighting the war and becoming generals, and while civilians like me were slapping the Japs, he was stuck with training-camp duty back home. And it has gradually soured his whole character."

"I'm glad there's some explanation," I said.

With vague misgivings, I reported to Colonel Daggett in his office, saluted as snappily as I could, and was immediately bawled out like a recruit. After the colonel had given me a lesson in the proper method of saluting, I got in a few remarks.

"Sir," I said, "there has been a mistake in my orders. Now the war is over, I'm supposed to be discharged, so I can return to a highly important civilian position as sales manager of the great Earthworm Tractor Company. I'm not supposed to be here. I'm not supposed to be sent back overseas."

A sergeant entered, saluted and said, "Sir, Lieutenant Brown is here."

Lieutenant Brown entered. "Sir," he said, "I wish to report on that tractor transmission you ordered replaced. Since disassembling the machine, we think we can repair the old transmission all right—"

"Your orders," said the colonel severely, "were to replace it."

"I know, but I thought—"

"You're not supposed to think. You're supposed to do as you're told."

"Yes, sir." The lieutenant withdrew.

"As I was saying," I resumed, "there has been a mistake in my orders—"

"It is not my habit," said Colonel Daggett, "to permit my subordinates to criticize military orders. You have been assigned to this organization. You will remain with this organization and accompany it overseas. The matter is closed. And I shall expect you, in your relations with the men under you, to inculcate in them the same habit of instant and unquestioning obedience that I require of you. That is all. You may go.

"Yes, sir," I said, and walked out.

Since then, my desire to get out of the Army has been even more acute than before. But the direct road of escape is hopelessly blocked in this Daggett bottleneck. That is why a detour is indicated through you, Henderson, and your Washington contacts. You may think you have got everything fixed. But you have not.

Inquiry among some of my fellow officers reveals that we still have our original orders to sail for Honolulu. All we are waiting for is word that a ship is available at the Army supply base and port at Cove Point on Puget Sound. This word may come at any moment. When it does, our plans are all prepared to drive the equipment over the twenty miles of forest roads between here and the port. It should take only one day to make this trip and load the stuff on the ship. And then we shall be on our way.

So I beg of you, Henderson, if you have any regard for me or for the Earthworm Tractor Company's postwar program—and if you want this batch of a hundred tractors—please shake yourself out of your lethargy and get those orders changed before it is too late.

> Yours, between hope and despair,
> ALEXANDER BOTTS.

———————————

FORT QUINAULT, WASH. SEPT. 27, 1945, 8 A.M.

TO GILBERT HENDERSON,
EARTHWORM BRANCH OFFICE,
SEATTLE, WASH.
FLASH! SHIP IS AT COVE POINT. WE HAVE OUR ORDERS TO
LEAVE HERE TOMORROW MORNING; EMBARK TOMORROW
NIGHT; SAIL THE NEXT MORNING, SATURDAY. PLEASE,
PLEASE, QUICK, QUICK, HURRY, HURRY, DO, SOMETHING
ULTRA SUPER HYPER, URGENT, RUSH.
> BOTTS.

SEATTLE, WASH. SEPT 27, 1945, 11 A.M.

MAJ. ALEXANDER BOTTS,
FORT QUINAULT, WASH.
HAVE TELEPHONED WASHINGTON. FIND YOU ARE RIGHT.
THROUGH SOME ERROR THE NEW ORDERS WERE NEVER
ISSUED. HOPE TO GET THESE THROUGH BY SATURDAY NIGHT.
CAN YOU DELAY SAILING TWENTY-FOUR HOURS?
       HENDERSON.

———————————

FORT QUINAULT, WASHINGTON.

Thursday evening, September 27, 1945

DEAR HENDERSON: Can I delay sailing twenty-four hours?
Honestly, Henderson, sometimes you think of the damnedest
things. I am not the captain of the ship, nor am I in command of
this tractor battalion. So my first reaction, on receiving your
wire this noon, was to reject this twenty-four-hour-delay business as an utter impossibility.

However, I am not one who easily gives up, even when things
seem hopeless. In this case, I hated to see all these tractors,
which are so urgently needed in the United States, being sent to
Honolulu, where they are not needed at all. I hated to see all these
overseas tractor drivers, who would presumably prefer to stay
in this country, being shipped far away. And, finally, I was completely outraged at the thought that I might have to waste an
indefinite period going to Honolulu and then trying to get back.
At the moment, my main, idea—as I may possibly have mentioned—is that I want to get out of the Army.

Stimulated by this desire, I resolved to concentrate all my
powers of intellect and all my aptitude for low cunning on the

one problem of finding some way to delay the embarkation of this tractor battalion. For a while, however, I was completely nonplused.

Early in the afternoon Colonel Daggett made a speech to his entire command. After explaining our orders for embarking, he pointed out that on our twenty-mile trip to the port we would follow rough, narrow, winding roads through dense forest. There would be many false turns. The weather prediction was for fog and rain, which meant poor visibility. Hence, there was danger of getting lost.

"Under these conditions," said the colonel, "it is highly essential, that the most rigid march discipline be preserved. The tractors will proceed in column. The first machine will be under my direct command. The driver of each succeeding machine will maintain an interval of one hundred feet. And at all times and under all circumstances he will follow the machine ahead. There will be no exceptions or modifications to this rule. Any disobedience will subject the offender to trial by courtmartial. Let me repeat—each driver will follow the machine ahead."

The colonel ceased speaking, and I reflected sadly that the old boy seemed to have worked out an absolutely ironclad system for getting those tractors to the port on schedule. This follow-the-leader system was completely foolproof. Then I began to wonder. I had a vague feeling that somewhere I had heard of a system like this that had gone wrong in a big way. I meditated a long time. Finally, I decided that the idea I was trying to recall was something I had read in a book—but I couldn't remember what book.

As you know, Henderson, my success in getting out of difficulties is often due to the fact that I have piled up ahead of time a vast store of the sort of knowledge that is useful in emergencies. Most of this knowledge comes from actual experience. But at times, in my efforts to improve my mind, I have actually gone so far as to read a book. You will remember that my information in the curious case of the Mobius strip came from a book on mathematics.

In the present instance, I was certain that somewhere, sometime, I had read something about somebody who had used a very simple strategem to render completely haywire a system very similar to Colonel Daggett's projected tractor convoy. Unfortunately, I could not remember anything definite about what it was or where I had read about it. All my efforts to jog my memory only made me more bewildered.

Finally, I decided to dismiss the matter temporarily from my mind, and get a little firsthand knowledge of the country through which tomorrow's march will proceed. Accordingly, I got into a jeep and spent the rest of the afternoon making a thorough reconnaissance of the terrain between here and the port at Cove Point. I took along a map, and examined every road and intersection in the entire area. As I have a natural aptitude for topography, I came back with a complete and detailed mental picture of the whole theater of operations.

So far, I have produced nothing in the way of a definite plan. But I will sleep on the problem tonight. And tomorrow I have every confidence that something will occur to me. If it is humanly possible to delay that column of tractors, I will do it. And I will let you know later how it works out.

In the meantime, keep working on those birds in Washington. I am depending on you.

Yours hopefully,
ALEXANDER BOTTS.

COVE POINT, WASHINGTON,

Friday evening, September 28, 1945.

DEAR HENDERSON: I have much to report. I have evolved a plan. I have put it into operation. But it is still too early to know whether it will succeed. The situation is tense, but hopeful.

When I got up this morning I was still in a mental fog. I was haunted by the feeling that the answer to this whole business was somewhere in the back of my mind. But I could not get it out. All I could do was go along and hope for an inspiration later on.

Instead of riding in one of the command cars, I decided I would be in a more strategic position if I drove one of the tractors. As soon as the machines had been formed in column, I started walking along beside them. I noticed that the driver of the fifth tractor from the front had a bandage on his thumb. At once I ordered him to ride with one of the other drivers, and climbed into the cab myself.

A moment later we started. It was six A.M. The trucks and auxiliary vehicles had gone on ahead and were soon out of sight. Colonel Daggett was in the lead tractor with complete road maps and a competent guide. There was no possibility of his losing his way. He was holding the speed down to two miles per hour; it being his idea that this is necessary to prevent the motors from overheating, although there is, of course, no reason why these Earthworms cannot hit it up to five or six miles per hour. Even at our slow speed, however, we would presumably reach the port according to schedule at four P.M. There was no chance of running out of fuel; each machine was carrying an extra supply.

The column rolled along. With our hundred-foot intervals, we were strung out for a distance of about two miles. It was foggy and it was raining. We entered the forest. The road became more winding, and so narrow that it would be impossible for the colonel to check our progress by sending anybody along the side of the column in a jeep or even a motorcycle. At sharp turns, the tractor ahead would be out of sight around the curve. When we reached a straight stretch, I would see it again, dimly visible through a hundred feet of mist and rain.

We passed a side road. I eyed it wistfully. It would be very easy for me to make a wrong turn. If, before doing so, I slowed down so as to let the tractors ahead get out of sight, it seemed reasonable to expect that the tractors behind would follow me without knowing they were leaving the column. I could then lead them far away. But this, I decided, would be too obvious. It would be impossible to conceal the fact that I was the leader of this unauthorized detour. And what the colonel would then do to me I did not like to contemplate.

I tried to think of something better. I thought and thought. The steady drone of the tractor motor began to make me drowsy. And then, with a sudden blinding flash of inspiration, I had the answer. I remembered that book.

It was "The Life of the Caterpillar," by a wise old Frenchman named J. Henri Fabre. In this excellent work the author tells of the Pine Processionaries—caterpillars which travel in a long line, like elephants in a circus parade, with each one hanging on to and following the one ahead. Apparently they do this automatically and without thought or reason. To find out just how automatically, Monsieur Fabre devised an experiment. He contrived to get the lead caterpillar turned around and hooked up to the rear of the procession—whereupon these witless creatures continued to travel around in a circle for seven days and seven nights, getting nowhere, until they finally collapsed from exhaustion.

The important point was that the Pine Processionaries' normal mode of travel was the same as Colonel Daggett's system for getting his tractors through the woods. And what Monsieur Fabre so aptly calls the "inconceivable imbecility" and "abysmal stupidity" of the Pine Processionaries is exactly comparable to what Colonel Daggett has described in such terms as "rigid march discipline," "unquestioning obedience," and "you aren't supposed to think; you're supposed to do as you're told."

"Eureka," 'I said to myself. "If Monsieur Fabre could cross up his Pine Processionaries for seven days and seven nights, I ought to be able to keep Colonel Daggett's Earthworm tractor processionaries similarly bewildered for a mere twenty-four hours."

At once I put my plan into operation. We were approaching an unusually sharp curve which I had noted on my previous day's reconnaissance. Beyond was a fork in the road, followed by more sharp curves. Just before reaching the first curve, I slowed down.

The machine behind me closed up to fifty feet and also reduced speed. The one behind that came into view. Cautiously I started around the curve. I noticed that the machine ahead had taken the correct turn—to the right—and was just disappearing around a bend farther on. As soon as it was out of sight, I speeded up. At the fork I turned left, into the side road. I kept on. The machine behind me followed. At a short straight stretch I caught sight of two more machines farther back. So far, so good. The colonel, with four tractors, was presumably rolling merrily on the way to the port. The rest of the pack was following me.

After three miles on the side road, I came to a place that I remembered from my reconnaissance of the day before. The woods were dense. And there was a pattern of intersecting roads exactly suited to my purpose.

By swinging two sharp corners and following dozens of

twists and turns in the narrow road, I was able to bring my tractor, with its long trail of followers, around in an irregular two-
mile loop, and head it back toward the side road I had been following.

As I approached this road, I slowed down. Ahead of me, dimly
seen in the mist, a tractor went by. This machine, I decided, must
be near the tail end of the procession which I was leading. I
stopped. I looked over my shoulder. The machine behind me had
stopped fifty feet away—too far for the driver to see what was
going on ahead. Another tractor went past on the road in front
of me. Then, for two minutes, all was quiet. The end of the parade had passed.

I started forward, swung the corner and drove rapidly after
that last machine. In five minutes I came in sight of it. I settled
down to the prescribed two miles an hour at the prescribed hundred-foot interval. The machines behind me followed in an orderly manner. The circle was complete, and only one more maneuver was needed.

At a blind hairpin curve near an intersecting road, I was out
of sight, for almost thirty seconds, from both the tractor in front
of me and the tractor behind me. With a quick, right-angle turn,
I sent my tractor off the road and into the concealment of a dense
thicket. I shut off the motor. I listened. The machine that had
been following me came roaring around the curve. It passed.
Then I heard the motor speed up. The driver had evidently noticed he was too far behind the machine in front of him. He was
closing up the interval. A second machine came by. Then another. I felt pretty good. The circle was once more complete—
this time with me out of it.

I started the motor. I drove cautiously through the thicket
to the intersecting road. I followed this for several miles. I got
back on the main road to the port. By speeding up to six miles

per hour, I finally managed to overtake the rear end of the little four-tractor convoy that the colonel was so confidently leading along at two miles per hour.

At four P.M.—exactly according to schedule—we reached the port at Cove Point. The ship was there. The trucks and auxiliary vehicles were there, but they couldn't be loaded, because all the tractors had to go in first at the bottom of the hold. So far, of course, there were only five tractors.

The reactions of the colonel were interesting, and, to me, both entertaining and delightful. My only regret, Henderson, is that you were not present to share in my enjoyment of the affair.

As soon as we had driven the five tractors onto the pier and shut down the motors, Colonel Daggett came striding back along the column. Spying me in the cab of the fifth machine, he at once opened up.

"Why are you driving this tractor?" he demanded. "What has happened to the regular operator?"

"Just as we were starting, sir," I explained, "I found he had an injured hand. As there was no time to get another operator, I drove the machine myself."

"Most irregular," he growled. "But what I want to know is what has happened to the rest of this convoy. Where are the other tractors?"

"I don't know, sir."

"You don't know! Why don't you know?"

"Sir," I explained humbly, "the orders were for each driver to follow the machine ahead, with no exceptions or modifications."

"But you are an officer. You should have assumed some responsibility for the man behind you. You must have noticed he wasn't there."

"I did indeed, sir. But at the time, I was driving the tractor. If I was to follow your orders and follow the man ahead, I could not at the same time go back and look for the man behind."

"All right," he snapped. "I'm going to find out what happened." He called one of the lieutenants and ordered him to drive back in a jeep, locate the tractors and hurry them along.

As the lieutenant departed, the master of the ship arrived to find out what was the matter.

"Even with these new improved methods of loading," he said, "it's going to take a long time to get a hundred tractors and all that other stuff stowed away. If we're going to sail tomorrow morning, we've got to get busy right now."

"The tractors will be here at any moment," said the colonel.

"They had better be," said the master. He walked away.

The rest of us waited and waited, while the colonel got madder and madder. At the end of almost an hour, the lieutenant returned in the jeep.

"Sir," he reported, "I drove all the way to Fort Quinault and all the way back, and I couldn't find a single one of those tractors."

"What?" roared the colonel.

"Sir, I drove all the way to Fort Quinault and all the way back, and I couldn't find—"

"You couldn't find even one out of ninety-five big tractors? Are you blind? Are you crazy?"

"Well—" began the lieutenant doubtfully.

"Move over," snapped the colonel. He climbed in behind the wheel. And by this time he was so mad he couldn't think straight any more. Apparently it never occurred to him that there could be any real difficulty in locating all these tractors. So he never stopped to organize an adequate searching party. "I am going to find those machines," he announced, "and I am going to find them in a hurry." And a moment later he and the lieutenant and the jeep disappeared up the road in the mud and the rain.

That was about five this afternoon. It is now nine in the evening, and I have been whiling away the intervening hours eating a good supper at the local officers' mess and writing this letter to you at the local officers' club. The master of the ship has called and threatened that if the tractors do not come pretty soon, he will load up with other material here at the port and sail without us. These threats, however, do not scare me at all.

As no news has come from Colonel Daggett and the lieutenant, I can only speculate pleasantly on what may be happening out there in the forest in the wind and the rain and the fog. As the rain has probably obliterated the tractor tracks, and as there are a good many side roads, with innumerable ramifications, it will presumably take them a long time to find anything. So it is my guess that they are still aimlessly driving about in their open jeep, cold and wet and hungry and mad—all of which grieves me, especially in the case of the unfortunate lieutenant.

As for the tractor drivers, a good many if not all of them have doubtless become aware by this time that they are traveling in circles. But what can they do? The colonel has so incessantly dinned into them the principle of unquestioning obedience that they will naturally hesitate a long time before doing anything sensible that is against orders. Besides, they have plenty of K rations and extra fuel for their machines. So I feel sure they are still dutifully playing at follow-the-leader.

In other words, while Colonel Daggett drives frantically here and there, that enchanted ring of processionary tractors, in its remote sylvan sanctuary, is doggedly and interminably going round and round and round, everlastingly chasing its tail and getting nowhere.

And with this beautiful thought, I will close for the present, adding a postscript to let you know how this comes out.

Yours,

ALEXANDER BOTTS.

P.S.: Monday, October 1. It is all over. On Saturday morning, the day after the above was written, Colonel Daggett came back, wet and cold and raging. He had found nothing. He got hold of a plane. By this time the weather had cleared. He cruised for two hours, and finally spotted the tractors; still rotating faithfully in a counter-clockwise direction. A rescue party was dispatched. The tractors were brought in. But by this time it was Saturday night. The ship had taken on another cargo and sailed. And, our new orders had arrived from Washington.

Thus I have been completely and gloriously successful in my tactics of delay, and you, Henderson, have been equally successful in stirring up the authorities in Washington. Unfortunately, however, through some ghastly error on the part of one of these armchair wonders in the War Department, what we have received is not the order to stay in this country—which you expected—but the previous order of August third, which had not, as you supposed, been canceled, and which directs us to proceed not to Honolulu, but to Manila. The result is that the entire outfit, after being promptly loaded onto another ship, is now steaming down Puget Sound, headed for a place much farther away than it was before we started our meddling. And all I can do about it is send this letter back by the pilot.

Moral: You and I can beat almost anything, but who can beat the United States Army?

> Yours, and I still want to get out,
> ALEXANDER BOTTS, MAJOR, AUS,
> APO #4739, Care Postmaster,
> San Francisco, California.

More enthusiastic than skilled, Alexander Botts practices driving his new sales item in this 1936 Earthworm Tractors film still. (Wisconsin Center for Film and Theater Research)

Botts Makes Magic

EARTHWORM TRACTOR COMPANY
INTERDEPARTMENTAL COMMUNICATION
To: GILBERT HENDERSON, PRESIDENT
EARTHWORM TRACTOR COMPANY
EARTHWORM CITY, ILLINOIS
From: ALEXANDER BOTTS, EARTHWORM SALES MANAGER
CARE GEORGE TYLER, EARTHWORM TRACTOR DEALER
TYLERVILLE, GEORGIA
Date: Saturday afternoon, February 12, 1949.

This will confirm my telegram asking you to ship me, double rush, one Earthworm 60-cycle A.C. 100 K. W. portable Diesel-electric generator set and one competent lawyer. I am in deep trouble, under circumstances that are well-nigh incredible.

This afternoon I was alone in Mr. Tyler's warehouse, checking over his stock of tractors and other machinery, when a very remarkable-looking man came in. He was tall and imposing. His mustache was black. His tweed suit was of a pattern which I can only describe as bold. His tie was even bolder.

He spoke in a rich bass voice. "Good morning, sir. Are you the proprietor?"

"No," I said. "Everybody has gone home for the Saturday afternoon holiday, but perhaps I can help you. I am the sales manager of the Earthworm Tractor Company, here for a few days' routine visit. Mr. name is Alexander Botts."

"Ah, Mr. Bottsl I am familiar with your reputation as one of the greatest salesmen in the world. I have a feeling that we can help each other."

We shook hands, and he gave me his card, which read as follows:

CYRUS AUGUSTUS CONWAY
OWNER AND GENERAL MANAGER
CONWAY'S COLOSSAL CARNIVAL
WORLD'S GREATEST AND MOST REFINED
AMUSEMENT ENTERPRISE

"I am delighted to meet you, Mr. Conway," I said. "What is on your mind?"

"My purpose, Mr. Botts, is twofold. First, I want to sell you some of my ideas on show business. Second, I want you to sell me that one-hundred-kilowatt electric set which is under a canvas cover in the parking lot beside the building here. I looked over the set this morning when your workmen were rolling it out. But it was only this afternoon that I decided to buy it. Perhaps you can give me the exact specifications?"

"Certainly, Mr. Conway. This set is powered by our eight-cylinder Earthworm motor, directly connected to the hundred-kilowatt, sixty-cycle, alternating-current generator. It is mounted on a sturdy rubber-tired trailer with tongue for attaching to a truck or tractor. The weight of the entire rig is approximately six tons. The price, delivered here in Tylerville, with standard accessories, including our completely automatic foolproof starting system, is around ten thousand dollars."

"Very good, Mr. Botts. I will take it."

"This particular machine," I said, "has been promised to Mr. Henry Hubbard, a personal friend of our Earthworm president, Mr. Gilbert Henderson. He runs the Hubbard sawmill and woodworking plant about twenty miles north of here."

"Does Mr. Hubbard have to get this machine at once?"

"Yes. His plant is more than five miles from the nearest power line. Up to this time he has made his own electricity with an ancient steam-generator plant, which has now completely broken down. He must have this Earthworm rig at once if he is to continue operations. That is why we trundled it out in the lot.

Mr. Hubbard is coming to get it with a big truck later this afternoon."

"Have you another rig you could sell me?"

"Certainly, Mr. Conway. I will wire your order to the factory this afternoon. I will have a duplicate machine here within two weeks."

"But I need it right now, Mr. Botts—this very afternoon."

"Why?"

"My carnival, with its merry-go-round, its swings and other amusement devices, has just been set up in a field about a mile south of town here. But not a wheel can turn. Not a light can shine. Why? Because at the last moment this afternoon, the electric company suddenly discovered that my carnival is across the state line in Florida. The power line is in Georgia, and the company's franchise limits their operations to this state. They refuse to do anything for me."

"There must be electricity in Florida."

"Yes, but the nearest line is several miles away."

"Couldn't you move your carnival into Georgia?" I asked.

"I have not been able to find a good location. Even if I could, I would waste a whole extra day by moving. Besides, I have had trouble getting electricity before. I have made up my mind to make my own. I want a generator set, and I want immediate delivery."

"Immediate delivery," I said, "is impossible."

"Nothing is impossible, Mr. Botts. And I am sure we can work this thing out satisfactorily if you will permit me to go ahead with the suggestion I made a moment ago. I want to demonstrate for you how my methods of conducting show business can be applied to your type of machinery business."

"I don't understand."

"You will," he said. "Kindly take a card, Mr. Botts." He reached into his pocket and pulled forth a pack of playing cards. I selected a card. It was the deuce of hearts.

Meanwhile, Mr. Conway had started a fluent stream of talk. "Kindly keep the card a few moments longer, Mr. Botts. Do not let me see what it is. I will now give you a demonstration of that particular division of show business which is known as magic, sleight of hand, prestidigitation or the *savoir-faire* of legerdemain."

"What has that got to do with the tractor business?" I asked.

"Please, Mr. Botts, do not interrupt the continuity of the procedure. Kindly place the card in this envelope. Now lick the flap and seal it up, being careful, as before, not to let me see the face of the card."

He handed me an ordinary paper envelope. I slipped the card inside and sealed it as he directed.

"Now, kindly write your initials on the envelope, so you can recognize it later. . . . That's fine. Our next move is to make a slight shift in the scene of our operations."

He grasped me by the arm and led me to the other end of the warehouse. He then handed to me a small silver box like a jewel case. It had a lock with a little key sticking out of the keyhole. Acting on his instructions, I unlocked and opened the box, placed the envelope inside, locked the box and removed the key.

"Mr. Conway," I said, "I still don't understand what you're trying to do."

"You will, Mr. Botts. You will. All you have to do now is examine the box closely and make sure that it is securely locked."

"It is," I said.

"Very good, Mr. Botts. Very good. You will now hold onto the key and hand me the box. I want you to take this little ball of string and unroll several yards. . . . Now hold onto the end of the string and throw the ball over that pipe up near the ceiling. One, two, three . . . there she goes! We now have the string over the pipe, with the two ends hanging down. Now watch closely. I twirl the string around like this . . . making a loop. In the loop I place the silver box . . . thus. The box, as you see, is now hanging on the end of the string, and the really big moment is about to arrive. I now start the silver box swinging back and forth. Watch it closely, Mr. Botts. That's right. Now we are both going to back away a short distance.... Careful, don't trip! Pardon me for grabbing you, but I didn't want you to fall. Don't let your gaze wander from the little box. All right ... halt!"

"Now what?" I asked.

"Now, Mr. Botts, I am about to pronounce an incantation which will cause the card, with its envelope, to vanish from the particular point which it now occupies in tridimensional space. It will reappear at an entirely different point in our universe. The process may be cryptic, but the result will be so obvious as to be indubitable. And now ... silence! I am about to pronounce the magic words: Old Bombastus, Theophrastus, Paracelsus, Hohenheim! Presto chango, fly away! Now's the hour! Now's the time!"

As he finished these words, Mr. Conway produced what looked like a revolver and pulled the trigger. There was a sharp crack.

"Nothing to worry about," he said. "This thing looks like a revolver, but it is really nothing but a cap pistol—just something to lend a bit of dramatic effect to the performance. And now, Mr. Botts, I would like you to walk over to the silver box, untie the string, insert the key in the lock and open the lid."

I did so. The box was empty.

"You see, Mr. Botts, the card is gone. Have you any idea where it is?"

"No."

"Feel in the side pocket of your coat."

I did so, and brought out the envelope. My initials were on the outside. The deuce of hearts was inside.

"It's a fairly clever trick," I admitted. "Probably you just slipped the card out of the box and into my pocket when I wasn't looking."

"Exactly, Mr. Botts. I see you have a quick, analytical mind.

You have, in those few words, 'when I wasn't looking,' put your finger on the basic principle which underlies all magic and sleight of hand. The only important factor in my little trick was the flow of language which I employed to divert your attention from what I did not want you to see."

"So all that foolish talk had a hidden purpose?"

"Yes, Mr. Botts. When I persuaded you, by purely verbal means, to concentrate on the job of throwing that ball of string over the pipe, I gave myself plenty of time to manipulate the false bottom in that box. Later, I used my skillful line of patter to make you think that I took hold of you merely to prevent you from tripping. Actually, of course, I was slipping the envelope into the side pocket of your coat."

"And what is all this supposed to prove, Mr. Conway?"

"It proves, Mr. Botts, that if you have a line of talk good enough to divert a man's attention from what you are doing, you can slip over almost anything. This is a basic principle. And I want to show you how it applies to your business just as much as to mine."

"You have a good line, Mr. Conway. It works all right for little two-cent card tricks, but it takes more than mere clever patter to get by in the tractor business."

"Don't be too sure of that, Mr. Botts. My next experiment will be a little more difficult. It will require a more effective line of patter. This, in turn, means that I must have a more complete insight into your character, Mr. Botts. Fortunately, I have made a study of graphology—the reading of character from handwriting. I must now have a sample of your handwriting." He reached into his pocket. "Kindly write your autograph on this piece of paper," he said. "Here is my fountain pen."

I wrote my name. Mr. Conway looked at it with great interest.

"I can see," he said, "that you have a remarkable personality, Mr. Botts. Kindly step this way."

We walked through the warehouse and out the door into the

parking lot. Mr. Conway called to a group of pedestrians who were passing along the nearby street.

"Hey, there! If you want free tickets to the carnival tonight, come in here!" Two young men with two girls came in. Mr. Conway gave them all tickets. "Sign your names and addresses on the attached coupons and hand them back to me. This will give you chances on the grand prize which will be given away next week."

As soon as the coupons had been signed and returned, Mr. Conway produced a small wand, waved it around and tapped on the canvas which had been thrown over the generator set.

"Ladies and gentlemen," he said, addressing the five of us, "I am about to perform a feat unprecedented in the history of prestidigitation. Within thirty seconds of the time I start my incantations, I am going to have this six-ton generator set installed safely on my carnival lot one mile south of town here.... Do you believe I can do this, Mr. Botts?"

"No," I said.

"If I can perform this seeming miracle, would you be willing to sell me the set, Mr. Botts?"

"Sell it? If you could do anything like that I would give it to you."

"I don't want you to give me your machine," said Mr. Conway. "I would rather buy it for one dollar."

"Okay," I said.

"Do you own this machine, Mr. Botts, or does it belong to the dealer here?"

"The title is still vested in the Earthworm Tractor Company, of which I am legal representative."

"All right, Mr. Botts. Let us get this straight: If, within thirty seconds of the time I start my incantations, the generator is installed on my carnival lot, you will sell it to me for one dollar. Is that correct?"

"It is," I said.

"All right. Here is the dollar. You can hold it while the demonstration is going on." He handed me a dollar bill. "Kindly take out your watch, Mr. Botts, and time me. Let me know when you want the thirty seconds to start."

I waited until the second hand pointed straight up. "Go!" I said.

Mr. Conway waved his wand and started his idiotic spiel. "Old Bombastus, Theophrastus, Paracelsus, Hohenheim! Presto chango, fly away! Now's the hour! Now's the time!" He jerked out his cap pistol, shot it off and bowed politely. "How long did it take me?" he asked.

"Ten seconds," I replied. "But nothing has happened."

"On the contrary, Mr. Botts, plenty has happened. I have the names and addresses of these four disinterested witnesses here. They can verify our verbal agreement—which has now been carried out. The generator set is now installed on the carnival lot. You have the dollar. The sale is complete. And I also have written proof. This is your signature, isn't it?" He produced the paper I had signed a few minutes before.

"That is my signature," I admitted.

Mr. Conway unfolded the paper. To my astonishment, I noticed that I had unknowingly signed at the bottom of what seemed to be a typewritten contract of sale. Before I could collect my thoughts sufficiently to comprehend what was going on, Mr. Conway walked out of the parking lot, stepped into a sedan that was parked at the curb and drove away.

A moment later I came to. I lifted the canvas. There was nothing under it but an old empty crate, the same size as the generator set. I sprang to action. I rushed to the nearest garage. I hired a taxi. I drove to the carnival lot. I fought my way through the front gate. I found the generator set parked at one side of the grounds. An electrician was connecting the wires, and a group of tough-looking workmen were assisting. Mr. Conway was bossing the job.

"You swindler!" I yelled. "Your line of patter was exactly what you said it was—only more so! I thought you were just distracting my attention so you could put over that card trick. Actually, you were keeping me occupied inside the building while one of your men hauled away this generator set with a truck or something and then put the canvas over that crate. All that hocuspocus out in the parking lot was just intended to give this thing a false appearance of being legal."

"False appearance, Mr. Botts? I can assure you that the whole transaction is completely legal."

"It is not!" I yelled. "And you're not going to get by with it!"

Mr. Conway turned to the group of tough-looking workmen. "This man is annoying me," he said. "Get him out of here."

"I'll come back here!" I told him. "I'll bring one of our tractors and take that generator away from you!"

I was thrown out the gate. By this time I had decided not to come back with a tractor. The taxi was waiting. I drove to town. I called at the residence of our dealer, Mr. Tyler. Then I looked up a lawyer whom Mr. Tyler recommended. I related everything that had happened and demanded action.

Unfortunately, the lawyer turned out to be a typical small-town product—timid and unenterprising. He agreed that I had been robbed. He recognized the urgent necessity of getting the generator set back at once, so that we could deliver it to Mr. Hubbard. But he was a complete defeatist as to the possibility of prompt action. "As the machine is across the state line," he explained languidly, "legal action would have to start at a Florida county seat many miles away. Besides, it is Saturday afternoon; nothing could be done till Monday."

"What's the matter with you? Aren't you interested in bringing this swindler to justice? If that's all you can do, I don't want you as my lawyer. You're fired. Goodby."

I walked out and came over to the hotel, where I sent you a wire asking you to rush me another electric set and a good lawyer. Since then I have been writing this report and conferring on the telephone with Mr. Tyler and with your old friend Mr. Hubbard.

Poor Mr. Hubbard is fit to be tied. I am afraid he will go completely crazy unless we take care of him. I shall therefore be eagerly and anxiously awaiting the arrival of another generator and competent legal talent.

Yours,

ALEXANDER BOTTS.

TELEGRAM

EARTHWORM CITY, ILLINOIS FEBRUARY 14, 1949

ALEXANDER BOTTS
CARE EARTHWORM TRACTOR AGENCY
TYLERVILLE, GEORGIA
YOUR WIRE HERE. YOUR AIR-MAIL LETTER HERE. ALSO WE HAVE SEVERAL HOT TELEGRAMS FROM MR. HUBBARD. I HAVE WIRED HIM THAT A NEW GENERATOR SET HAS BEEN SHIPPED AND THAT I AGREE AT LEAST IN PART WITH HIS COMMENTS ON YOUR MENTALITY. WE ARE NOT SENDING YOU A LAWYER, AS OUR ATTORNEYS HERE FEEL THE CASE CAN BE HANDLED BETTER BY A MAN DOWN THERE. HOWEVER I AM GLAD YOUR WIRE CAUSED ME TO CONSULT OUR ATTORNEYS, WHO ASSURE ME THE EARTHWORM COMPANY NEED NOT SUFFER ANY LOSS IN THIS MATTER. THEY FEEL YOU ARE LEGALLY RESPONSIBLE AND THAT WE SHOULD CHARGE AGAINST YOUR FUTURE SALARY THE DIFFERENCE BETWEEN THE ONE DOLLAR RECEIVED AND THE TEN-THOUSAND-DOLLAR PRICE OF THE GENERATOR SET. PLEASE GIVE ME YOUR REACTION TO THIS.

GILBERT HENDERSON, PRESIDENT
EARTHWORM TRACTOR COMPANY

TYLERVILLE, GEORGIA.

Tuesday, February 15, 1949.

DEAR HENDERSON: Thank you very much for your telegram, which arrived yesterday, and which was most helpful because it made me so mad that it stimulated me to devise a plan of action which, although it did not work out exactly the way I had planned, was nevertheless a whole lot better than anything that could be thought up by any lawyers, particularly the kind you seem to have up there.

To put it briefly, as soon as I finished reading your telegram late yesterday afternoon, I knew I was through with lawyers. I decided to return to my former idea of rescuing the generator with a tractor. But this time I would act with finesse.

I got hold of Mr. Tyler, our local dealer. After considerable argument, he lent me one tractor driver and six of his best mechanics, one one-hundred-fifty-H. P. Earthworm tractor, fifteen hundred feet of high-grade, one inch, wire hoisting rope and a .45 revolver. We loaded the rope in a wagon hitched behind the tractor and drove south. As soon as we were out of town we turned off the road, crossed a pasture and nosed the tractor into a clump of tall bushes about a quarter of a mile from the lot where Mr. Conway's carnival was operating. We unhitched the wagon and swung the tractor so its rear end was pointed toward the carnival.

By this time it was dark. We unloaded the rope. With much grunting and sweating we managed to get it laid out across the pasture field. We hitched one end to the tractor drawbar. The other end, with forty or fifty feet of slack, we coiled up just outside the north fence of the carnival grounds. This end had a hook on it.

The fence was a portable affair with canvas panels to prevent nonpaying customers from enjoying the outdoor part of
the entertainment. Squinting through a crack between two
pieces of canvas, I was pleased to note that the generator set
was in the same place I had seen it on Saturday—with the tongue
pointing toward the fence. Cautiously, I poked the end of the
wire rope, with the hook on it, a few inches under the fence. Then
I withdrew a short distance with my seven helpers.

"You will go back to the tractor and wait," I said. "I will sneak
into the carnival and watch for a chance to hook the cable onto
the generator set. Then I will fire Mr. Tyler's pistol as a signal.
The tractor operator will drive north a quarter of a mile and stop.
This will bring the generator set to the clump of bushes where
the tractor is now. You mechanics will be waiting for it, ready to
defend it in case any of Mr. Conway's tough guys pursue it."

Once inside, I wandered casually past the electric-generator
set. One of the electricians was seated right beside it. And the
whole neighborhood was so brilliantly lighted that I did not want
to take a chance with the rope. I therefore concealed myself behind some boxes in a corner of the fence and waited for several
hours.

About midnight the crowd started to go home. A little after
one o'clock the attendants began urging the few remaining
stragglers toward the gate. By half past one the customers were
all gone, but the lights still burned. Finally the electrician beside the generator cut off the engine. As the generator slowed to
a stop, the lights gradually dimmed and went out, the merry-go-
round and the Ferris wheel slowed down and stopped, and the
music ended with a dismal squawk. All at once the whole carnival was covered by a pall of darkness and silence.

Swift and sure as a panther, I crept from my hiding place,

felt my way along the fence, found the hook on the end of the rope, dragged it across the intervening twenty-five or thirty feet and hooked it in the ring on the end of the tongue of the generator rig.

I reached for the pistol in my pocket, then hesitated. People seemed to be coming toward me from all directions through the darkness, yelling as they came. They were complaining that they had not finished their work. They wanted the lights on again.

In an emergency I always think clearly. I decided it would be safer for me to get out of the center of this crowd before I fired my signal shot. It also occurred to me that it would be wise to remove the key from the generator starting switch. I felt my way along the side of the rig. My hand reached the box containing the control mechanism. My fingers closed eagerly on the key—just a little too eagerly, as it turned out. In my haste to pull it out, I must have turned it. And as this particular Diesel-electric set has our completely automatic foolproof starting mechanism, the engine began turning over.

I was startled. I jumped back. I tripped over a toolbox. I sat down. Before I could get up, the engine had reached its full speed. The lights came on. Several people grabbed me. I looked around. It was Mr. Conway and his tough guys. I noticed that Mr. Conway was carrying a steel box.

"Well, well!" he said. "If it isn't my old friend, Mr. Botts! Is there anything I can do for you this evening?"

As I have a quick mind, I realized that the situation was rapidly deteriorating. These ruffians were holding me so tightly that I could not get at my pistol to signal the lusty lads with the tractor. At any moment one of the carnival workers might notice the wire rope. Even though it was partially concealed in the grass, the lights were so brilliant that it would not remain undiscovered for long. The occasion seemed to call for a line of talk or patter such as Mr. Conway had previously used.

"Mr. Conway," I said, "suppose I were to tell you that I have perfected a feat of legerdemain better than anything you can perform. Suppose I told you that I could pronounce an incantation which would cause this big generator rig to move away from here before your very eyes, would you believe it?"

"Frankly," said Mr. Conway, "no." He laughed derisively.

"Are you going to turn me loose so I can perform this experiment?" I asked. "Or are you a mere second-rate magician who is afraid, even in the midst of your friends, to give a rival performer the chance to prove his superiority?"

"Turn him loose, boys," said Mr. Conway. "It will be amusing to see what the poor yokel tries to do."

As soon as I was released I stepped up on the toolbox and looked over my audience, which had now been augmented by a lot more of the carnival people, including several freaks and a group of Oriental dancing girls. "Ladies and gentlemen," I said. "You are now about to witness—"

"Make it short," Mr. Conway interrupted.

"O. K.," I said and recited Mr. Conway's silly little nursery rhyme: "Old Bombastus, Theophrastus, Paracelsus, Hohenheim! Presto chango, fly away! Now's the hour! Now's the time!" Jerking the pistol from my pocket, I held it aloft and pulled the trigger.

This was supposed to be the big moment. But it was not. Instead of the healthy report which one would expect from a .45 revolver, there was only a weak little snap.

"I don't know exactly what you are trying to do, Mr. Botts," said Mr. Conway, "but it may interest you to know that when we grabbed you I noticed that bulge in your pocket. As I did not want you to hurt yourself or anybody else, I quietly removed the dangerous weapon you had brought along and substituted my own little cap pistol."

"I guess you win, Mr. Conway," I said sadly. "Probably the trick is just too hard for anybody—even you, Mr. Conway. I will bet you a hundred dollars that you can't go through this same routine and move the generator even ten feet. And here is the money."

Mr. Conway opened his steel box and pulled out a roll of bills. "Here is a hundred dollars," he said. "I take you up on that."

We gave the stakes to the merry-go-round operator to hold. Then Mr. Conway, still carrying the steel box, got into one of the big trucks parked beside the generator, drove it around, and stopped with the front bumper of the truck about six feet from the rear of the generator rig. He took a big logging chain from the truck toolbox and connected the front bumper of the truck with the rear axle of the generator rig.

"Hey," I protested. "Using a truck like that is cheating."

"No, Mr. Botts. There was nothing in the bet to prohibit using a truck. There is plenty of slack in the electric wires to let me move it the ten feet, so I have won my bet."

"That's right," said the merry-go-round operator.

"Wait a minute," I said. "He hasn't gone through the routine yet."

Mr. Conway climbed back in the truck, gave me his smug smile and pronounced the incantation, "Old Bombastus, Theophrastus, Paracelsus, Hohenheim! Presto chango, fly away! Now's the hour! Now's the time!" He pulled out the revolver he had filched from me and fired it once toward the sky. The report was loud and clear.

Mr. Conway put the revolver back in his pocket and started slowly backing the truck. The logging chain tightened. But the generator rig did not follow. Instead, to the surprise of every-body but myself, it moved forward toward the fence, dragging the truck behind it. At once I resumed the patter technique which Mr. Conway had so highly recommended. To distract the atten-tion of the carnival people from the wire rope out in front, I pointed at the logging chain and yelled, "Look at that chain! Mr. Conway is using a six-foot logging chain as a pusher! It's the best trick he ever did!"

By this time the generator rig had crashed through the flimsy wire-and-canvas fence. The truck, with Mr. Conway still in it, followed. The mouths of the spectators opened in aston-ishment. To a student of psychology like myself, it was clear they had all been shocked into a condition of semihypnotic trance.

Taking advantage of this condition, I kept right on with my patter, "Don't move! Don't spoil Mr. Conway's wonderful trick by following him! Stay right where you are until he gets back! In the meantime, I'll take that money and pay the bet!"

The merry-go-round man was too flabbergasted to resist. I jerked the two hundred dollars out of his hands just as the elec-tric cables pulled out by the roots. There was a shower of elec-tric sparks, then darkness.

I stumbled through the newly made gap in the fence. Mr. Conway had snapped on the truck lights. I ran after him and climbed over the tailgate into the truck body. I rapidly sized up the situation. And it suddenly occurred to me that a man like Mr. Conway, who had used such doubtful methods to acquire our generator set, might well have used similar methods to ac-quire other property; such, for instance, as the truck. I decided to try a bluff, ornamented with a little more patter.

By this time we had reached the clump of bushes where I had ordered Mr. Tyler's six mechanics to wait. We stopped. The six mechanics swarmed in over the truck, grabbed Mr. Conway and took the gun away from him before he knew what was happening.

"Well, well, Mr. Conway," I said, "fancy meeting you here. You are now back in the state of Georgia. And it may interest you to know that the sheriff of this county has a warrant for your arrest, and an attachment for this truck, which I understand you acquired in a rather unusual way."

Mr. Conway reacted as I had hoped he would. "How on earth did they find out about this truck?" he demanded. "I thought I had covered my tracks perfectly."

"You don't have to worry," I said, "provided you do as I say. I suppose you have the day's receipts in that box?"

"Yes."

I rapidly counted out enough of the larger bills to make a thousand dollars and handed the rest back to him. In the bottom of the box I found the one-dollar sales contract which I had inadvertently signed. I tore it up.

"Now, Mr. Conway," I said, "you are going to sign a regular order here for an electric set at ten thousand dollars. I will keep this thousand dollars as a cash deposit. The rest you will pay C. O. D. The set here goes to Mr. Hubbard. You will get a similar set which is now on the way from the factory. I will keep the two hundred dollars we put up on our bet; it was our tractor and not you or your truck which did the moving. Do you agree to all this?"

Mr. Conway started to argue. I repeated my threat to turn him over to the sheriff. And he must have had even more of a sense of guilt than I had supposed. He wilted completely and accepted all the terms.

As none of his thugs came to rescue him, we made him help us gather up our wire rope and other equipment. When we finally started back toward town, I turned him loose in his truck and wished him a cordial good-by.

"Mr. Conway," I said, "I thank you from the bottom of my heart for encouraging me to use the sort of show-business patter which has brought me such complete success in this little deal—and, incidentally, saved me exactly nine thousand nine hundred and ninety-nine dollars."

In closing, Henderson, I might suggest that the Earthworm Tractor Company could save even more by getting rid of a lot of useless attorneys.

     Most sincerely,
     ALEXANDER BOTTS.

Botts' Folly

EARTHWORM TRACTOR COMPANY
EARTHWORM CITY, ILLINOIS
OFFICE OF THE PRESIDENT

Friday, March 8, 1957

Mr. Alexander Botts
Sales Manager, Earthworm Tractor Co.
Jungle City Hotel
Jungle City, Florida

DEAR BOTTS: I hear you are in Jungle City. Please call as soon as possible on Mr. G. Dudley Montgomery, president of the Jungle City Trust Company. This bank owns a large block of Earthworm common stock. I want you to do everything you can to persuade Mr. Montgomery to vote this stock in favor of the present management of the Earthworm Company at the annual meeting to be held in Earthworm City, March 19. All he has to do is sign the enclosed proxy and mail it to us.

This is of vital importance. I also enclose a report explaining the entire situation.

Very truly yours,
GILBERT HENDERSON,
President

———————

JUNGLE CITY, FLORIDA

Monday, March 11, 1957

DEAR HENDERSON: Your letter and the report have arrived. As I am too busy to take care of a routine matter of this kind right now, I have turned it over to our local dealer, Mr. Ben Wiggins.

And now I will give you some really important news. As you may remember, I have, for several years, been carrying on preliminary research and working out tentative plans for a completely new and revolutionary piece of equipment which I have named the Earthworm Super-Jungledozer. Unfortunately, owing to your unreasonable opposition, Henderson, I have never been granted the funds to assemble a pilot model at the factory. However, by the use of cogent arguments and brilliant salesmanship, I have recently succeeded in selling this idea to Ben Wiggins. And I am happy to announce that by combining my brains and mechanical ingenuity with Ben's monetary resources, we have finally put together the first Super-Jungledozer in the history of the world.

This mechanical marvel consists of four of our big XX88 Earthworm tractors, placed side by side and assembled into a heavy jointed-steel frame equipped with various tree pushers, rooters, shredders, rock crushers and giant subsoil plows. The machine is designed to advance through any type of jungle or forest, cutting a swath fifty feet wide, knocking down and chewing to pieces trees and brushwood of all sizes, crushing rocks or other refractory obstacles, and finally plowing the chips and fragments deep under the ground and leaving a clean, smooth surface for the seeding of grass or other crops, or for the construction of roads and buildings The entire apparatus is the last word in land-clearing machinery—a veritable masterpiece of mechanical engineering.

Ben Wiggins and I have arranged to demonstrate our Super-Jungledozer next Friday to Mr. Ralph Dixon, a Florida millionaire, who has investments all over the world. Recently he has bought, near Jungle City, a tract of land consisting of many square miles of dense, junglelike forest.On this property Mr. Dixon is planning a tremendous real-estate development—miles of streets, hundreds of homes, several small lakes, a shopping center, a big hotel, half a dozen motels, a golf course and many other features. Before he can get started, he must, of course, clear away the jungle. And that is why we have put together our sensational Super-Jungledozer. It will do the job better, quicker and cheaper than any other piece of equipment in existence. And, after the land clearing has been finished, it can be disassembled and the tractors used in the subsequent construction work. We have created exactly the sort of machine Mr. Dixon needs—which means the sale is practically in the bag.

I should like to point out, however, that our success, when it comes, will be well deserved. In the planning, building and testing of our machine, we have encountered, and overcome, many difficulties. We started out by testing the various component parts in a big vacant lot behind Ben Wiggins' establishment. In this way we proved that our giant subsoil plows would turn over the earth to a depth of six feet. We also proved that our equipment can plow up almost anything buried in the top six feet of soil. On the very first day we broke off and pulled up a section of twelve-inch water main, which resulted in flooding that whole section of town. This, of course, was not our fault; the main had been very carelessly buried only two feet below the surface. However, citizens whose property had been flooded joined with the City Water Department in threatening to sue us. And it took many hours of diplomacy and a certain amount of cash to quiet things down. Later, when we cut off a telephone cable, we had the same sort of difficulty with some very unreasonable officials of the telephone company.

The entire Super-Jungledozer is too big to move over the roads, so the final assembly had to be done outdoors at the edge of the jungle. This caused more trouble. At times the sun was too hot. At other times we had heavy rains—in one of which I got soaking wet and contracted a bad cold.

There were inevitable minor accidents, since none of our workmen had ever seen a machine like this.

As our operations proceeded we attracted more and more of an audience from the local population. Loafers and idlers would congregate and amuse themselves by making witless comments—most of them of a derisive character. They began referring to the machine as "Botts' Folly," and to me as "Botts the Bungler." But it takes more than ridicule to stop me. I merely reminded myself that plenty of wise guys had laughed at Robert Fulton. And I kept on working.

The Super-Jungledozer is now completely assembled, and we plan to spend most of the coming week tuning it up and getting it ready for the big demonstration next Friday—at which time Mr. Dixon is expected to arrive from Venezuela, where he has been inspecting some of his properties.

At the close of the demonstration I feel sure that I shall be able to report that we have sold our beautiful machine to this very important customer.

With all best wishes,

Most sincerely,

ALEXANDER BOTTS.

TELEGRAM

EARTHWORM CITY, ILLINOIS
MARCH 13, 1957

ALEXANDER BOTTS
JUNGLE CITY HOTEL
JUNGLE CITY, FLORIDA
I HAVE YOUR LETTER TELLING HOW YOU TURNED THE
MONTGOMERY PROXY MATTER OVER TO BEN WIGGINS. I
ALSO HAVE A LETTER FROM BEN STATING THAT HE CALLED
ON MR. MONTGOMERY LAST MONDAY AND FAILED TO AC-
COMPLISH ANYTHING. AS I PREVIOUSLY INFORMED YOU,
THIS IS A MATTER OF VITAL IMPORTANCE. YOU WILL THERE-
FORE DROP YOUR FOOLISH SUPER-JUNGLEDOZER PROJECT AT
ONCE. YOU WILL GIVE CAREFUL STUDY TO MY REPORT. AND

YOU WILL THEN BEND ALL YOUR ENERGIES TO SECURING
MR. MONTOOMERY'R PROXY. THIS IS URGENT. THIS IS AN
ORDER.

                    GILBERT HENDERSON

JUNGLE CITY, FLORIDA

Wednesday, March 13, 1957

DEAR HENDERSON: Your telegram arrived early this afternoon.
I had been working very hard getting the Super-Jungledozer
ready for the great demonstration. Everything about the machine was in perfect shape. I had just gone to bed in my hotel
room to nurse the very severe cold I had contracted last week. I
was dosing myself with my favorite cold medicine. And Ben
Wiggins had dropped in to discuss a few last-minute details.

After all the work I had been doing for the good of the Earthworm Company, I found the peremptory tone of your telegram
most annoying. And I was not in any mood to study a long and
tedious report from you, Henderson. Fortunately, however, it was
not necessary for me to waste my time in this manner. Ben had
read your report. And he very kindly explained the salient points.
Our conversation ran approximately as follows:

"A man by the name of Fox," said Ben, "has been quietly
buying up common stock in the Earthworm Tractor Company.
And a couple of weeks ago he began sending out a whole series
of letters to all Earthworm stockholders urging them to give him
their proxies for the annual meeting."

"And just what is this Mr. Fox trying to do?"

"He is trying to grab control of the company. He wants to
elect his own board of directors, so that he can kick out Mr.
Henderson and the entire present management."

"You mean he might even fire me?"

"Certainly."

"But if he fires me, he might wreck the whole company."

"Apparently, Mr. Botts, that is just what he plans to do. From what I hear, the man is a crook. And he is trying to put over the same sort of deal that he has worked on other companies in the past. He buys as much stock as he can, and tries to line up enough independent stockholders to give him a majority. Then he moves in, robs the company by paying out tremendous dividends and exorbitant salaries to himself and his henchmen. And finally he unloads the stock and moves on."

"And you really think he has a chance to do this to the Earthworm Company?"

"Apparently so."

"Then why hasn't anybody told me about it before?"

"It was all in Mr. Henderson's report. But you were too busy to read it."

"I'm afraid you're right," I said. "The whole trouble is that my power of mental concentration is too great. When I once start working on an important project like this Super-Jungledozer, it takes a real jolt to switch me off onto anything else. I hope Henderson is putting up a good fight against this man Fox."

"He is sending letters to all stockholders. And the more important ones are receiving personal calls. That is why he wrote you in the first place and asked you to see Mr. G. Dudley Montgomery. And that is why he still wants you to see him. Now that I have failed to accomplish anything, he apparently thinks you might have better luck."

"You say you got nowhere with Mr. Montgomery?"

"Nowhere at all, Mr. Botts. He had already sent in his proxy to Mr. Fox. And in spite of everything I said, he refused to sign a new proxy for me. So finally I had to give up."

"And you reported all this to Mr. Henderson?"

"Yes. I tried to tell you about it, but you were too busy to listen. So then I wrote to Mr. Henderson. I gave him the whole story. In the first place, I told him how Mr. Montgomery had heard so many people making fun of our Super-Jungledozer that he had made up his mind it was no good—and, hence, that the Earthworm management is no good."

"When he sees that machine in operation," I said, "he'll change his mind."

"Maybe so," said Ben. "But that's not the only difficulty. Mr. Montgomery's whole mind has been poisoned by the false but clever propaganda put out by Mr. Fox."

"And what exactly is this propaganda?"

"Mr. Fox claims he wants to save the Earthworm Company from being ruined by the present management. He says Mr. Henderson is too old. He is hopelessly senile. He dwells in the past. And he is almost completely devoid of energy and initiative. Mr. Fox promises a complete house cleaning. He will throw out all the deadwood, replacing such people as you and Mr. Henderson with a group of competent young men full of new ideas, inspired with the spirit of progress and ready and anxious to lead the Earthworm Company to new advances in production and vast increases in profits and dividends."

"But all this is pure idiocy," I said, leaping out of bed and starting to get dressed. "I will call on Mr. Montgomery at once. When I will tell him that this talk about the Earthworm management being senile is nothing but a pack of lies. Even though Henderson may be getting old and a bit doddering in his ways, he still has enough sense to keep me on the payroll. This means that the Earthworm management has the benefit of all my energy, drive and enthusiasm. Such a management is, of necessity, progressive in the best sense of the word."

Ben did not think I would have any chance of converting Mr. Montgomery. But I persisted. And finally he agreed to take me around and introduce me.

By this time my cold had induced a fever of approximately 102 Fahrenheit. Although I had no thermometer, I was able to make a very close estimate by checking on the state of my mental processes. By long experience I have learned that a temperature of 102 has a tendency to stimulate my mind to a much greater brilliancy than is normal. My imagination and my creative powers are increased. I begin to think much more clearly and much more accurately. I am able to generate a veritable torrent of new ideas. And at the same time my judgment remains cool and collected.

So it was on this occasion. As Ben and I walked down the street, it suddenly came to me in a flash of inspiration that my first plan of attack had serious drawbacks. It might be very difficult, in a short interview, to convince Mr. Montgomery of the tremendous effect of my own personality in inspiring the entire Earthworm management to a high level of achievement. As an outsider, Mr. Montgomery would naturally assume that the management would reflect the influence of the president of the company. I decided, therefore, that I would stretch the truth and give you, Henderson, complete credit for everything.

Mr. G. Dudley Montgomery turned out to be a self-important little runt. He was seated behind a large desk in a luxurious office. And even though he was not an inspiring audience, I was able—partly because of that 102 degrees of fever—to make one of the most eloquent appeals of my entire career. I built you up, Henderson, as a veritable superman. I explained how your financial wizardry had always kept the company on a sound fiscal basis. I extolled your high moral character. I praised your tact and understanding in dealing with men. I dwelt at length on your unerring instinct for the proper approach in advertising and in sales. And finally I opened up with a glowing tribute to your achievements as an engineer and an inventor.

"Mr. Montgomery," I said, "you have no doubt heard of the great Earthworm Super-Jungledozer which is to have its premier performance on the outskirts of this city next Friday. This remarkable piece of equipment, Mr. Montgomery, is the brain child of that mechanical genius, Mr. Gilbert Henderson, president of the Earthworm Tractor Company. His was the brain that conceived this engineering masterpiece; his the mechanical skill that integrated the various working parts into a harmonious whole; his the determination that pushed this mighty monster through to completion. The Earthworm Super-Jungledozer, Mr. Montgomery, is one of the greatest achievements of modern science—one of the wonders of the world. And yet Mr. Fox has the effrontery to claim that the creator of this boon to mankind is senile. Such a statement, sir, is false!"

"Maybe so," said Mr. Montgomery; "maybe 'senile' is not the proper word. In my opinion, the Super-Jungledozer is an idiotic monstrosity. If Mr. Henderson, as you say, actually designed it, he is not so much senile as crazy—which is another good reason why I shall continue to vote against his management of the Earthworm Company. My mind is made up. I do not care to discuss the matter further."

Ben Wiggins gave me a look which seemed to say, "I told you so." But I was not discouraged. "Mr. Montgomery," I said, sonorously and magnanimously, "I understand completely your point of view. I sympathize with your attitude. I do not expect you, as a competent businessman, to believe any of my claims. All I ask is that you give me a chance to back up my words. My only request is that you attend the great demonstration next Friday and make up your own mind."

"All right, Mr. Botts. I will be there. Your demonstration might be good for laughs, if for nothing else."

"Thank you," I said.

Following this interview, I decided, in spite of my wretched cold, that I will spend every single daylight hour from now until Friday in completely re-examining, readjusting and retesting our beautiful machine. The situation is now critical. Any failure in our demonstration might result not only in losing the sale to Mr. Dixon but also in losing Mr. Montgomery's votes—which, in turn, might result in our losing control of the Earthworm Company. To prevent any such unbelievable disaster, Henderson, I am resolved to fight to the last. Yours with calm and hopeful determination,

ALEXANDER BOTTS.

TELEGRAM
EARTHWORM CITY, ILLINOIS MARCH 15, 1957

ALEXANDER BOTTS
JUNGLE CITY, FLORIDA
YOUR DELAYED EFFORTS TO INFLUENCE MR. G. DUDLEY
MONTGOMERY HAVE TURNED OUT TO BE WORSE THAN
USELESS. AFTER RECEIVING THE REPORT OF WIGGINS'
FAILURE, I WROTE MR. MONTGOMERY A LONG LETTER,
WHICH HE WILL PROBABLY RECEIVE THIS MORNING. I TOLD
HIM THAT THE EARTHWORM COMPAN Y AND ITS PRESIDENT
DISCLAIM ALL RESPONSIBILITY FOR THE MONSTROSITY YOU
CALL A SUPER-JUNGLEDOZER. I ASSURED HIM THAT THE
PRESENT EARTHWORM MANAGEMENT IS COMMITTED TO A
POLICY OF ENERGETIC BUT SENSIBLE PROGRESSIVISM, AND
I MADE A STRONG APPEAL FOR HIS SUPPORT. YOU WILL
APOLOGIZE AT ONCE TO MONTGOMERY AND TELL HIM YOU
WERE IN ERROR IN BLAMING THE RIDICULOUS SUPER-
JUNGLEDOZER ON ME. THEN YOU HAD BETTER GO TO BED
AND TAKE CARE OF THAT COLD. YOUR FEVER, INSTEAD OF
STTMULATING THE CLARITY OF YOUR THOUGHTS, HAS
APPARENTLY MADE YOU DELIRIOUS.
GILBERT HENDERSON

JUNGLE CITY, FLORIDA,

Friday evening, March 15, 1957

DEAR HENDERSON: Your telegram arrived about noon today, just before our big demonstration, and I am compelled to report that I was definitely nonplused to learn you had written Mr. Montgomery contradicting everything I had told him about your alleged contribution to the building of the great Super-Jungledozer.

However, in spite of the bad news from you, and in spite of my very severe cold, I remained undaunted. And, in order that you may appreciate my Herculean efforts to overcome incredible difficulties, I will give you a complete account of the events of a very trying afternoon.

The demonstration started auspiciously. Out of a blue and cloudless sky the sun shone down in lordly grandeur on the complicated machinery of our colossal Super-Jungledozer. Every moving part had been carefully inspected, adjusted and lubricated for the great demonstration. Mr. Ralph Dixon was on hand, in jovial and friendly mood. A crowd of townspeople had arrived. The great moment was upon us.

I waved my hand. The roar of four powerful diesel engines filled the air. The four mighty Earthworm tractors, integrated by the huge all-embracing steel frame into a single unit, moved majestically forward. The tree pushers, the rooters, the shredders, the rock crushers and the subsoil plows went into action with a magnificent grinding, crashing and crunching. In the face of this stupendous onslaught, the jungle was completely pulverized and plowed under.

After the machine had traveled about half a mile, cutting a swath fifty feet wide, it made a sweeping turn and came back toward its starting point, cutting another fifty-foot swath.

The performance was so successful that the crowd of onlookers—most of whom had come to jeer—burst into spontaneous applause. Mr. Ralph Dixon was visibly impressed. And I began to hope that Mr. Montgomery—who had arrived late—might also show a favorable response. Such, however, was not the case. As soon as he spotted me in the crowd, he walked up and addressed me in denunciatory terms.

"I have just received a letter from your Mr. Henderson," he said. "It indicates that one of you people is a liar. First you tell me that this Super-Jungledozer is a wonderful machine and that Mr. Henderson should have all the credit for it. Then Mr. Henderson tells me that he considers it a mechanical monstrosity and denies all responsibility."

I started to explain. But I was interrupted by a cry of alarm from the crowd. The Super-Jungledozer had come to a sudden stop. A number of people were examining the freshly turned earth behind it. We rushed over and found that a somewhat unusual accident had taken place. Someone had parked a car behind a thicket of brush where it could not be seen by the operators of the Super-Jungledozer. As a result, the car had been chopped, crushed and shredded into small fragments and then plowed under without a trace.

It was indeed a remarkable performance. And Mr. Dixon was much interested. Naturally, I lost no time in making the most of the occasion, pointing out that a machine which so easily disposed of a complete motorcar could be relied upon to dispose even more easily of large trees, rocks and other obstructions.

My satisfaction over this lucky break was a bit spoiled, however, when some of the workmen started digging to find the fragments. Almost at once they turned up a license plate, which proved conclusively that the car, an expensive foreign model, belonged—or rather, had belonged—to Mr. G. Dudley Montgomery. The accident was his own fault, of course. I tried to tell him that he never should have parked his car where it was sure to be run over. But he would not listen. He flew into a rage. He yelled. He threatened to sue me. And he repeated his previous statement that he would never vote his Earthworm stock in favor of what he called "the present egregiously incompetent management."

This was definitely the low point of the afternoon. Most people, in my place, would have given up hope. But not Alexander Botts. As I have previously explained, my fever had considerably stimulated my mental processes. Furthermore, I am always at my best when faced with seemingly insurmountable difficulties. And I rose to the occasion in what I can describe as a magnificent manner.

In one of my most brilliant flashes of inspiration, I suddenly came to realize something that had been buried in my subconscious mind for some time, but which I had been unable previously to bring up into my conscious mind. It was so simple that we both should have thought of it before. But we did not. And, as far as I know, you haven't even yet.

What came over me was the thought that a modest bank in a small town would be very unlikely to invest its own funds in a large block of common stock. Obviously, then, that Earthworm stock registered in the name of the Jungle City Trust Company must be held in a trust fund. And, if it was a large block of stock, it must be a very large trust fund, set up very likely by the town's wealthiest citizen. All this, of course, was a mere assumption. But it was such a plausible assumption that I acted upon it at once.

After assuring Mr. Montgomery that our insurance would pay for his car, I addressed Mr. Dixon—who turned out to be a man of quick decisions.

"Sir," I said, "are you going to buy this Super-Jungledozer?"

"Yes," he said.

"And you will need additional Earthworm equipment?"

"Yes. I'll need a lot of it."

"You like the Earthworm Company?"

"Yes."

"You want to keep on doing business with the present management, including myself?"

"Absolutely."

I then explained about the proxy fight, and asked if we could have the proxy for the Earthworm stock in his trust fund at the Jungle City Trust Company.

"How," he asked, "did you know I owned that stock?"

"I didn't know," I said. "I just guessed it."

"Well, you're right," he said. "Normally, Montgomery votes all my stock without bothering me. But in this case I am going to take charge myself." He turned and spoke to Mr. Montgomery. "You will send the Earthworm Company a new proxy in favor of the present management. You will send it right away, air mail, registered."

"Yes, sir," said Mr. Montgomery.

"And one more thing," said Mr. Dixon: "Don't forget that my trust fund is revokable. If you want to keep on doing business with me, I would suggest that you vote any other Earthworm stock you may hold in favor of the present management."

"Yes, sir," said Mr. Montgomery. He hurried away.

After thanking Mr. Dixon, I returned to the hotel, where I have been writing this report. I will now mix up an unusually large dose of my favorite cold medicine, and retire for a much-needed rest.

> Yours,
> ALEXANDER BOTTS.

TELEGRAM

EARTHWORM CITY, ILLINOIS MARCH 19, 1957

ALEXANDER BOTTS
JUNGLE CITY, FLORIDA
CONGRATULATIONS. THE MEETING IS OVER. DIXON'S PROXY
SAVED THE DAY. WE RETAIN CONTROL OF THE COMPANY. I
HOPE YOU CAN ARRANGE TO HAVE A SEVERE COLD AND A
FEVER ON ALL FUTURE OCCASIONS WHEN YOU ARE CON-
FRONTED WITH CRITICAL PROBLEMS.

> GILBERT HENDERSON

Botts and the Bag of Tricks

EARTHWORM TRACTOR COMPANY
EARTHWORM CITY, ILLINOIS
OFFICE OF GILBERT HENDERSON, PRESIDENT

Tuesday, March 24, 1959

Mr. Alexander Botts
Sales Manager, Earthworm Tractor Co.
Canterbury Hotel
San Francisco, California

DEAR BOTTS: I have recently received a call from a representative of the Scientific Sales Advisory Service of Los Angeles, an organization which offers a complete program of instruction in modern dynamic sales methods. I have been so impressed by this program that I have arranged for a trial subscription starting at once for young Bob Preston, our new dealer in El Centro, California. Bob has recently been having trouble in his sales operations, and I trust the SSASOLA program will provide the assistance he needs.

I suggest that you call on Bob at your early convenience and help him to get the greatest possible benefit from this new service. Some of the SSASOLA methods are so novel and progressive that you may find difficulty in reconciling them to your somewhat old-fashioned ways of thinking. I must caution you, therefore, not to disagree with these methods merely because you yourself did not think of them first.

Most sincerely,
GILBERT HENDERSON

Friday, March 27, 1959

DEAR HENDERSON: When I called on young Bob Preston this afternoon, he met me in his outer office and assured me that all his troubles were over.

"I know what you mean," I said. "But I want the full story of your difficulties just the same. Tell me from the beginning."

Bob explained—what I already knew in a general way—how he had inherited the Earthworm dealership upon the death of his father a year ago, how he left college, got married and plunged into the business with the greatest enthusiasm—but soon found himself in trouble.

"I never had any experience in selling," he said. "I didn't know how to handle the customers. I began losing business to my competitors. And every month I sank deeper into the red. In the meantime I had gone heavily in debt for a new showroom, repair shop and a lot of other stuff. So I decided I had to make more sales or I would be sunk. I became so worried I was almost paralyzed. Last week when I heard about a man who might buy a lot of tractors, I was afraid to go after him."

"Why?"

"This man is so important. He is Mr. Vedder Van Cortlandt— a big capitalist from New York City. He has been buying a lot of mining and mineral properties in the mountains around here. Last week he arrived in El Centro and set up an office. And I understand he plans to reopen an abandoned mine somewhere in the mountains west of here. It produces a rare mineral that has recently become important. And he needs a tractor to work inside the mine—pushing material around and loading ore."

"Just one tractor?"

"That's all he needs for this one mine. But when he opens up a lot of his other mines he will need half a dozen or more."

"He sounds like a good prospect," I said.

"I know," said Bob. "And that's what scared me. This sale was going to be so important to me that I just went into a panic. I had already lost so many sales that I had no confidence in myself. I was afraid I would say the wrong thing or make some blunder that would spoil everything. But probably you can't understand this."

"On the contrary," I said, "I understand perfectly. Even though I myself never worry, I have the greatest sympathy for those who do. So you can relax, Bob. As you yourself said when I came in, your troubles are now over. I have arrived on the scene. I will take charge of everything."

"But that's not what I meant, Mr. Botts. My troubles were over before you came in. Mr. Henderson has sent me a man from the Scientific Sales Advisory Service of Los Angeles—they call it SSASOLA—and he and I have been working out a sales campaign which is going to solve all my difficulties."

"So that's it," I said.

"I want you to meet this SSASOLA representative," said Bob. "You might learn something."

He took me into his private office and introduced me to a dapper little man named Cedric Something-or-other. "Delighted to meet you," said Cedric. "In our sales counseling work we have often found that it is the sales managers of large corporations rather than the salesmen themselves who need our help the most. The lower ranks of salesmen are in close touch with the customers; this keeps them alert and progressive. The higher executives tend to become a bit—shall we say ossified? If you'll sit down I'll be delighted to go over the points I have been explaining to Bob here."

Note: I will admit that at this point I was considerably irked by the remarks of this young whippersnapper. Most sales managers, under these circumstances, would have walked out and had nothing further to do with the proceedings. But I am by nature modest. I am emphatically not the type—as you erroneously suppose—to reject an idea merely because I did not think of it myself. I am always ready to learn.

"You are very kind," I said humbly. "I shall consider it an honor to sit at your feet and pick up such crumbs of wisdom as you may let fall."

Little Cedric launched into his subject with enthusiasm. "Our entire system," he said, "is based on the Six Scientific Secrets of Successful Selling. You are, of course, familiar with them?"

"No," I said.

Little Cedric was incredulous. "You are the sales manager of the Earthworm Tractor Company and you never heard of the Six Scientific Secrets of Successful Selling?"

"No."

He handed me a small card. It read as follows:

SSASOLA–SSSOSS

PLAN PRESENTATION

PLAY UP PROSPECT

PLAY UP PRODUCT

SUPPRESS SELF

AVOID ARGUMENT

WIN WITH WORDS

"This may mean something to you," I said, "but it means nothing to me."

"You should use your mind, Mr. Botts. You should snap out of this lethargy that seems to have possessed you. SSASOLA–SSSOSS stands for the Scientific Sales Advisory Service of Los Angeles and the Six Scientific Secrets of Successful Selling."

"I'm afraid I never was much good at puzzles," I said.

Little Cedric went on expounding. "The first Secret—Plan the Presentation—means of course that in any sales interview you must have a plan of campaign. We divide this into three subheads. First comes the Initial Impact—you attract the prospect's favorable attention. Next comes the Slow Softening—you overcome sales resistance by an inexorable piling up of fact upon fact. Then comes the close—the Winning Wallop that gets the name on the dotted line. Always remember this triple-threat plan—the Initial Impact, the Slow Softening and the Winning Wallop."

"That's very interesting," I said. "But how would it be if we forget all this theory and call on Mr. Van Cortlandt? Then we could find out what's on his mind and maybe sell him a tractor."

"Before we make any hasty moves," said little Cedric, "we must be sure that our plans are sound. We must master the theory before we attempt to act. The second Secret—Play Up the Prospect—is the most important. You concentrate on the head man."

"You butter him up?"

"I don't like your choice of words, Mr. Botts. What you do is treat the prospect with courtesy and consideration. You make sure, for instance, that you have his name right; people are always sensitive about their names. You discuss his hobbies."

"That's plain enough," I said. "And so is the next one—Play Up the Product. You just claim the Earthworm is the best tractor in the world. But what's this about Suppress Self?"

"As a salesman, you should refrain from exploiting your own personality. You should keep yourself in a subordinate position."

"You crawl in on your hands and knees?"

"Certainly not, Mr. Botts. You merely refrain from discussing your own personal affairs. It's a sensible rule. So is the next one—Avoid Argument. Don't discuss controversial subjects like politics."

"What about this Winning With Words?"

"You would be surprised, Mr. Botts, at the tremendous results you can attain by the proper use of words. Through research and testing and endless experiments, our organization has evolved literally thousands of Sentences That Smile, Sentences That Sing, Sentences That Shout and, above all, Sentences That Succeed. I have a short motion picture here that shows exactly what I mean."

"I don't want to see any motion picture," I said. "I think we ought to go over and call on Mr. Van Cortlandt and try to sell him a tractor."

Little Cedric paid no attention. He switched off the lights and started running a 16-mm film. It showed a school which the SSASOLA people had set up for the service-station attendants of a certain oil company. First we saw whole groups of these attendants repeating over and over what were called Scientific Selling Sentences: "Pardon me, sir, this radiator hose is pretty soft. It may give way at any moment. I can change it for you in a jiffy." Next we saw a few scenes with actual customers being given the works by alert young attendants. The film closed with a lot of statistics showing that during the first month after the introduction of these selling sentences the company's sales of radiator hose increased by 752½ per cent.

Note: I ran into this particular trick myself last summer. I was buying some gasoline. The attendant gave me these same selling sentences. And, sure enough, I bought a new hose. The next day at the same filling station another attendant gave me the same sentences. I did not buy another hose. Two days later at another filling station run by the same company, still another attendant handed out the identical words. Since then I naturally avoid all filling stations of this particular oil company. They made one extra sale, but they lost a lifetime customer. I was tempted to explain this to Bob and Cedric, but they were so completely wrapped up in their childish schemes that I decided it would be useless at the time.

"Let's go and see Mr. Van Cortlandt," I suggested.

"Very good," said Cedric. "We are ready. I have given Bob complete instructions for a dynamic scientific sales interview. He has rehearsed it until he is letter-perfect. I will go along to back him up. And we should be delighted to have you come too,

Mr. Botts, so that you may see an example of our advanced SSASOLA methods."

"Always glad to help out," I said.

"I'm sorry," said Cedric, "but we don't exactly need your help. In fact, I must insist that you take no part in the proceedings. If you, with your old-fashioned methods, try to interfere, you might spoil everything."

"Very good," I said. "I will be as inert and as silent as an oyster."

Bob went into another room, came back with a small beagle hound on a leash, and we started walking down the street.

"Why the dog?" I asked. "Are you going to hunt this prospect like a rabbit or a partridge?"

"Of course not. You'll soon see what we're going to do."

In due course we arrived at the office of the intended prey, and Bob put over the Initial Impact.

"Mr. Van Cortlandt," he said, "I have, learned that you are a great fancier of beagles. I also am a fancier of beagles. I have here one of the finest specimens of the breed in the entire state of California, and I hope you will accept it as a free gift from one beagle enthusiast to another."

"Thank you," said Mr. Van Cortlandt. He was visibly impressed. The dog was indeed a beautiful animal.

Bob followed up his advantage with some skillful Slow Softening. He said he had heard that Mr. Van Cortlandt had acted as toastmaster at the annual banquet of a group of beagle lovers and he asked him to repeat some of the jokes which had rolled the audience in the aisles. Mr. Van Cortlandt obliged, and Bob laughed uproariously. Mr. Van Cortlandt seemed pleased. Between jokes Bob inserted a lot of propaganda in favor of Earthworm tractors. He refrained from talking about himself. He ducked several chances to argue about politics. And he used plenty of Sentences That Smile and Sentences That Sing. He also suggested that Mr. Van Cortlandt would do well to buy not only the single Earthworm that he needed for his immediate purposes but also a whole fleet of Earthworms for future work.

"There is one point," said Bob, "that I wish to stress above all else. Your operating and maintenance problems will be tremendously simplified if you use just one make of tractor for all your present and future needs."

All this time I was standing in the background, putting on my imitation of an inert and silent oyster. As you may well imagine, Henderson, it is almost unheard of for Alexander Botts to be present at a sales interview and take no part. But I was sure that the time was not yet ripe for me to interfere. By a tremendous effort of will power I controlled myself.

Little Cedric sidled up to me and started whispering, "We now have him softened up," he said. "It's time for the kill. I am going to present the order blank and the fountain pen. Bob will pick up the dog and set it down so its nose points directly to the dotted line. For a dog lover like Mr. Van Cortlandt, that will provide the real Winning Wallop."

Little Cedric stepped forward. He laid as order blank on the desk. Bob lifted up the dog. He set if down and pushed its nose toward the dotted line. Little Cedric presented the fountain pen. Mr. Van Cortlandt automatically extended his hand. But the dog was too quick for him; he grabbed the pen, chewed it in two and dribbled ink all over the desk.

By the time the mess had been cleaned up Mr. Van Cortlandt had been diverted from the dotted line. But he was still in an affable mood. He thanked Bob again for the dog, said he was favorably impressed with Earthworm tractors and would make a final decision just as soon as he had time to consult with his chief engineer. "I will call you as soon as I have any news," he said.

Bob and Cedric and I walked back to Bob's office.

"I hope you observed," said little Cedric, "how perfectly the SSASOLA methods worked out. We had the man completely sold. If it had not been for that unfortunate accident with the fountain pen, he would have signed the order before he had time to think. But there is nothing to worry about. The sale is in the bag. Mr. Van Cortlandt will soon receive the approval of his chief engineer and call Bob up. In the meantime I shall return to Los Angeles, where I hope to receive the good news in the very near future."

Little Cedric departed. Bob and I had lunch in the hotel. Back at his office Bob had a telephone call—at the end of which he sank back in his chair with a groan of despair.

"It was Mr. Van Cortlandt," he said. "He called up his chief engineer, who told him the tunnel into this mine is four feet in diameter. Our smallest Earthworm tractor is five feet, ten inches high and five feet, two inches wide. So he has decided to buy a machine called the Weasel tractor, which he has tried out and which goes through the tunnel fine. But even that is not the worst of it."

"No?"

"As long as he's getting a Weasel tractor for this one mine, he says he's going to get Weasels for all of them."

"But that's absurd," I said. "I am familiar with this Weasel tractor. It's all right in its way. It's a special job designed to get into tight places. They use Weasels in small aqueduct tunnels and in various mines where they are cramped for room. They even use them to haul bat guano out of narrow passages in caves—like at Carlsbad. But nobody in his right mind would use one of these long, low, narrow Weasel monstrosities on any job where he had room for a normal, standard-sized Earthworm."

"That's what I started to tell Mr. Van Cortlandt," said Bob. "But he got ahead of me. He said that in my sales talk I had proved to him conclusively that all his maintenance and repair problems would be simplified by standardizing on one make of machine. If he buys this first Weasel, he will buy nothing but Weasels from now on."

"You might suggest that he enlarge the opening of his mine," I said.

"He has thought of that already, and his engineer tells him it would be impractical."

"There must be something we can do," I said.

"Maybe so, but what?"

"At the moment," I said, "I haven't the faintest idea. I'll try to think of something."

"All right, Mr. Botts. While you, in your futile way, are trying to think, I will go into action. Mr. Van Cortlandt is leaving right away to fly to New York. He will be back next Wednesday, at which time he plans to sign up with the Weasel Tractor Company. In the meantime I am going to Los Angeles to confer with Cedric and the other SSASOLA experts. When I get back I'll have a complete plan for a second attack on Mr. Van Cortlandt. I'm sorry you can't help me, Mr. Botts, but I'm glad that Mr. Henderson has put me in touch with some people who can."

As I could not think of any good reply to this, I merely wished Bob a pleasant good afternoon and came back to the hotel— where I have been writing this report.

I am sure, Henderson, that it was lack of time for investigation, rather than stupidity, that caused you to endorse this absurd SSASOLA organization. Fortunately I will have several days to look into the matter. And, although the situation has me temporarily baffled, I am not discouraged. In the course of the next few days I am sure to think up some plan for rescuing Bob from his unfortunate infatuation with little Cedric's cheap tricks and corny devices. Hence you may have complete confidence in

Your progressive Sales Manager,
ALEXANDER BOTTS

TELEGRAM
EARTHWORM CITY, ILL. APRIL 2, 1959

ALEXANDER BOTTS
EARTHWORM TRACTOR AGENCY
EL CENTRO, CALIF.
YOUR LETTER IS HERE. ALSO A LONG AND FRANTIC TELE-
GRAM DATED YESTERDAY FROM BOB PRESTON ACCUSING
YOU OF RUINING ALL CHANCES OF PUTTING OVER THE
HIGHLY IMPORTANT VAN CORTLANDT SALE. IT SEEMS
OBVIOUS THAT YOUR ACTIVITIES IN EL CENTRO ARE WORSE
THAN USELESS. CONSEQUENTLY YOU ARE DIRECTED TO
LEAVE TOWN AT ONCE AND TO SEND ME AN EXPLANATION OF
YOUR CONDUCT.

GILBERT HENDERSON

CARE EARTHWORM TRACTOR AGENCY
EL CENTRO, CALIFORNIA

Thursday, April 2, 1959

DEAR HENDERSON: Your wire is here, and I am compelled to admit that I really did cause Bob Preston a lot of unnecessary trouble and grief in his unsuccessful efforts to put over the Van Cortlandt sale. I do not blame him for sending you that violent telegram. And in order that you may understand exactly what has been going on, I will give you a complete account of recent developments.

When Bob and little Cedric got back from Los Angeles yesterday morning, I was waiting for them at Bob's office, all ready to tell them about the ideas I had evolved during their absence. Before I could explain anything, however, they launched forth on an enthusiastic description of their own plans for dealing with Mr. Van Cortlandt.

"We'll mow him down," said Cedric.

"We'll chop him up and feed him to the birds," said Bob.

"The Initial Impact will be twice as powerful."

"This time, instead of just one dog, we're going to give him two."

"We've learned a lot more about his hobbies."

"We'll talk about how his father's family settled New Amsterdam and how his mother's family came over in the Mayflower."

"We've got a lot of new Sentences That Smile and a lot of new Sentences That Sing."

"And for the Winning Wallop," said Bob, "I'm going to tell Mr. Van Cortlandt that my little sister is collecting autographs of leaders in American commerce and industry. I'll say she's just dying for his autograph. We'll have him write it on a card. This will put him in the mood for signing his name, so he'll go ahead and sign the order before he really knows what he is doing."

"Just a minute," I said. "You've been talking so fast that I had forgotten one of the main points. Suppose Mr. Van Cortlandt were to object that our tractor is too big for his mine. What had you planned to say about that?"

"We won't say anything," said Bob. "We're going to talk so fast and so continuously about other matters that he won't have any more time than you did to think up objections. We have a system that is bound to win. And we are now going to Mr. Van Cortlandt's office to try it out. If you want to come along we'll show you just how it works."

"You're a little late," I said. "Mr. Van Cortlandt got back from New York yesterday morning–a day earlier than he had expected. So I went over and called on him myself."

"You did? What did he say?"

"About what I expected. He was still convinced that he wanted a tractor that would go through that narrow mine tunnel in one way or another. Also he had decided to buy fifteen more tractors for his other properties, and he thought it would be a good idea to standardize on just one make. Naturally I agreed with him."

"What! You didn't give him an Earthworm sales talk? You didn't make any attempt to get him to change his mind?"

"Of course not," I said. "The man had made a decision that from his point of view was very sensible. His chief engineer had approved. The order for the whole sixteen machines was right there on his desk. I advised him to sign it. And he did."

"This is terrible!" said Bob.

"It's ghastly!" said little Cedric. "But maybe he hasn't sent in the order yet. Maybe we still have time to give him the Earthworm sales talk. We must get over to his office right away."

"It won't do any good," I said. "Mr. Van Cortlandt left for Australia last night. He will be away for two months."

For a moment Bob and Cedric were speechless. Then they opened up with a torrent of abuse, accusing me of virtual treason for agreeing with Mr. Van Cortlandt's idea that he should have tractors capable of entering his narrow mine tunnel, and demanding why I had not telephoned them in Los Angeles, so they could have hurried back and handled Mr. Van Cortlandt themselves before he left for Australia. They made so much noise yelling that I had no chance to answer. Finally Bob went into his office and started dictating that telegram to you. And I walked out.

After a good lunch at the hotel I decided—as explained at the beginning of this letter—that I really had caused Bob a lot of unnecessary trouble and grief. So I went back to his office and apologized to him and to little Cedric.

"Everything I told you this morning was true," I said, "but I never got around to telling you the whole story. This was partly because you kept interrupting me—and partly because I was annoyed at the way you assumed that I am old-fashioned and out-of-date and that you know more about selling than the old master, Alexander Botts."

"If you have any further explanations," said Bob rather stiffly, "we are listening."

"The SSASOLA system of selling," I said, "is nothing but a bunch of cheap tricks. My own system, on the other hand, is sound and sensible."

"Go on," said Bob.

"To make a successful sale," I said, "all you have to do is find a situation, or create a situation, where the prospective buyer wants your product, needs your product and can't afford to get along without it. If you have such a situation, you don't need any tricks. If you do not have such a situation, all your tricks will do you no good."

"Does all this have anything to do with Mr. Van Cortlandt?"

"Certainly. Last week the situation was wrong. The mine tunnel was too small for an Earthworm. So Mr. Van Cortlandt did not want an Earthworm, he did not need an Earthworm and he felt he could get along fine without an Earthworm. Under these circumstances your tricks did no good. And all you could think of was to go to Los Angeles and try to work out some more tricks."

"That's right," Bob admitted.

"While you were gone," I said, "I thought I would forget about the tricks and try to change the basic situation. I took one of your Earthworm tractors up to the mine. I talked with Mr. Van Cortlandt's chief engineer. I studied his operations. And I decided there was no reason why the tractor had to go through the tunnel all in one piece. Working with a crew of his mechanics, I disassembled the tractor, dragged the parts through the narrow tunnel and reassembled them in the more spacious chamber inside. Here the machine did all the work they needed—bulldozing material and loading it into small cars, which are pulled through the narrow tunnel by cables. I then drew up an order for sixteen Earthworms. The chief engineer sent it to Mr. Van Cortlandt's office with his enthusiastic endorsement. And when I called on Mr. Van Cortlandt yesterday the situation was so favorable that there was no need for any tricks."

"You mean," said Bob, "that the order he signed was for sixteen Earthworms?"

"Certainly," I said. "I never told you any different. Here is the order. I hope it may prove an object lesson in sound selling methods, and that in the future Cedric may be able to give his clients a little better advice, and Bob may follow up this successful sale with so many more that he will eventually become one of the best and finest of all Earthworm dealers."

Cordially yours,

ALEXANDER BOTTS

The relentless salesman Botts wheedles his way into a yet another impressive Earthworm tractor demonstration.